SACRIFICE PLAY

SACRIFICE PLAY

Conrad Haynes

SEVERN HOUSE PUBLISHERS

This first world edition published 1991 by
SEVERN HOUSE PUBLISHERS LTD of
35 Manor Road, Wallington, Surrey SM6 0BW.

Simultaneously published in the U.S.A. 1991 by
SEVERN HOUSE PUBLISHERS INC of
271 Madison Avenue, New York, N.Y. 10016.

British Library Cataloguing in Publication Data
Haynes, Conrad
  Sacrifice play
  I. Title
  823.914 [F]

  ISBN 0–7278–4119–X

Printed and bound in Great Britain
by Bookcraft [Bath] Ltd.

Dedication: To the staff of the *West Linn Tidings* and
                the *Lake Oswego Review* – a deeply,
                deeply strange bunch of folks.

Acknowledgements: To Detective J. Grant of the Lake Oswego Police Department for his help in matters of substance. And to Professor Curtis Keedy of Lewis and Clark College for his compound interest.

CHAPTER ONE

It was a dark and stormy night. And that was at noon.

Throughout the previous day, fat, blackened clouds had begun to amass over the Pacific Ocean, building intensity, elbowing and jostling each other for room, skirting around a high-pressure zone just off the coast of central Oregon and rotating clockwise toward Portland and Southern Washington. By three that morning the front reached the city, where a good portion of it hunkered down inside the Willamette Valley, snuggled in for the duration and began dumping buckets of rain.

Professor Henry Bishop stood by his office window and tried to discern any moving shapes behind the curtain of water that washed down the pane. Nothing was stirring, so far as he could tell, on the campus of John Jacob Astor College. A gust of wind dumped a particularly heavy curtain of rain against the window, which rattled and creaked. Harry flinched and an ounce of Scotch whisky splashed out of his mug.

Harry cursed the tragic loss of the amber liquid and gulped the last fingerful, lest another wind gust cost him another drop. One can never be too careful.

With a self-pitying sigh, Harry returned to staring out the window at the waterlogged liberal arts campus. It was the end of the first week of summer break and Portland was doing its impression of Atlantis.

It could be worse, he thought. The library was open. There was still half a bottle in the lower left-hand desk drawer. And from where he stood, Harry could just see his department chairman, Lyman Bledsoe Jr., step into a massive puddle of rainwater.

Who could ask for anything more?

This was, of course, before Harry was aware of either murder.

CHAPTER TWO

Once the storm broke – and summer storms in the Northwest, like residents of Oz, come and go quickly – the call went out to the main tower at Portland International Airport to resume take-offs and landings.

Korean Air Lines Flight 156 was cleared for immediate landing, since it had been circling the longest. Inside the crowded terminal, agents Johnson and Jenson checked their Rolex watches simultaneously. Shannon adjusted his tasteful tie. Brock smoothed back his jet black hair.

The pilots were scheduled to unload, reload and head out immediately for San Jose, so they wasted no time taxiing up to the boarding ramp, the windshield wipers pacing furiously back and forth, the whining turbos sending up a comet's tail of water behind the tubby 747. Soon, exhausted vacationers and business people began streaming up the ramp. Some were met with the waiting arms of impatient loved ones. Others weren't. One Korean social worker carried an eight-month old child and was met by a giggling, cheering and *Aaaaahing* mob that represented the little one's new adopted family. Flash bulbs popped around the tyke who screamed in terror.

A small man in a severe blue suit and graying temples limped out, near the back of the throng. He was followed, one pace right flank rear, by an equally small woman wearing her hair in bangs and fastened at the back. They were Japanese, and neither spoke to each other.

Agents Shannon and Brock nodded to each other then

3

stepped forward.

"Mr. Nakano?" Agent Shannon bowed curtly.

"Ms. Ishii?" Agent Brock bowed equally curtly.

"Sheppard," the small woman nodded in return. "Kimiko Ishii Sheppard. And yes, this is Mr. Nakano."

Mr. Nakano bowed to the two agents, then shifted his valise to his left hand, proffering the right. The agents shook his hand.

"Sorry for the delay, sir," Agent Shannon said, his voice as brittle as chipped ice. Allowing an early summer storm to brew obviously had been his fault.

Mr. Nakano turned to his young associate, who translated into Japanese. She turned back to the agents. "Mr. Nakano speaks no English, I'm afraid. I'm to translate for him at the Astor conference. Shall we gather the luggage?" Her clipped tone indicated that the apology was neither required nor appreciated.

"Luggage," Agent Shannon nodded.

"Done," Agent Brock replied.

It was dim and gray in the terminal, and both men wore Foster Grant sunglasses.

Christopher Detweiler splashed bourbon into a heavy, masculine glass and held it out to his companion, then poured one for himself. Both tumblers held three fingers of the liquid.

"To timber," cried L.C. Noraine, lifting his glass.

"To profit," replied Detweiler. Both men sipped.

The weather was kicking up again and the Hotel Trafalgar's shatterproof glass bowed against the pressure. Detweiler watched his own reflection distort in the concavity, only to straighten out after the gust subsided. "If things go well, L.C., then there's no reason on God's good Earth why you'n me won't be swimming in dough by Christmas."

"And won't that be fine!" L.C. replied, taking a hefty swallow of the bourbon then sighing contentedly. L.C. Noraine looked like an extra in a made-for-TV Western. He wore snakeskin boots and a black leather vest, unbuttoned. The tips of his shirt collar were gilded in gold arrow points. His belt buckle looked

4

like a hubcap and his slacks were embroidered in a flourishing white top stitch around the pockets. He had been a meaty, tough man a few decades earlier, but much of the muscle had turned to fat and the wind-chapped redness of his face had been replaced with the purplish glaze of someone who's too familiar with the bottle. L.C. finished his drink in a gulp and slammed down the glass.

Detweiler nodded approval and hauled the decanter over to the end table, readily refilling his guest's glass.

"When're these Japanese supposed to get here?" L.C. asked, diving into the glass almost before Detweiler had finished pouring.

"They're here now, if the airport's open," Detweiler replied, hoisting himself up on one of the three barstools that lined the counter separating the kitchenette from the living room. It was a spacious apartment with tasteful furniture, a neutral, shag carpet and several fine, framed posters touting art festivals in other countries. If the Hotel Trafalgar couldn't afford one thousand, two hundred and fifteen rooms filled with real art, at least they could advertise a few real art galleries.

Detweiler sipped his drink slowly and retrieved a leather-bound calendar book from his breast pocket. "Let's see. Nakano was supposed to land this morning, about an hour ago. He'll be stayin' here. I hear he doesn't speak any American, so there's a translator here for him."

L.C. frowned. "That means an intermediary, of sorts. I don't like talkin' through nobody else, Chris."

Detweiler's mind thought up four or five sharp retorts, but he smiled and shrugged and sipped his bourbon. "Who does, L.C.? That's the breaks, I guess. Still, I figure this fellow's here to dicker, and we've got the timber to dicker with. Am I right?"

"You're right as rain," L.C. laughed and emptied his glass. He pulled himself to his feet, a tad unsteadily, and stuck out a thick hand, mottled with liver spots. "I'd best get dressed for dinner, Chris. I'll see you tonight?"

"Bet on it," Detweiler replied and shook vigorously, squeezing a bit as a man's supposed to do.

L.C. winked and strolled out the door with a sailor's bowlegged gait. Once the door was closed, Detweiler uncorked the decanter and carefully poured his bourbon back in. He reached for the telephone and dialed the front desk.

"This is Christopher Detweiler in 1443. I'm expecting the Nakano party. Have they arrived yet? No? Fine. Thank you."

All trace of the good ol' boy inflection was gone from his voice. Detweiler popped a breath mint in his mouth, as if to wash away the flavor of the affected drawl.

Phoebe Pogue said thank you and returned the telephone receiver to its cradle. Pulling up the hood of her poncho, she hunched her shoulders, took a deep breath and slammed open the telephone booth's accordion doors.

The wind hurled a sheet of water at her, splattering against the cheap plastic poncho she'd picked up for a dollar ninety-five at a sidewalk sale three years earlier. The water was mean-spirited and cleverly sought out the five inch gash in the material, soaking into the sweatshirt beneath. Rain oozed out of her holey tennis shoes with each step as she raced for the dark green Buick parked half a block away.

Joshua had kept the engine running and the insides of the windows were frosted over with fog from his breath. Phoebe yanked open the passenger side door and Joshua shouted "Hey!" as the rain splashed in.

She crashed down onto the ripped seat, slamming the door behind her. The fifteen year old Buick came with all the latest options, including the looped piece of twine attached to the floor brackets beneath her seat. Phoebe deftly snatched up the loose end and looped it over the passenger door handle, to make sure the door stayed shut.

"Hell of a day," Joshua intoned, staring at the sheets of water rolling down the Buick's windshield. He pulled a hefty, forty-two ounce Styrofoam cup out of a Plaid Pantry bag and handed it across to his wife.

"Did you get through? Are they here yet?"

Phoebe pried off the plastic lid and inhaled the aroma. The coffee was oily and only lukewarm, but she was so cold it smelled like heaven. The couple sat almost four feet away from each other in the vast expanse of the Buick. A puddle of rain water was forming on the seat around her rump, seeping into the already moulding cushion stuffing through the gash in the upholstery. Phoebe slurped a little coffee noisily. "I don't know, Josh. The hotel wouldn't say one way or another."

Joshua Pogue ran a hand through his thick beard (a sign that he was thinking furiously, Phoebe realized). He removed his round, wire-rimmed glasses and wiped the filthy lenses against the equally filthy shirt tail that hung out below his olive drab, army issue sweater. "Piss up a rope," he muttered, then turned back to his wife. "Did you tell 'em you were related?"

Phoebe lowered her head and glowered at him through her eyelashes. "Joshua, do I *sound* like someone named Takeshi Nakano?"

He thought about it for a moment then nodded. "Not much, no."

"Right. So what do we do now?"

The ignition switch and housing were disconnected from the Buick's massive steering column and hung by two wires, swinging slightly by Joshua's knee. He reached down and inserted the key into the unit. It took almost two minutes before a puff of blue smoke farted from the tailpipe and the engine kicked over.

"Now?" he said, rolling down his window and squinting to see if he could pull away from the curve, "Now, we take matters into our own hands."

"Right," Phoebe said, replacing the plastic lid and holding the cup in both hands for warmth. "We can't let them do this, Josh."

Joshua leaned across the wide seat and patted her damp thigh. "We won't, Sweets. We'll stop 'em. You'll see."

The receptionist returned the telephone to its cradle and went back to sorting Visa and American Express receipts.

"Pardon me."

She looked up and smiled at the devastatingly handsome black man who smiled back at her. His hair was clipped short and ended in a widow's peak, which she had always found an attractive feature. It tended to make a man look a little dangerous.

"Can I help you?" the receptionist asked, then mentally kicked herself when she heard the slight varnish of lust in her words.

"Yes. I'm wondering if the Nakano party has checked in yet?" he asked, his voice resonant and warm.

She smiled. "That's funny. I just got a telephone call asking about the same party. I'm sorry, sir, but I can't answer that. It's, um, a policy I'm afraid. I'm terribly sorry." She realized glumly that she hadn't been nearly that solicitous to the woman who had just called.

"Ah." The tall man replied and bequeathed unto her a dazzling smile that absolved her of all guilt for not being able to answer the question. "In that case, may I have my mail? I'm Neil Keiter, room 1322."

"Yes sir." She turned and retrieved two envelopes from the appropriate pigeonhole. "Here you go." Again she received the golden smile. "And, um, the Nakano party is a bit delayed."

The smile went from warm to scorching and the receptionist started thinking of ways to cancel that night's date.

American Airlines flight 502 out of Denver was given clearance to land. As the captain made the final loop into the approach pattern, Daniel Todson McMurdo folded his table into the seat ahead of him and replaced the book marker in his well-thumbed paperback copy of "To Kill A Mockingbird." He dug into his vest and pulled out the antique pocket watch.

About damned time, McMurdo thought. Chances are, Nakano and that Sheppard woman were already on the ground. Well, he was landing now. There'd be plenty of time to take care of a little business, then maybe get away and head up to Mount Hood for some summer skiing.

Who knows? He might even find a moment to drop in on old Henry Bishop. The thought made Daniel McMurdo grin. Old Henry – Harry to his bosom friends – would faint dead away at the sight of him. Faint dead away.

CHAPTER THREE

Harry popped a Tic Tac in his mouth and waited a moment to see if he would get a bang out of life.

Shrugging, he pulled open one of the glass doors that lead into the library. The magnetic anti-theft device clicked as he passed through and for the umpteenth time he wondered why an anti-theft device had been installed for the in-coming door.

Several summer-school students – mostly graduate students – hailed him in passing. Harry had many faults but his rapport with the students wasn't one of them.

The building was very modernistic and thus, to Harry's eye, ugly as sin, with no two walls ever meeting in right angles, pastel colors that blended into each other to lessen eye strain and brick columns spattered indiscriminately throughout the floors, supposedly to hold up the ceiling but actually, he suspected, to act as sound baffling. Harry had always loved libraries and even one designed to "make a statement" was pleasing to be in.

He found Kate Fairbain in the first room he looked. She was sitting in one of the comfortable wood and fabric chairs, settled sideways relative to the long study table which was almost covered in piles of news magazines, photocopies, text books and Kate's telltale powder-blue legal size pads. There were no liquids allowed in the library and a cup of Constant Comment perched nonchalantly at her elbow. None of the library staff or work-study students dared quote rules to Professor Fairbain.

She wore a turquoise cable knit sweater with a long, plaid skirt and sat with her knees together, both feet on the next chair over, the soles of her flats resting on the seat cushion. A thick, dusty book rested on her knees. She chewed a pencil and peered through the wide, round glasses that perched on the end of her slightly-upturned nose.

"Zing" went the strings of Harry's heart.

Harry cleared a space on the table and sat down, keeping his rain-sodden shoes on the floor. "Pardon me, ma'am, but me 'n the boys're drivin' cattle through t'Montana. Don't s'ppose y'all got a cup of java and some grits, wouldja?"

Kate didn't move her head but peered over the tops of the reading glasses at Harry's childish grin. "Go away," she said around the pencil.

"And what are we working on today, little girl?" Harry ignored the order and began browsing through her notes.

Kate slipped the pencil behind her ear and closed the massive tome, then stretched like a cat, fingers locked, arms over her head. "A history of tariffs and trade agreements for timber sales from the Northwestern states and British Columbia to Pacific Rim countries, specifically Japan and South Korea." she replied.

Her voice indicated she was data-heavy – a disease Harry recognized instantly from himself and his own students: That patina of fatigue which settles over the brain after an influx of too much raw knowledge.

"How long have you been at it?" he asked. "Three hours? Four?"

Kate grabbed Harry's wrist and twisted it to look at his watch. "Four. Lee Connar asked for some help before his Trans-Pacific conference gets under way." She nestled the glasses in her silvery hair. Kate was only a few weeks younger than Harry – he personally had planned her fiftieth birthday, a few months back. Yet she looked easily ten years his junior.

Harry glanced through some of the papers and realized the subject was outside his range. Like most political science professors, he tried to keep up in a marginal way with a thousand relevant issues, but international trade was pretty low on his study list. "You're exhausted, fair Kate. Can I buy you some lunch? The weather's starting to break."

"I can't. I should really finish this project."

"You've got hours to go, am I right?"

"Yes, but—"

Harry stood up and took a deep bow. "M'lady's table is waiting. M'sieu Dutch has prepared a *magnifique* selection of delectables for your enjoyment. May I escort Madame?"

Despite herself, Kate smiled. No one on earth ever made her as angry as Harry Bishop, a radical old Roosevelt liberal with a blind eye toward anything Republican or conservative. For a woman who had served in the Office of Management and Budget during the Ford administration, that tended to rankle. Nonetheless, there were times when he actually managed to dent her deflector screens.

I really must be tired, Kate thought. Harry actually looks good to me today. "I can't. Really. Lee's waiting for this information."

"Then how about dinner?"

"Sorry. I've got to be at that banquet tonight, at the Trafalgar." Then – even before she was aware of saying it – Kate amended, "But you're welcome to come."

Harry's jaw dropped. Hers did too.

"Hi, honey. I'm home."

It always made Lee Connar feel a bit like Ward Cleaver to say that, but it also felt a bit good. Lee was nothing if not domestic.

Three years earlier, through sheer luck and a bit of persistence, Lee and Penny Connar had landed a two-story split level home in the Sunburst IV neighborhood of West Linn, within walking distance of the John Jacob Astor campus. His job as dean of the faculty often meant an endless procession of business luncheons or noon meetings with this faculty group or that administrative task force. And Penny's two occupations – she was a free-lance tax preparer and donated endless amounts of time to local good causes – also tended to keep her out of their home at lunchtime.

But every now and then, maybe once a month, maybe less often than that, Lee and Penny had a noontime free and would meet at home for tuna fish or grilled cheese sandwiches and iced tea, which they would eat on the formica counter in the kitchen.

Lee counted those rare lunches among his most cherished moments.

This was not one of those times.

"Lee? Are you home for lunch?" Penny's voice sang out from her den. It had stopped raining an hour earlier so Lee slid his dry, folded umbrella into the hallway stand and slipped off the dry raincoat, hanging it on the wooden peg by the mirror. His wife would be itemizing someone's life, he knew, though how anyone could think about taxes in June was beyond him.

"Penn, have you seen my brown satchel? The one with the initials, you gave me?"

Penny Connar stepped out of the double glass doors that separated the den from the family room. The space had been designed as a solarium or indoor garden, but as soon as they moved in she adopted it as her office. As always, Penny wore pink sweats and Nike tennis shoes, her hair piled atop her head and held in place with a rubber band. And, as always, there was a pencil smudge on the bridge of her nose. Lee often wondered how she managed to make the same smudge three or four times a week.

"It's on the end table in the dining room, by the phone." she replied, circling the couch to peck him on the cheek. Lee wiped the smudge off her nose and returned the kiss, then hurried into the kitchen for the satchel.

"Is everything all right?" Penny asked, following him.

Lee held his hand out, palm downward, and made a wobbling motion. "There's a million and one things to do before tomorrow and I'm supposed to meet with the conference members this afternoon. And I think someone forgot to get the fact sheets and agenda over to the Public Information Office in time for the newspapers." He spoke quickly, rummaging through the folder. He found the papers he wanted and his shoulders sagged. "And I think that someone was me."

Penny was a slightly chubby woman with freckles and a quick smile. She rubbed Lee's back with one hand and leaned against the grass green and white wall paper. "Will Christopher be there?"

Lee looked up and smiled. "He's already in town. Called me from the Trafalgar about an hour ago. Everything's set and all the conferees are in town. He's got the old Detweiler luck running full strength, I think."

"It'll be good to see him again."

Just then, a vision of utter chaos shambled into the dining room and crashed down on one of the matching mahogany chairs, a yawn of epic proportions contorting its face, the rest of the body hidden behind holey jeans and a much-too-large International News sweatshirt.

Lee and Penny studied the monstrosity for a moment, smiling. Their daughter, Mary Beth, was doing what every good student does during the first week of summer break. She was hibernating.

"Hi, princess." Lee said, not sure it would register.

"Hommm." Mary Beth Connar replied, rubbing at the pillow creases that lined her face.

"I take it the job hunt is going well?"

His nineteen-year-old daughter glared at him through her eyelashes and rested one elbow on the dining room table, her fist mashed into her cheek to support her head. "Nummm."

"That's good." Lee tucked the satchel under his arm and tousled her brown hair in passing. Penny walked him to the door and asked what she should wear for the dinner that night.

Mary Beth was asleep on the table before her dad was out the door.

CHAPTER FOUR

Some people enter a building. Others *make an entrance.*

Takeshi Nakano was president and chief executive officer for The Kuroshio Group Limited, one of the five largest import and export companies listed on the Japanese Exchange. He didn't enter the Hotel Trafalgar with flashing strobe lights or a red carpet or a fanfare of trumpets. He simply stepped into the plush, two-story tall lobby and nodded his head an inch or so at the doorman. It was nonetheless *an entrance.*

The lobby of the Trafalgar is an oblong room dominated (to distraction, some said) by a rich carpet in intricate floral designs, five hanging chandeliers of crystal and brass, and rows of rectangular pilaster columns lining the two long walls. The lobby was circled by a mezzanine-level restaurant and lounge, held up by marble pillars staggered in two rows that stretched from the main door on Broadway to the grand stairway at the north end. The stairway was wide enough at the top for a Busby Berkeley musical number and mushroomed out even wider at the base, making it resemble a lava flow that had hardened conveniently into a stair step pattern.   '

Takeshi Nakano said not a word, yet several people on the restaurant level turned and peered over the wrought iron railing at the small Japanese man in the severely cut, dark blue suit. Patrons of the first floor bar were scattered along the periphery of the lobby in tables that clustered around the pillars. They, too, found themselves drawn to him.

Takeshi Nakano walked calmly down the center of the vibrant carpet, trailed by Kimiko Ishii Sheppard, who carried an attaché case and shoulder bag and wore a suit of the same severe tailoring and somber tone as Nakano's. Two men in grey suits and sunglasses marched behind them, their heads pivoting slowly and steadily like automatic lawn sprinklers.

Halfway toward the grand stairway, the entourage came to an abrupt halt as Christopher Detweiler emerged from the bar, a warm but not overbearing smile on his face. He stepped into their path and bowed with his head and shoulders only.

Without a pause, Takeshi Nakano stopped and returned the bow. His companion followed a beat later.

Johnson and Jensen exchanged glances but didn't bow.

Detweiler turned directly to the young woman. "You must be Miss Sheppard? I'm Christopher Detweiler, Detweiler Farms Timber. How do you do?"

Judging from her western surname, Detweiler extended a hand. Sheppard smiled and switched the attache case to her left, then shook hands.

Nakano also extended his hand and the men shook. His leathery, well-wrinkled face bore almost no emotion.

Detweiler kept his eyes on the old man, but his words were aimed at Sheppard. "Welcome to Portland and the United States." By the word "Portland," Sheppard was translating in a soft murmur, watching Detweiler's lips. Like the American, her eyes were on one person while her words were aimed at another. Nakano betrayed no reaction at all.

"We have great expectations for this conference." Detweiler continued. "Our countries are tied together through a love for peace and democracy, and through the intimate ties of commerce. We feel quite sure that the results of this weekend's conference will enhance that relationship."

Sheppard stopped speaking a second after he did. Nakano nodded his head, then murmured in Japanese.

"Mr. Nakano also is pleased with the prospects." Sheppard translated. "Japanese companies need timber and Americans need markets for timber. What could be a more complimentary relationship? Mr. Nakano asks."

Nakano and the American both bowed their heads in unison, then shook hands again.

L.C.Noraine stood well back near the teak bar and watched the procession. He downed a gulp of straight whiskey and slapped the glass down on the bar, marking the need for a refill. Things couldn't look better, Noraine thought.

Neil Keiter sipped from his glass of sherry and rested both arms on the wrought iron railing that lined the balcony. Leaning over, he could see that Detweiler and Nakano had made first contact and, in the manner of all businessmen the world over, were sounding each other out, searching for weak spots and strong suits.

Keiter sipped his drink again, only tangentially aware that his strong, chiselled frame was drawing glances from every woman and a few of the men in the restaurant and lounge.

He tipped his drink toward the party below, in silent toast. Things couldn't look better, he thought.

Joshua and Phoebe Pogue stood on the sidewalk and stared through the glass doors at the figures inside. The doorman in his black hat, red coat and epaulets glanced at them meaningfully, but they ignored him.

The business people inside were nodding and shaking hands and smiling. (At least the American was. The Japanese had their backs to the door). From all outward appearances, a business deal was in the making.

Things couldn't look much worse, they both thought.

Across the street from them, Daniel Tadson McMurdo stood at a phone kiosk and thumbed rapidly through the White Pages directory which hung from the phone box by a chain. "Bishop, Bishop, Bishop?" he muttered, then found the page he wanted and ripped it from the book.

(Fifteen minutes later, using the stairs rather than the elevator, Dodge managed to avoid almost everyone in the ritzy hotel. So far, so good. After all, it wouldn't do at all to answer a bunch of questions. Wouldn't do at all.)

(Smiling, Dodge added a few more scribbles to the pocket-sized, wire bound note pad. The perfect place for the "unfortunate accident' was now settled. *Thing to do* number two: Contact the victim.)

CHAPTER FIVE

Some deity somewhere flicked a switch and the rain stopped, the clouds parted, the heavenly orb broke loose and a chorus of herald angels laid down a mean bit of scatting.

Harry, grinning like an idiot, hurried out of the library and smiled at the incredible double rainbow that appeared over Portland.

"Pretty, huh?" A student stopped beside him and stared at the spectacle.

Harry nudged the student, whom he had never met. "D'you know Professor Fairbain? Economics?"

"Yeah."

"I've got a date with her! Isn't life grand?"

Humming something vaguely like a tune, Harry hurried up the hill toward the Alice Joan Weymouth-Hyde Memorial Administration Building. Even the limp caused by his bad knee – he had popped a tendon several months earlier – wasn't bothering him today. Harry bade everyone he passed a good morning and marched resolutely through, rather than around, the puddles.

The Administration Building was a renovated manor house with gabled roof, stone turrets and actual ivy-covered walls; (the enrollment office was forever using photos of the building on school brochures, along with shots of handsome, smiling students of ethnic diversity sunning themselves and plucking guitars on the Western Lawn). Once inside the grand structure, Harry hurried down the stone stairs to the Admissions Office, as per the note he had found in his pigeon hole that morning.

The office was jammed with excited, new students and cynical grad. students, all trying to secure places in the greatly-reduced roster of summer classes. Much to his dismay, Harry had been assigned one of the Summer Sampler classes this year. The program was designed to give community college transfers and recent high school graduates a (relatively) inexpensive taste of liberal arts education, in hopes of luring them into the regular school year. Harry had whined and wheedled incessantly during the past few weeks, hoping to escape the Summer Sampler class, which was only five weeks long and two days per week, thus, he pointed out repeatedly, insufficient amount of time to teach anyone anything of any conceivable importance. His protestations were to no avail.

Harry's sunny disposition was wearing a bit thin by the time he had elbowed his way to the front of the line and gained the attention of a bedraggled secretary in half-glasses and an attractive skirt and blouse, over which she wore a too-small JJAC sweatshirt (part of the administration's efforts to make the Admissions Officer "user friendly" and "accessible" to the new students).

"Professor Bishop," she nodded curtly. Harry couldn't remember having ever met the woman before.

"Lovely day, isn't it?" he replied. His weird accent – Scottish born, London raised, Princeton education, West Coast rooted – boomed in the crowded room.

The secretary stared at him over the tops of her glasses.

"Er, yes." Harry searched through his pockets until he found the note from his department chairperson. "I'm apparently teaching a brief course in Comparative Political Systems. Class code . . . er, L-119?" He turned the note around and showed it to the woman.

"That's looks like an 'L'," she concurred. "No way to be sure. Our computers have been down all morning and we're hand-sorting everything." The secretary shuddered at the concept then searched through a wire basket before coming up with the paperwork.

"Right. L-119. You've got fourteen students signed up."

19

Harry's attitude brightened a bit more. "That's a manageable size. Have you the class list?"

She handed it over the formica counter. "You're meeting in the gym, third period."

Harry's jaw dropped. "In the gym?"

"The gym," she replied.

"The gymnasium?"

"That's the gym."

"There must be some mistake."

"Nope. I've been in the gym. It's a gymnasium all right. *Next!*"

He shouldn't have been surprised. Harry was forever finding himself with a roster of thirty students and a classroom the size of a walk-in closet, or with six students assigned to one of the science lecture pavilions. Grumbling a bit, and temporarily forgetting that evening's date, he pushed his way back out of the crowded room, up the stairs and back out into the sunshine, where, indeed, his spirits picked up some of their battered gleam.

As so often in the past, Harry marveled at the chameleon-like ability of JJAC's students to mirror their surroundings. That morning the students had been an unending line of rain slickers and umbrellas, many decked out in fiery, Day-Glo colors. Now, a few hours later, mini-skirts, tank tops, jogging clothes and sandals were de rigeur.

Harry had left his old doctor's bag in his office. He jammed his hands into his pants pockets and ambled lazily down into the heart of the campus, still more than an hour away from his first class. Harry had been trying to "make points," as the students might have put it, with Kate Fairbain for many years. Sometimes their relationship was similar to that of Eisenhower and Khrushchev. Other times it warmed up to tolerance. Kate rarely agreed to a full fledged *date*.

Since his wife died, far too many years ago, Harry's romantic interests had been few and far between. He was looking forward to that evening as he had looked forward to few evenings of late.

Harry stopped in front of the spanking new sports complex

which housed an Olympic sized swimming pool, full weight room, twin racquetball courts in the basement and a basketball court with retractable backboards and accordion bleachers. The western wall was made almost entirely of glass doors and he tested the nearest. It was locked.

"Hey."

Harry turn to find a student sitting on a concrete step, knees at chest height, arms folded across his knees. Even sitting, the boy looked tall and lanky, like Harry himself.

"Hullo," Harry replied. "They've locked us out."

"A janitor came by 'bout ten minutes ago. He said it'll be open soon," the student replied. He had a soft, southern accent and wore his ice blond hair severely short.

"Are you in . . . L-119?" Harry asked, taking a seat on the steps and stretching out his bum leg, which twitched slightly.

The boy reached inside his letterman's jacket and pulled out a crinkled pink slip, studying it for a moment. "Yes sir. They told me there'd be about a dozen of us."

"That's what I hear." Harry leaned back with his elbows on the next higher step above his butt. "My name's Henry Bishop."

"How do you do," the student replied politely and reached over. Harry shook his hand. "I'm Wes Kiley from Texas."

"How d'you do, Wes Kiley from Texas."

The boy smiled shyly. "I have to say, sir, you're not what I expected. No offense intended."

"None taken. What did you expect?"

He shrugged. "Don't know, sir."

"I see. Tell me, Wes Kiley from Texas, why Astor? What brought you to our sun-swept shores?"

Again with the shrug. "I heard you had a good summer program. I'm going to Texas A&M, starting next winter, but I've got to raise some money first."

Harry thought about that for a moment. "We do, indeed, have a good summer program. And what, pray do tell, is your weakest area, would you say?"

The boy leaned back and stretched out his legs, crossing at the ankles to subconsciously mimic Harry's posture. "Well . . .

I suppose defense. To be honest, sir, I don't always understand some of the intricacies."

Harry smiled warmly. It was so rare to find a student who was aware of his own shortcomings and could acknowledge them so openly. He drew his long, thin legs back in and stood, brushing himself off. "You and almost everyone else, Wes Kiley from Texas. We'll definitely focus on defense in the next few weeks. In the meantime, let me leave you with a thought: Walther Rathenau, German minister of reconstruction after World War I, said that the country forced to disarm after one war will have an advantage in the next. 'The army which is least hampered with obsolete material will have a great advantage,' quoth Herr Rathenau."

The student looked up at Harry, squinting in the sunlight. "I'm not so sure I follow that, sir. Unless, what you mean is, the guy who loses this year will bounce back faster next year?"

"Right. Think about it a bit, my friend. We'll discuss defense at length. I'll be back in an hour or so."

"Yes sir," the student nodded, brow furled in serious consideration.

If that young man is any indication, Harry thought, this group is going to be wonderful.

CHAPTER SIX

Dean of Faculty Lee Connar didn't trust his driving on Portland's grid of downtown streets, all one-way and none of them ever going his way. Thus, at a little past noon, Lee stepped down off a Tri-Met bus on the corner of Clay and Park and took stock of his image in a store window: leather satchel and folded umbrella with collapsible handle tucked under his arm, black plastic horn-rimmed glasses firmly in place, male pattern baldness marching on.

It was only half a block to the Trafalgar and Lee approached it from the rear, on the Park Blocks side. He stared up at the 31 floors with their balconies overlooking the long, narrow park that stretched all the way past Burnside, more than a mile away.

Lee noticed the shiny, white stretch limousine taking up two parking spaces on this side of the building, with City of Portland canvas hoods placed over the parking meters, making the spaces free. Lee sensed Christopher Detweiler's string-pulling talents.

He circled the monumental, pre-World War II building, entering from the Broadway side. He had been in the monumental lobby a half dozen times in the past but its elegance never failed to impress him. This time, before he could marvel at the marble, Christopher Detweiler burst out from the first floor bar, a smile spreading across his square features, hands jammed into his pants pockets, tweed jacket folded back behind his arms. "Lee! Howsa boy!"

Lee smiled and nodded, feeling self-conscious as the big

man's voice boomed throughout the lobby. "Hello, Christopher. How's the war?"

Detweiler folded his arm around Lee's shoulders and led him to a table hidden behind one of the pillars. A chubby man in a leather vest and plaid shirt with bolo tie was finishing off a tumbler of amber liquid. "Never better. How's Penny? And Mary Beth? I can't begin to tell you how excited I am by this whole project. Lee, do you know L.C. Noraine?"

"I don't believe so." Lee shook the sitting man's hand.

"L.C., this is Lee Connar, dean of the faculty at Astor. Connar's an old friend of mine. He was my legislative aide a thousand years ago when I served in the state legislature. Lee, L.C. here is that most disreputable of scoundrels: a timber man."

"Ha!". The comment seemed to strike L.C. as funny. He waved to catch the bartender's eye then made a circular motion toward the table, calling for another round.

Lee sat down and shoveled his arm-load beneath the chair. "Do you own timber land in Oregon?" he asked L.C.

"Some. Mostly in Washington and the Idaho panhandle, though. Ol' Chris here, him and me go way back."

There was something forced and rehearsed about the bad English and the colloquialisms, Lee thought. He guessed that L.C. Noraine held a business degree from some big university back east and had concocted the good ol' boy mannerisms in order to do business in the Northwest.

Detweiler leaned back and let the waitress set down three glasses before the men. Lee had no idea what was in his but politely shoved his aside and asked for a cup of coffee, decaf. "Lee," Detweiler said, "L.C. and I feel that this trans-Pacific trading agreement could revolutionize the timber industry in the Northwest. Now I've met with our Japanese counterpart, Takeshi Nakano, and I'm convinced he's here to do business."

"Great," Lee could smell the rich, heady aroma of good bourbon and his stomach muscles tightened. He had been dry for almost a decade, but no one ever fully recovers from alcoholism.

"And here's the kicker," Detweiler continued. "The Japanese

24

have no interest in establishing just one more business conduit into the U.S. They've got all of that they can handle."

"What are they looking for?"

Detweiler leaned back and smiled like a poker player laying down a pat hand, a card at a time. "They want cultural ties with the States. And that's what Portland can offer. First, by tightening the tourist industry that already exists. I've met with officials from the Port of Portland and the idea of doubling or even tripling the number of direct flights from Japan to Portland International – bypassing San Diego and SeaTac entirely – appeals to them."

"Damn right it does!" L.C. cut in, raising his glass in salute and draining it.

Lee's coffee arrived and he thanked the waitress, who seemed slightly surprised by the politeness. Detweiler seemed not to notice either interruption. "Second, we need to strengthen the educational ties with Japan. As you know, Lewis and Clark College beat you to the punch in its Pacific Rim relations programs, including the ISALC language institute and the undergraduate exchange programs. But that's okay. See, their programs are geared to International Affairs and foreign language. Not business or law. That's where Astor can grab a slice of the PacRim pie, so to speak."

Lee nodded. He had known Christopher Detweiler for years, had worked for and with him in many capacities. But the man's fantastic ability to rivet himself into a project, to drive like a military commander and to engage all around him with that same all-absorbing enthusiasm, never failed to enervate Lee. Christopher Detweiler was a televangelist of business and marketing, and Lee was tempted to leap to his feet and shout "Hallelujah!"

"And third," Detweiler spread out his hands, palms upward, "is business. The Japanese need timber and we need reliable markets for timber. It's a win-win situation."

"Damn straight." L.C. hoisted a glass again and drained it again. Lee noticed it was the drink he had turned down.

Lee lifted the brittle china coffee cup and saluted as well. "I don't know about tourism or timber, Christopher, but I can assure you the Astor Board of Trustees is more than enthused about the educational exchange end of the business. President Eckersley and I talked to them two nights ago and the reception was good. Very positive. If we start slow, a handful of students at a time, I think we can make a go of this."

Detweiler's eyes twinkled and he slid a hand into his pants pocket, jiggling his spare change. "Not to put too fine a point on it, Lee old son, but I have a feeling L.C. and I are about to get rich, and your John Jacob Astor College is about to get famous. Who can ask for anything more?"

L.C. Noraine asked for another drink.

CHAPTER SEVEN

Kimiko Ishii Sheppard scanned the three pages of correspondence that appeared on her lap-top computer's screen. It
was her final read-through, looking not for typos this time but
for the over-all image of the letters – the professional spacing
from all four edges, the proper font, the lack of widows at the
end of paragraphs.

Satisfied, she leaned as far back as the could, bending her
vertebrae against the wooden chair back. The stretching motion
felt good. She stood and pushed back the chair, then quickly
folded herself in half, pressing the heels of her hands into the
thick carpeting between her bare feet. She held the position for
a few seconds, not bouncing but letting the tension ebb out of
her bones and muscles. She stood up right and twisted her torso
far to the right, then far to the left.

Sighing, Kimiko knelt on the single bed and reached for the
telephone, dragging it back to her side. She dialed zero zero
zero and listened to the tone generator. The hotel had graciously
allowed Mr. Nakano's staff to install a modem in the main
switchboard. Now, with the press of a few buttons, she fitted the
telephone receiver into matching slots in her computer console
and punched the transmit codes. The three letters disappeared
from her screen, to be replaced with a quick scroll in Japanese.

*Letters received, Hokkaido. Today's mail X-mit to you.
Further instructions? End*

She thought about it for a moment, then typed *No. End
message* to the staff back in The Kuroshio Group headquarters

in Hokkaido. Thanks to the switchboard modem and the laptop, no matter where they were, Mr. Nakano could access the company's main frame and send and receive electronic mail.

The Kuroshio Group had perfected the communications technology. Take that, Sony, she ungallantly thought.

Kimiko found her leather-bound pad and pen and made a careful, graceful check mark beside the word "letters." There were a dozen more things to do on the day's list, which was printed in English, not Japanese. She already had made a considerable dent in the list. Mr. Nakano was sleeping in the next room and wasn't to be disturbed for another hour yet. With time to kill, she decided to take the porter's suggestion and locate the observation room on the thirty-first floor.

She slipped out of her sweats and into something more proper, then washed her face and hands and combed her fine, black hair, securing it back away from her cheeks with a tortoise shell clip. Kimiko checked her image in the spacious bathroom's mirror. Casual yet professional, she pronounced. She slipped the hotel room key with its thick wooden fob into her skirt pocket and tossed a sweater over her shoulders, before strolling out into the hallway and into a conveniently open elevator.

"Hold it!" She heard the voice and automatically sliced her hand across the door opening, breaking the electric eye beam and halting the door. A tall black man in a blazer and turtle neck sweater jogged through and smiled at her. "Thanks."

Kimiko nodded and stepped back, hands folded in front of herself. The big man took a step back and to his right. Like elevator-riders the world over, Kimiko Sheppard and Neil Keiter according each other their own space. And like beautiful women and handsome men the world over, they were instantly aware of the subtly uncomfortable electricity in the confined space.

Kimiko had punched the button for the observation deck. She restrained a smile when Keiter made no effort to select any other floor.

Ernie deSidrio finished the last dregs of his beer and took the three darts handed to him. "So what is it you do?" his opponent asked.

"I'm a driver," deSidrio replied, taking careful aim, wrist at shoulder height, hand swinging back and forth in small pendular arcs like a python getting set to strike.

"Bus?"

"Nope." DeSidrio let fly and the dart hit home in the triple-slot of the eighteen. He grinned and winked at his opponent.

"Shit," the other man said, then motioned to the bar tender for another round, peeling a wadded five dollar bill out of his jeans pocket.

"Thanks," deSidrio accepted the new beer. "But to answer your question, buddy, I'm a chauffeur."

"Yeah?"

"Yeah. I drive a stretch limo." He slipped the brew, American, of course, and let his eyes wander to the waitress' shapely legs. "Man, you should see that mother on the road. Eight banger under the hood, more horses than you can use in a lifetime."

"Yeah?"

"Yeah. Y'know, I once out-ran a cop car?"

"No shit?"

"No shit. Flat out, onna freeway, just fucking blew him away. Y'see, limos, they're big, right? And they can't turn for shit, right? But people always figure any boat with that much metal has gotta be like driving an aircraft carrier with wheels. But the drive train is awesome."

"Yeah?"

"Oh yeah. I'm telling you. Another match?" DeSidrio waved the darts at his new-found friend.

"You bet. So you working this week?"

"Sure." He handed the three darts over. "I'm booked to drive this old Japanese fart around. I brought 'im in from the airport this morning. He's got this fantastic looking young thing with him, you know what I mean?"

"Do I!"

"Oh yes, indeed. And this guy's gotta be a hundred and twenty if he's a day. Personally, I think she gave me the eye this morning. I mean, I can usually tell with women. You know?"

"Oh, hell yes. So where you taking this guy? The zoo. OMSI? The usual touristy stuff?"

DeSidrio snorted. "Hell, no. You're not going to believe this. This old guy wants to go to some fucking tree farm in Wilsonville."

"You're shitting me. Wilsonville?"

"God's truth, man. So you going to throw that dart or what?"

"God's truth."

Harry finished the last of his paperwork and slid it into the in-basket on the desk of the poli.sci. department's secretary, who arched her eyebrows and asked what was wrong. The paperwork was done on time and correctly. She sensed impending doom.

Unruffled, Harry checked his pigeonhole and found another pile of the never-ending paperwork, plus a post card from San Salvador that bore Tucker Nelligan's tell-tale chicken scratchings. The card showed a row of dancing girls decked out in Carmen Miranda hats and bikinis. On the other side, Tucker had scrawled *Having great time. Wish you were queer.*

Grinning, Harry gathered his massive raincoat and his much abused blackstone bag and headed toward the gymnasium. This last-day-of-the-week introduction was designed as a welcoming session, and there would be time enough when class truly began on Monday to find a better location for such a small class.

Harry felt supremely confident. He had met only one member of the class, Wes Kiley, but that young man had shown a keen interest and a ready wit. Young master Kiley had said he lacked an understanding of defensive systems and their intrinsic place in a society, and why not? Harry wondered. So rarely in homo sapiens history had anything been built expressly so it would not be used, yet in the twentieth century much of the defensive hardware of the first- and second-world countries was specifically keyed to not being used, most obviously the nuclear strike forces of the world. Mutually Assured Destruction. The Reagan administration had even re-introduced poison gas, that bogyman of World War 1, back into the U.S. defensive arsenal. Why? So no one else would feel inclined to deploy poison gas.

Wes Kiley of Texas has reason to wonder about the complexities of defense, Harry thought.

Whistling, he hobbled up the stairs and entered the now-unlocked doors into the sports center. Halfway down the wide corridor, lined with glass and steel trophy cases, the wooden doors to the gym stood open. He could hear basketballs ricocheting off backboards and the telltale squeak of tennis shoes coming to abrupt halts on the hardwood floor. Harry frowned. He wasn't bloody thrilled about teaching in a gym, even for Summer Sampler classes, but the least they could do was counter-program the phys.ed. classes away from him.

He entered the gym and set down his back and coat, then looked around.

Fourteen young men stood or sat around the key on the nearest end to him. A couple of them were shooting. The others were chatting. All were dressed in tank tops, shorts, tube socks and sneakers.

Harry's heart rose into his throat.

Wes Kiley came down from a jump shot and smiled at him. "Hey, guys. I'd like y'all to meet Coach Bishop. He said he's going to be focussing on defense for us."

CHAPTER EIGHT

"Hey Sailor. Got candy bar?"

Kate Fairbain glanced up from her mailbox cubby hole – one of many lining one corridor wall in the Student Union Building – and rolled her eyes. "Nice, Harry. Give the students a good impression."

She closed the square, metal door with her department key, then studied Harry closer. That look of utter weirdness which only Harry Bishop can manage dominated his long, angular face. "Are you all right?"

As she so often did with Harry, Kate spoke in Russian.

Harry made an elaborate shrug, as they started off together down the hall. "I'll explain later. Are we still on for tonight?" His Russian was decidedly less fluid than hers.

Kate smiled warmly. Harry's knees quivered at the sight. "Yes, but I've still got to run through some of this information I'm presenting on ways for Astor to maximize international relations and international law."

"Oh." Harry tried hard to make his voice sound resigned.

It seemed to work. "But that doesn't mean we're off!" Kate quickly added. "It just means I'll have to get there a little early. Say sixish? Does that still work for you?"

Harry sighed. "Of course, Katarina."

"Good. Shall I pick you up?" She knew about Harry's fear of driving the dilapidated Datsun any time after regular garages were closed.

Harry smiled and perched on the edge of his desk. The

humiliation of facing his "class" suddenly evaporated. "If you wouldn't mind."

"Of course. Five-thirty, your place?"

"Done."

They stepped out of the building and into a ring of cement seats, called Speaker's Corner. The center of the miniature amphitheater was dominated by an inlaid time capsule and a memorial plaque from the class of 'sixty-six – the year Kate gained her master's degree from Astor.

Kate blushed as they passed the marker, as Harry had noted her do before. Everyone fantasizes about their youth, he realized. Now, however, she stopped, stood on tip toe, and gave him a quick kiss on the cheek. It wasn't much more than a slight pressure of her lips against the edge of his zygomatic bone, all very chaste and proper really. Harry damn near broke out in a baritone aria and attempted to dip her, but somehow found the will to restrain himself. "Sure, fine. Five-thirty it is. *Das skorova*."

Kate waved to him. "*Das skorova*, Harry."

Kate hurried left and Harry strolled to the right, his heart arrhythmic.

Singing off-tune snatches of "S'wonderful," Harry swung by his department head's office to leave a note, informing him of the grievous error that had occurred in his class assignment and asking steps must be taken, first thing Monday morning, to rectify the situation. "*Elsewise*," the note continued, "*I shall be forced to call my associate, Bruno the Knuckle, who deals exclusively in misconstrued social contracts and their ramifications, a la broken kneecaps. Yours, etc., etc., HB.*"

With his coat over one arm and the over-stuffed bag in the other hand, Harry bade the poli. sci. personnel a good weekend and headed out to his car. So happy was he that Harry didn't have the vaguest notion that he was being followed.

CHAPTER NINE

Kate weaved her new Saab expertly through the downtown streets, Harry hanging on for dear life in the passenger seat. The sleek, silver car slid effortlessly, like Mercury, and Harry suddenly found himself in a parking structure, Kate saying something witty and releasing her shoulder harness, Harry's life already having passed before his eyes.

By the time they were out on the street and on foot, less than a block from the Hotel Trafalgar, he had regained his equilibrium. Harry had put on his better gray suit and best gray tie for the evening but he looked as disheveled as always. The suit fitted a bit too tight here, hung too loose there on his tall, angular frame. The tie refused to hang straight. All the polish in the world couldn't reverse time and de-scuff his shoes. Kate was dressed to the nines as usual, wearing a long black skirt, slit up the back, and a gold lamé blouse with matching earrings and a bracelet of heavy, beaten gold. She wore black shoes with very high heels and Harry heard a nightingale sing in Berkeley Square.

Outside the Trafalgar they were surprised to find half a dozen pickets, carrying signs referring to the U.S./Japanese trade situation. *KEEP OREGON JOBS IN OREGON!* one said. *DON'T UNDO GOD'S WORK!* quoth another.

"Lovely," Kate muttered.

"Are you with the trade consortium?" A young woman heard Kate's comment and stepped in front of them.

"We're from Astor, yes," Harry replied, touching Kate's elbow and attempting to lead her around the blockade.

"Don't you realize what they're doing?" The woman stepped in front of them again. She was tall and lanky, wearing a Navy pea coat over a plaid work shirt and jeans, her stringy brown hair pulled back and held with a rubber band. "Our forests are being destroyed! There's so little left. We can't let them defoliate the Northwest!"

"Your grasp on forestry and trade is somewhat limited," Kate replied, stepping up toe-to-toe with the taller woman. Harry sighed. Kate Fairbain loved nothing so much as trolling for liberals. "There are thousands of people in Oregon looking for employment. The economy of Klamath Falls and other cities to the south is deplorable. No one – no one at all – wants to 'defoliate the Northwest.' But only a fool would want to ignore the vast potential of the Northwestern forests. If you'll excuse us."

"You bitch!" the protestor hissed. "The whole nation is becoming a toilet thanks to your kind. You—"

"Phoebe!" a bearded man in a matching pea coat reached across her chest and grabbed her arm, holding her back. "Stop it. They're too greedy to see."

"Yes," Kate smiled sweetly at them both. "Surely that's it. We're too greedy to see. Shall we, Harry?" She swept past them.

Harry leaned toward the couple *en passant* and whispered, "Good for you. Keep at it."

They were more than an hour early for the reception and the gilded meeting room was being set up by the hotel staff. Kate lead Harry upstairs to room 1401, which JJAC had reserved as a hospitality suite and a meeting place for the symposium. Lee Connar greeted their knocking. Papers and manila files were spread across the double bed. A small manual typewriter rested on one table with a box of files on the floor. In no time Lee and Kate got down to business. Harry excused himself and went in search of the bar.

Once the door was closed, Lee shoved his glasses up into his thinning hair and raised both eyebrows.

"What?" Kate asked, hearing the defensiveness in her own voice.

"Well?"

"Well, what?"

"Well, well."

"*Well, well what!*" she snapped at Lee, who simply grinned. "Lee Connar, don't you even think it! I simply needed an escort for the evening and—"

There was a knock on the door. Lee breathed a sigh of relief. Kate glowered at him, then turned to open it. "Yes?"

An amiable-looking man with a ruddy complexion and close cropped, silver hair smiled at them. "Are you the Astor party?" he asked, a strong New England twang in his voice.

Lee stepped up beside Kate and introduced himself.

"How do you do? Daniel Tadson McMurdo, State Department. I'll be running interference for the conference."

The mezzanine-level bar was all brass and deep, dark wood, with a woman behind the baby grand piano playing innocuous show tunes. Harry hoisted himself onto the red leather stool and perched his shoes on the brass foot railing before ordering a scotch, rocks.

The liquor was top drawer and he sighed. It was the first time in months he had been out for a social evening. Harry Bishop liked to think of himself as a gregarious sort of fellow but as he sat in the half empty bar, he thought back to how many nights in June he had spent at home, alone except for his cat, Niccolo. And how many nights in May? In April? Too many.

He ordered another drink, hoping one of his morose periods wasn't about to start up. He made a mental note to call his daughter in Florida on Saturday.

"You're here for the symposium?" A voice jarred Harry out of his self-pity.

"Hmm? Ah, yes."

The stranger, a handsome, black man with a dazzling smile, sat on the adjacent stool. Noting Harry's confusion, he pointed to the blue three-fold pamphlet the professor was using as a coaster. "You've got one of the brochures from that college, Astor. I take it you're with the symposium. Am I right?"

"Not quite." Harry proffered a hand, which was met with a vigorous grip. "Henry Bishop, professor of political science at Astor. I'm just here escorting a friend to the reception."

"How do you do. I'm Neil Keiter, ITEU rep."

"Ah, International Timber Employees' Union. Are you speaking tomorrow?"

Keiter sipped his martini. "Yes, briefly, in the evening. But mainly I'm here to see if this damned thing can be knocked off track."

Harry twisted his stool so as to face Keiter. "You mean the symposium? I'm a tad surprised, Mr. Keiter. I'd have thought the unions would be ecstatic over anything that offered more work."

Keiter carefully fished the twist of lime out of his drink and set it on the napkin. "There's more to it than all that, professor. It's a complicated situation." Like Harry, Keiter had a deep, mellifluous voice. Unlike Harry, he also had an air of quiet power to him. If this man is a contracts negotiator, Harry thought, then heaven help any employer facing him across a dickering table.

"The U.S./Japan negotiations look great on paper," Keiter continued. "But there's more to it than that. What old man Nakano – he's the sole Japanese business negotiator here – what Nakano wants is a deal where our workers cut down the trees, shave off a couple branches maybe, then ship the wood to Japan, where Japanese workers turn the wood into lumber products; boards and planks and anything they desire. The finished product then will be exported from Japan to any other country needing wood products, and that includes the United States. No, professor, our lumberjacks are happy to be working, and there's more than enough timber available to cut down, but we also represent the men and women in the lumber mills and paper mills, and those folks are going to be left high and dry by this agreement. Moreover, fully a third of our members are Canadians, like me, working in the timber industry north of the border. They want to know where they fit into this picture."

"And you're here to scuttle the symposium?" Harry interjected.

37

Keiter studied him for a moment, before smiling again. "Why, no. Not at all. I'm a negotiator. My job is to explain the position of the American and Canadian workers and ameliorate any portion of the agreement which would have a negative impact on the union."

Harry made note of Neil Keiter's expensive pin-striped suit, Rolex watch with gold linked band and massive gold ring on his right hand. "I must say, Mr. Keiter, you don't look like the heir-apparent of the Wobblies. I half expect union representatives to wear plaid shirts and carry axes."

Keiter laughed – it was an infectious, deep-timbred sound. There were only a few female patrons in the bar but Harry noticed their eyes turn frequently to Keiter. "With a red bandana and a cheek-full of tobacco, right? Sorry to disappoint you, professor. I've got an MBA from McGill University and a law degree from Willamette. I drive an Audi and the only calluses on my hands are the ones I get from playing hand ball."

"The times they are a'changing," Harry added. "So how do you go about altering the agreement?"

Keiter finished his drink and pulled a bill out of his hip pocket, nodding thanks to the bartender. "I talk to all sides and convince them to make the finished products in the U.S., rather than just shipping trees across the Pacific. And speaking of talking, I'm late. Nice to have met you, professor."

"You too, sir." Harry watched Neil Keiter button his jacket and stride out of the bar. He had a feeling that – calluses notwithstanding – the plaid shirt and axe were buried just under Keiter's Brooks Brothers surface.

He turned back to his drink and scanned the pamphlet Kate had given him, but a disturbance at the far end of the bar snagged his attention. An over-weight, middle-aged man slammed a fist into the bar and roared: "I'm paying big money for a God-damned room in this flea-circus hotel and I God-damn expect some service. Now pour me that God-damned drink!"

The young bartender's eyes were as wide as saucers and he groped for a reply. A gray haired man in a much-stained apron burst quickly out through the kitchen's swinging doors and stepped up to the bar. "Mr. . . . .?"

"L.C. Noraine, sunshine," he shot back, his words slurring, "and I'm staying at this over-priced cathouse for more money that it's worth, I don't mind telling you! Now I want a drink!"

But by that time Harry had lost interest in the drunk. He finished off his scotch and paid for it then wandered out into the hall, wondering what Kate and Lee were up to.

(Dodge watched the lanky Englishman saunter out of the bar, trying to decide if he was a "player." Dodge had a hard and fast rule about never ignoring anyone remotely connected to the job. That included The Plan.

He made a mental note to watch Professor Bishop.)

CHAPTER TEN

The administration of John Jacob Astor College arrived in all their splendor for the small reception at the Trafalgar Hotel. College President L. Charles "Chuck" Eckersley somehow managed to wear the perfect combination of businesslike and casual attire, with a wool, burgundy sweater under his $500 sports jacket. He was a tall, silver-maned man with a flashing smile and matinee idol eyes to die for. His wife was equally handsome and equally at ease in the opulent surroundings of the mezzanine-level lounge.

Lee and Penny Connar also were good at these affairs, since the politics of education is a necessary evil. They circulated the dark, wood-panelled room and conversed with administrators and their vaguely-remembered spouses, both keeping mental Rolodexes with one or two interesting facts and opinions on every conceivable topic of conversation. The national debt? Sports? The Oregon Art Institute's new exhibition of works by Graciela Rodo Boulanger? Name it – Penny and Lee Connar could chat about it.

Kate faired well at social gatherings as well, but Harry retreated into himself. He had a horrible time remembering anyone's name for more than ten seconds and his opinions on most subjects of national importance were so far to the left of the businessmen in the room that he soon isolated himself from most of the conversations. He and Kate dove into a whispered but heated argument over the European Economic Community and the viability of a pan-Europic currency. The argument reached its best point when Kate called him a "pinhead." They both enjoyed the fight immensely. Secretly, Harry always feared that, if she ever agreed with him on any point, his unrequited lust for her might diminish.

Both Connars knew Kate and Harry and gave them a wide berth. They also noticed that, through much of the party, Christopher Detweiler kept L. Charles "Chuck" Eckersley occupied in conversation, their heads bent, L. Charles "Chuck" nodding from time to time.

Surprisingly, Takeshi Nakano was not the center of attention, although by all rights he should have been. When the elderly man entered with his translator and the two Secret Service men, in their severe suits and Dick Tracy jawlines, the dynamic of the room turned instantly to them. There was a polite smattering of applause and Nakano bowed politely.

But after Kimiko Sheppard – who wore a simple yet elegant gray jump suit with a crimson sash at her waist and no jewelry – intercepted half a dozen polite questions and translated their answer, Nakano seemed to fade into the background, answering any and all questions with a few brief and always complimentary responses, but initiating no conversations. Ms. Sheppard, holding an unsipped glass of champagne throughout the evening, never left his side, although she entered several conversations on her own.

Johnson and Jensen scanned the audience like automatons at Disneyland.

At one point in the evening, Christopher Detweiler untangled himself from a three-way conversation and nudged Lee's shoulder. "Nakano's not what you'd expect from a man with ad hoc ambassadorial status, eh, Lee?"

Lee sipped his seltzer and studied the wizened man, who stood perfectly still on the far side of the room, smiling gently. "I know what you mean. He seems almost totally apolitical. But I guess I'm comparing him to Western business leaders, who always use these occasions as perfect forums for that fine but oft' neglected art of sucking up to potential clients."

41

Detweiler's left eyebrow arched and a quick grin flashed across his square face. "Never one for mincing words, are you?"

"Nope. I have a pretty good understanding of the physics of businesses." Lee rubbed his fingers and thumb together in the international symbol of money.

Detweiler squeezed Lee's shoulders in a powerful embrace. "Lee, I'm about to embark on a business venture that will help deflate the American trade deficit. U.S./Japanese relations will improve if my program is successful and more forestry workers will have jobs and Astor College will gain international acumen and all good things will come to all good people. But the bottom line—" Detweiler clinked his glass against Lee's and whispered conspiratorially – "is that I'm gonna get me a wad of dough, brother!"

Lee clinked his glass in return. "To Christopher Detweiler, winner of the 1990 Albert Schweitzer Award for altruism at all costs."

"Hallelujah." Detweiler drifted away and entered another polite conversation.

Meanwhile, Harry finished one glass of very fine scotch and retrieved another from the barman, along with a white wine for Kate. He had had only three drinks that night but he already felt a slight buzz. This was better hooch than his metabolism was used to.

On his way back through the crowd he noticed the tall union leader, Neil Keiter, holding an intense conversation with the elderly Japanese man whom Kate had earlier identifed as Takeshi Nakano. A very pretty young woman was translating for Keiter. Harry (ever the romantic) thought he noted a trace of more-than-professional interest in her eyes. Keiter cut a fine figure, after all.

Harry also noted the drunk he had seen in the bar earlier, this time engaged in a too-loud and ribald story with several Astor administrators. Harry handed the long-stemmed wine glass to Kate and gestured toward the overweight man. "D'you know him?"

Kate was adept at the arcane science of cocktail parties and her glance was a study in unobstrusiveness. "Yes, his name is

Noraine. He owns a string of lumber mills and a great deal of timber land, I understand. That security fellow from Washington pointed him out earlier."

Harry sipped his drink. "Security fellow? Which branch?"

Kate smiled at Harry, eyes suddenly twinkling. "Oh, yes. I'm always forgetting that you used to be C.I.—"

"A long time ago, in a galaxy far, far away," Harry cut in, the color in his gaunt cheeks draining a bit. Kate lied: she *never* forgot that Harry had served with the CIA and was liaison to the National Security Council, during the Kennedy and Johnson years, just as she never managed to associate the peacenik, ultra-liberal professor she knew with The Agency. But she sometimes forgot how little he liked to talk about that era.

"Anyway, I think he said he was with the State Department," Kate replied. She tried to remember McMurdo's name and couldn't.

Harry nodded. "'State' makes sense. Mr. Nakano has ambassadorial status, I'm told. Did you notice the twin pillars of salt flanking him? I believe the goverment buys those steely, gun-fighters' eyes wholesale for all operatives. So, do the negotiations begin tomorrow?"

Kate shook her head, her hair swaying in a gentle fan on either side of her face, the silver complimenting the black. The gold lamé blouse shimmered with her every move. "As I understand it, Lee and the timber bigwigs are going to give Nakano a brief tour of the city – probably the Washington Park Zoo or the Japanese Gardens, I assume. Lee had some notion of taking the Japanese delegation down to that . . . um, that market under the Burnside Bridge. You know the one?"

"Saturday Market?"

"Right, whatever that is."

Harry paused in mid-sip. "You've never been to Saturday Market?"

Kate blanched. "No, I haven't. It's supposed to be very counter-culture and oh so Bohemian, as I understand it. Not my style, Harry."

"Nonsense!" Harry replied a bit too loud and several heads turned. "D'you know what your problem is, Fairbain?"

43

"No, but I'm sure you'll tell me," she replied, hackles at the ready.

"You are a bookworm. And a workhorse."

"You turn a girl's head."

"I'm serious! You're the classic over-achiever. Kate, dearest Kate, please be ready around ten tomorrow morning." His voice had taken on an unusually concrete tone of finality.

"What?"

"Wear blue jeans and tennis shoes, please. You can borrow them from somebody who has fun – surely you know someone who has fun."

"I've got a ton of research to do tomorrow, Henry Bishop. I am not walking through any open-air market and rubbing elbows with the great unwashed. Understood?"

"We'll see."

Before Kate could snap back, President Eckersley used his innate ability to find the focal vector point of any room and placed himself where everyone could see him. He rapped his champagne glass with an hors d'oeuvre fork and all eyes turned in his direction. The string quartet stopped playing and the murmur of conversation died away. Standing to his right were Detweiler and Takeshi Nakano, with Kimiko Sheppard and the Secret Service handlers behind them. Daniel Tadson McMurdo sidled into the room, unseen by most everyone.

As the rumble of conversation began to die down, Lee produced a hand-held tape recorder with mini-cassettes, thumbing the dial to maximum volume pick-up.

Neil Keiter squeezed past Harry and touched Lee on the shoulder. "You're Dean Connar, right? Neil Keiter, ITEU."

Lee smiled at the man and nodded.

"A word to the wise," Keiter spoke softly so only Lee, Harry and a handful of others could hear him. "Ditch the recorder."

"Why?"

"Look at it, friend. It's a Sony. Sony is the numero uno competition for Nakano's people, The Kuroshio Group. Trust me, he won't be thrilled to see that."

Lee exhaled and slipped the recorder back into his pocket. He gripped Keiter on the shoulder and squeezed. "Thank you, sir. Thank you, sir. That kind of political blunder we don't need."

"My dear and good friends," Eckersley began, his natural orator's voice carrying throughout the room. "We welcome you all today to this most momentous kicking off point in an effort to establish – nay, re-establish and enhance – in a growing manner, that valued and important relationship the United States of America enjoys with its historic ally, Japan. Truly, our countries are like two peas in a pod, society-wise, in terms of capitalism and a hunger, or perhaps thirst, for world peace, which our friends across the Pacific share with us, as well you all know. But it is not a matter of war or peace or even conflict of a peaceful yet warlike manner which brings us forth today, but rather, indeed, a matter of economic maturity and entrepreneurial endeavors which, if successful, and we all, I feel certain, are certain of its success, will enhance the economies of both these great nations as well as the people of each country and the businesses therein, which, of course, are owned and operated by those self-same people, if not by the governments themselves, in some instances. Yes, this ship of commerce which we launch tonight will set sail for both profits and improved international relations for all men and women, especially those who like wooden things – and don't we all? – which our natural resources have bequeathed unto us. With that, allow me to introduce our esteemed representative from the government and business world of Japan, Mr. Ambassador Takeshi Nakano."

Harry and Kate dove toward the hors d'oeuvre table to muffle their snickering. Kimiko Sheppard had struggled valiantly to translate the blizzard of words for the first few seconds before giving in and staring, awestricken, at L. Charles "Chuck." Nakano, luckily shielded by his lack of understanding, stepped forward and smiled when the people began applauding, turning in a semi-circle and gracing the local trade and education representatives with a series of short bows. His eyes all but disappeared when he smiled and fault lines fractured outward from his eyes across the leathery skin of his temples.

Sheppard stepped forward as well, though still a half-step behind her employer. Nakano spoke in soft, undulating tones which the crowd could barely hear, his eyes circling the room, the smile omnipresent. Sheppard spoke with the crisp, well-articulated voice of one trained for the opera.

"Thank you, everyone," she sang out. "It is a great honor to be in your country. I will now do you the honor of not making a long speech." The laughter was obligatory. "As many of you know, I am president of The Kuroshio Group Limited, named for the Kuroshio Ocean Current which flows from the Philippine Sea to the North Pacific. Just as – soon, we believe – more timber goods will flow from Oregon ports to Japan and back again.

"Let me add that my country has a great desire to develop even stronger business ties with America and a great need to be considered an active, vital partner in Pacific Rim trade and international relations. If our countries can, indeed, reach "economic maturity" by aiding each other in this quest, then our actions will benefit everyone. That would be a noble endeavor. Again, thank you for your warmth and hospitality."

The crowd applauded and Nakano bowed his head an inch or two. Sheppard stepped back. Johnson and Jensen canvassed the room with their eyes.

Christopher Detweiler now took center stage, hoisting his glass and panning the crowd. "Folks, many of you, like me, are just businessmen. So when I invited you here, you figured there'd be a quick buck to be made." This laughter was less obligatory. Sheppard spoke softly to Mr. Nakano, translating steadily. The old man didn't laugh.

"But others in the room are educators from John Jacob Astor College, and it's to them that I offer this toast: May the negotiations we undertake this weekend bear the fruit of education and international understanding as well as profit." Glasses were raised and clinked around the room. Detweiler flashed one of those all-encompassing grins. "I've spoken to representatives of the Japanese importing infrastructure and they assure me that our esteemed Mr. Nakano has the authority to okay whatever deal we strike. This means the market for Northwest timber will expand at least three-fold this year, with more increases expected. It also means the Port of Portland and the Port of Seattle will receive the lion's share of the new importing and exporting business. And, thanks to a discussion I've had with my good friend Charles Eckersley, here, I also can announce tentative plans that will make Astor the focal point of this project."

Kate nudged Lee, her eyebrows raised. He replied with a barely perceptible shrug.

"If all goes according to plan – and those of you who know me know my plans *always* go accordingly – beginning this fall, Astor will participate in an exchange of both students and faculty with Japanese colleges. Within three years we hope to have a permanent undergraduate program exchange, with up to one hundred American students spending an *entire year* in Japan and their Japanese counterparts spending a year here. Faculty also will be exchanged for one-and two-semester durations. This will be the most wide-ranging educational consortium agreement in Oregon history."

There was a round of applause. Lee Connar's jaw dropped open. Kate and Harry exchanged glances. "That's amazing!" someone gushed.

"That's ridiculous," Lee replied under his breath. Kate leaned close and whispered, "Lee? Do you know about this?"

"No!" he spat back, trying to whisper. "Kate, this would devastate every other international exchange program Astor has! There's no way we could authorize that kind of wide-ranging agreement! What is he, nuts?"

By that point, L. Charles "Chuck" Eckersley and Christopher Detweiler found themselves in a circle of well-wishers, laughing and explaining details of the inchoate agreement.

Lee wedged his way through the crowd, Harry in his wake out of morbid curiosity. Lee shouldered past Sheppard and Nakano, and tapped Detweiler on the shoulder. The stocky man turned and winked. "Pretty good stuff, huh?"

"Chris," Lee spoke softly, his teeth set. "We've got to discuss this. Astor is in no shape to agree to such a program. We've already got recip. programs with fifteen other countries and they stretch our finances and faculty to the limits. Come on, let's step over in the corner so I can explain this to you."

Detweiler didn't move an inch, his grin never wavering.

"Christopher?" Lee tried again.

Detweiler bent his head low by Lee's ear and hissed. "Listen to me, Lee old boy. This is a done deal, see? This *is*. Forget about what you've done before or hoped to do soon. *This* is what Astor *will* do. Got it, friend?"

The dean stepped back a pace, his face ashen. Christopher reached over and straightened Lee's tie. "Don't you cross me, buddy," he said through the omnipresent grin. "Don't you do it. Fair warning."

CHAPTER ELEVEN

The party broke up soon afterward. The business types patted each other on the back and savored the good booze. The Astor administrators looked at each other with a mixture of excitement and fear in their eyes. They all knew that such a project as the one proposed by Christopher Detweiler could solidify John Jacob Astor's reputation across the country, but that it also would mean a phenomenal drain on the college's faculty and financial resources. The risk was great but the possible pay-off was beyond description.

Harry was surprised to find Lee Connar standing by the food table, gulping a Calistoga seltzer. Harry had figured Lee would be opposed to jumping head-long into such a project and would fight it all the way. But there he was, whispering to his wife and avoiding eye contact with everyone else.

"In theory, this could be great for the college," Kate Fairbain tried to put the best face on Detweiler's proposal, but she wasn't even convincing herself, let alone Harry. "After all, the Pacific Rim is where it's all at."

"Questionable at best," Harry muttered. "I just hope Lee can get a hold of the trustees and the other administrators before anything is written down and signed. Surely he realizes the folly of this thing."

Kate retrieved her jacket and bade good night to several people. As they left the beautiful meeting room, she stifled a yawn. "God, I'm tired, Harry. I'd buy you a nightcap but I don't think I'm up to it."

"Never mind," he replied (surprising Kate enormously). "After all, we'll want to be refreshed and ready to go at ten tomorrow."

Kate began to argue with him but discovered she couldn't find the energy for it. Instead, she slipped her hand into the crook of Harry's arm and let him escort her to the bank of elevators.

Harry's soul soared.

They talked about the surprise announcement all the way down to the lobby and out onto the street. The protestors had called it a night. The downtown street traffic was as heavy as always but the sidewalk traffic of business people and shoppers had been replaced by loud, tough-looking young people. Little old Portland had come of age and the streets at night were not particularly safe.

That morning's monstrous thunderstorm was now somewhere near Idaho and the stars were shining over Portland. The night was warm and Kate carried her jacket over one arm, her other still linked with Harry's.

When she had tipped the parking lot attendant, Harry leaned forward and kissed her. Much to his surprise, she kissed him back. "It was a lovely evening. Thank you," Kate said.

"Ah. Foof. Um. Yes," Harry replied. He hadn't stammered after a kiss since about 1952. It made him feel like a moron, but it also made Kate smile and blush a bit. She hadn't made anyone stammer with a kiss since about that same era. "Get in, I'll drive you home."

Harry held the driver's door open for her. "Can't. I'm worried about Lee. His reaction to Detweiler's plan was . . . wrong, somehow. I'd like to have a word with him."

Kate was too exhausted to argue. "You're sure? All right. I'll see you on Monday."

"That's true," Harry said as she climbed behind the steering wheel. "You also shall see me tomorrow, at ten a.m. sharp."

"Harry, really, I can't."

"Right. See you tomorrow."

"Harry!"

He depressed the locking mechanism then closed the door and waved at her through the window.

Kate put the Saab in gear and pulled away into the night. Harry sighed and smiled and then grinned and decided that there was, indeed, a supreme being who was benevolent and in a charitable mood. Yes indeed.

The cat call snapped him out of his reverie. Harry didn't think he liked the implication in the two whistled notes – especially the prolonged down-beat note. He turned back into the cavernous opening of the parking structure and scowled.

"You can believe me, boyo, that's a fine figure of a woman."

Harry stood for a moment, blinking, suddenly feeling dim and light headed. Alfred Hitchcock used to do a cinematographic trick in which the camera operator zoomed in tight onto a character's face while physically pulling the camera away. The person in the foreground remained in focus and unmoving while the background appeared to fall away, as if sucked into some monstrous black hole.

Harry saw that happen all around him now.

The man stepped closer, his hands jammed into his pockets, a wide and wicked grin spread across his ruddy face. Harry blinked again as if to clear his vision.

"As I live and breath," the man winked. "If it isn't Harry himself Bishop, the Mad Hatter."

Harry spoke but the word came out as a coarse whisper, jagged and corroded by memories. "Taddy?"

Daniel Tadson McMurdo waggled his eyebrows and clicked his tongue against his teeth. "Give us a hug, then."

Harry took two tentative steps backward, his hands bunched into fists at his side. His heart beat in staccato, without rhythm. He turned and rushed out of the parking garage, his vision sizzling around the periphery of his eyes.

(Dodge chatted to a few people, pretending to enjoy the stupid party as it was breaking up. Something had queered the night – it was obvious from the strained joviality and hushed but vigorous whispering all around the room. Yeah, something had set everyone off, all right. What? Hard to say. Probably it was nothing to worry about.)

(That thought made Dodge smirk. Yeah. Right. And since when did anyone get rich by ignoring the angles? *Probably* the tension in the air didn't affect the Plan, but *possibly* it did and that *possibly* was way, way too much of a risk to take. After all, we're talking murder here.)

CHAPTER TWELVE

The high pressure bubble which had chased off Friday's monumental storm hovered over the western half of Oregon and Washington, and Saturday dawned bright and beautiful. From Kate's new River Place condo on the Willamette River, she could stand on her balcony and watched the sun rise over Mount Hood, a plume of snow climbing like a volcanic steam vent off its western face, its perennial snow tinted pink in the morning air.

Upon waking that morning, Kate exercised, showered, then made a quick run to the grocery store. Back at the apartment, she unfolded the antique mahogany writing desk, lowering the writing surface to its horizontal position, and quickly wrote three letters to family members, then addressed envelopes, adhered stamps and set the letters by the wrought iron stand next to the door.

She cleaned the apartment thoroughly, ground the next week's worth of decaf coffee beans and finally turned on the television and rewound the tape she'd made the night before of *Wall Street Week*. She kept a powder-blue legal pad on her lap and made notes while Louis Rukeyser quizzed his guests.

When she answered the door at ten, Harry beamed at her, his eyes puffy, a yawn contorting his features. "Ah, Kate. Good, you're up already."

Kate said Saturday Market was within walking distance and Harry pointed out that it was at least *ten blocks!* Rolling

53

her eyes heavenward Kate climbed into Harry's much abused Datsun B-210 and let him drive along Front Street toward the megalithic Burnside Bridge and the huge White Stag neon sign, twin harbingers which dominate the Old Town district.

The trip took them almost an hour, since they soon ran into cordons and a twenty-minute wave of joggers, most dressed in shorts and sneakers but some wearing such unusual running attire as hoop skirts, clown outfits and Spider-man costumes. "It's part of the Rose Festival," Kate explained. "A fun run."

"Make up your mind, *Katarina*. Are they running or having fun?"

The wave finally passed and police pulled back the cordons. Harry rolled around the historic Old Town district until Kate spotted a parking space. From there, it was a simple matter of walking past Portland's burgeoning homeless – many of whom are scary looking but few of whom are dangerous – until they arrived at the sprawled Saturday Market.

The market was a twentieth century version of a Renaissance fair, With brightly colored tents set up in parking lots and rows and rows of produce and hand-made goods stacked beside abandoned warehouses, chic, gentrified restaurants, crusty old bar rooms, and, for those who know where to look, brothels.

Like Kate, Harry had worn comfortable sneakers, which were mandatory since the Market was knotted and bunched, with tables of ceramics jutting one way and snarled cul-de-sacs of woven goods curling another way, like the contours of a human brain. The Market took up only about six square blocks but touring it thoroughly meant covering a great deal more space.

They strolled past dozens of flower merchants and a few glass blowers, browsed over basket weavers and rug makers, racks of tie-dyed skirts and hand-knit shawls, home-made myrtle wood wind chimes and wooden toys, wind socks and banners, clay pots and instant-portrait caricature artists, potpourri incense burners and proud displays of rock and mineral collections.

One row of tables had been set up for the liberal agenda and Harry accepted pamphlets from NARAL, Cascade AIDS Project, Physicians for Social Responsibility and the American

Socialist Party. Kate accepted a pamphlet from the Aryan Nations neo-Nazi movement, just so she could take the opportunity to flay the pamphleteer with five minutes of invectives and insults, while a crowd gathered to watch. As she summed up her withering tirade, the impromptu audience applauded.

Real conservatives loath the New Right, Harry noted.

Street musicians stood at every intersection – fiddlers, guitarists, dancers, singers, one-man bands, dulcimer players and mandolin players. Most kept hats or boxes or violin cases at their feet and patrons threw them coins or dollar bills.

Next came the food, and the aroma drove them both over the edge. Carts had been set up with steam rising from them all. Proprietors hawked genuine, spicy Thai dishes along with authentic Pakistani, Mexican, German, Korean, East Indian, Native American and Greek foodstuffs. Harry bought them an elephant's ear, a flat, warm piece of fried dough like an over-sized pancake, covered in butter and cinnamon. Harry held the floppy thing in two hands, paper napkins absorbing the extra oil, while Kate tore off a bite-sized strip for herself and then one for Harry.

Mostly they ogled the fine art pieces and intricate, hand-made items, many reawakening near-dead and ancient crafts.

Throughout the morning, Harry kept glancing over his shoulder and jerking abruptly whenever anyone shouldered past them. Kate noticed it, but had become used to his multitude of idiosyncrasies.

Sometime around noon, Kate realized they were holding hands. She didn't know who instigated it or how long it had been going on, but she didn't stop it, either.

(Back at the Hotel Trafalgar, Dodge waited until the corridor was empty then knelt beside the door of Room 1314, carefully jimmying the lock. It gave easily. So much for hotel security.)

(Dodge slipped into the room – knowing everyone else was on their way south to that Wilsonville tree farm – and pulled the power tool out from the gym bag, along with a pillow to muffle the noise. There was time enough to do it right. A really good murder isn't something you do lightly, after all. A thing like that takes planning, consideration, timing. Only an idiot depends on luck or brute strength.)

(Dodge was no idiot.)

CHAPTER THIRTEEN

Harry dropped Kate off at her condo and watched her carry the loot upstairs – a macramé plant hanger for her sister, a small stained glass tableau for an up-coming wedding shower, and a toy train, hand-carved from myrtle wood, for Kate's own book case.

Harry hurried to his Sellwood home as fast as the old Datsun would take him, checked the empty mail box, quickly fed the cat, then showered and changed into a gray suit and gray tie. Kate had agreed to take him to the tree farm, where the Americans were showing off modern reforestation programs to their Japanese counterpart. Harry remembered the odd look Kate had given him when he asked to come along. "Since when did you care about reforestation?"

"Since now," Harry had lied.

So why indeed he now asked himself. Because he wanted to talk to Lee Connar about this proposed, massive exchange of students and faculty with Japanese colleges. Such a program could be highly advantageous for any school and Astor wouldn't be harmed by a bit of good publicity in the States and broadened ties with Japan. But such a program would decimate the budgets of many departments, including his own beloved poli. sci. and Kate's econ.

But as he tied his tie, realized it was five inches too short and untied it, Harry admitted to himself that this was not the main reason he wanted to attend the symposium party at the tree farm.

His tertiary purpose was the future of John Jacob Astor College.

His secondary purpose was to spend more time with Kate Fairbain.

His primary purpose was to see if yesterday's unexpected encounter with a ghost was a coincidence or somehow tied into the symposium. Harry prayed for a coincidence.

This time they took Kate's car and, once on the highway, she cranked up the Saab and let it loose, swinging the low-slung Saab from lane to lane. Harry hung on for dear life.

"How's your Summer Sampler?" she asked as they blasted past Lake Oswego and Tigard, heading south toward Salem on 1–5.

Harry groaned and explained – as well as he could – about the mess-up with his class. Before he was done, Kate was laughing so hard she had to daub at her eyes with a Kleenex. "Oh God, Harry. That's wonderful."

"Anyway, we'll get it sorted out on Monday," he replied.

"I mean, I just can't see *you* coaching a basketball camp. Of all people."

Harry bristled a bit. "Why 'of all people'?"

"Oh come on!" Kate burst out in another gale of laughter, driving one handed and fifteen miles over the speed limit. The Saab's engine purred. "No one on Earth knows less about sports than you do, Harry! Really, this is the funniest story I've heard all month."

They drove for a few miles without speaking. "I s'pose you're right," Harry said after a while. "I'm not the typical American male with a penchant for football and baseball and what have you. Of course, I'm not totally knowledgeless about basketball. I have watched the sport."

Kate guffawed and rubbed her eyes again. The Saab jerked erratically as she laughed.

"Really, Kate! God knows I don't want to have anything to do with Summer Sampler, and I loathe to think who's got my real class, and I will get it all put a'right on Monday. Still, it's not so funny as all that. I mean, I'm certainly no one's first choice for a basketball manager—"

"Coach."

"—coach. But neither am I *completely* incapable."

"No, no," Kate struggled to get a hold of herself. "Of course not, Harry. I didn't mean . . . that is . . . " Peels of laughter broke out again.

They rode the rest of the way in silence. Harry truly had no intentions of ever coaching any sport and he had no delusions about his own lack of knowledge when it came to basketball. He tried to remember how many men played on each side and thought that it was something like five, although an uneven number seemed unlikely. Still, he found himself wishing Kate hadn't enjoyed the story quite so much.

Kate kept the speedometer at seventy until they reached the second Wilsonville exit, then down-shifted and swung off the highway toward Lower Boones Ferry Road, tooling around the southern edge of the town that was metamorphosing from rural to suburban as Portland's urban sprawl oozed southward. Lee Connar had given her directions to Detweiler Farms, which – being Kate – she had memorized. The Saab ate up the miles and they soon found themselves taking a sharp left off the macadam road onto a private drive. They passed through a wide gate that separated two very high, aluminum fences. A curved, wooden sign over the road identified the area beyond as Detweiler Farms Timber Land.

Harry and Kate glanced at each other. About thirty protestors huddled outside the property, waving signs and yelling at them as they passed through. The signs were painted with slogans such as *Save Oregon's future* and *Preserve the Old Growth Timber*. A young couple seemed to be in charge, Harry noted. It was the same couple who had confronted Kate the night before.

A jeep stood on the other side of the fence, complete with two men toting shotguns. For some reason, they didn't challenge Kate. Maybe, Harry thought, conservationists don't drive Saabs.

Beyond the high fence and the protesters was a newly blacktopped driveway that curved to the right. On the left was a steep cliff, overlooking a series of out-buildings and a service road thirty feet below and spaced along the banks of the Willamette River. On their right was a copse of fir trees, primarily Douglas and noble. This was no forest, Harry noted. The trees were all of about the same height and all spaced evenly apart. They looked like thousands of giant chess pieces set off in rank and file.

Kate followed the curved blacktop into a gravel parking lot. More than two dozen pick-ups and vans were there, and Harry guessed they belonged to the farm hands. One corner of the lot was dedicated to city vehicles: sedans and sports cars, along with one stretch limousine for the visiting delegate. A freshly washed and waxed mini-van with *Detweiler Timber* emblazoned on the side was parked next to the limo. That was Detweiler's personal vehicle, Harry guessed.

Kate parked with the city folks and climbed out, smoothing her long, suede skirt and adjusting her matching Eisenhower jacket.

They started off down an even, level path of small stones. Harry had never been much of an outdoors person. He rather despised hunting, fishing, camping and that sort of activity which, modern times being what they are, he found totally unnecessary. If a person could afford a roof and a warm meal, why on Earth would they want to sleep under the stars, he often wondered. Still, there was something so utterly unnatural about being on a tree farm that Harry actually longed for something – anything – to be out of place. A branch here, a dead log there, anything would do.

But no. The Detweiler Farms acreage was only pretending to be the woods. The land here was controlled, corralled, absolutely tamed. It reminded Harry of a television show shot on a sound stage, with the floors of "caves" and "forests" perfectly flat and each actor properly lighted.

They found the symposium party easily since there was no unruly undergrowth to block sound or sight. The group stood in a perfectly round clearing dominated by massive picnic tables under a wide, wooden roof supported by broad beams. The tables were rough-hewn, but self-consciously rough-hewn, Harry thought.

About half a dozen administrators from the college were present, outnumbered two to one by people Harry recognized from Friday night's banquet. The heavy-set man in dude ranch apparel – L.C. Noraine, Kate had identified him – stood beside Mr. Nakano and his translator, grinning ear to ear and wearing a cowboy hat that showed not the slightest bit of wear, dust or sweat stain. Neil Keiter of the International Timber Employees Union was present and occupied in deep whispers with some of the business types. He looked absolutely right in demin jacket and jeans, as he had looked absolutely right in the double breasted suit on Friday.

Harry looked around for Lee Connar. He eventually located the dean of faculty up front by the Japanese representatives. Makes sense, Harry thought, since poor Lee had been saddled with running the symposium, or – as L. Charles "Chuck" Eckersley had put it – taking the point position on this inchoate but important roughed-out yet front-burnered project, logistically speaking.

Harry kept looking around, and suddenly felt his spine stiffen. His stomach muscles contracted the way they do before one throws up.

"*Shto eta?*" Kate whispered in Russian, touching him on the arm.

Harry turned to her and smiled. "Oh, nothing. My knee's just acting up a bit."

Across the clearing, Daniel Tadson McMurdo slouched nonchalantly against one of the beams. He winked at Harry and grinned.

Christopher Detweiler stood on a picnic table's bench, facing the crowd of about twenty. He was wearing a Levi jacket, jeans and a red plaid shirt today, open at the throat. Where L.C. Noraine's costume looked like Central Casting wardrobe, Detweiler looked perfectly at home on the tree farm.

A man in matching grubbies stood on the bench beside Detweiler and was explaining to the city-slickers the process by which trees are harvested in Oregon, along with the reforestation process run jointly by the U.S. Forest Service, the Bureau of Land Management and private entrepreneurs. According to the expert, more trees were growing in Oregon today than during the Lewis and Clark Expedition and this astounding plethora of forests actually had to be shaved back occasionally so as not to overpopulate some species.

Harry thought the argument carried the reliability of a love note left on a prostitute's pillow. Apparently he wasn't alone, judging by the protestors at the main gate.

The ranch hand/tour guide finished by outlining the forty-year plan for the tree farm and touching briefly on Oregon's burgeoning Christmas tree export trade. The businessmen and college administrators applauded as he stepped down and Detweiler waved to gain their attention.

"Ladies and gentlemen, that's just a brief description of the state of modern timberland management in America. As I said last night, we have the means and the know-how to provide timber for the rest of the world, and it's time this often-ignored cash crop is used properly."

Harry listened intently, actively ignoring McMurdo. His face felt hot and his heart was beating too quickly. He could hear the incessant buzz of whispered Japanese coming from the young female translator.

"And now," Detweiler waved one arm in the best Ringling Brothers style, "some of my boys will demonstrate for you all the state of the art in technology. There was a time when working with timber meant gigantic, metal monsters that tore up the earth and left gouges in the sides of the hills." Detweiler pulled a Radio Shack walkie-talkie out of his jeans' back pocket and said, "Let 'er rip."

An engine snorted behind the crowd and a small, yellow tractor pulled into the clearing. Two men hung on to the outside of the cab, wearing hard hats and heavy boots with steel toe caps. Goggles hung loosely around their necks. The driver maneuvered the tractor like an expert, dodging between the trees and entering the clearing, then turning on a dime to face the trees he had just weaved through.

The tractor was really just a glassed-in driver's cabin atop two massive wheels. The front of the vehicle was dominated by a jointed arm, much like a snow plow's. Instead of a curved shield for scooping up snow or dirt, this one held a yellow metal device shaped in a half circle. The teeth of a buzz saw, at least four feet in diameter, protracted from the mouth of the half-disk.

The two side-riders jumped off the tractor and moved apart, flanking one tree. Gears ground as the driver positioned the tractor and two thick legs descended in the rear, accompanied by the whine of hydraulics. When the legs were in place and the tractor fixed to the spot, the driver manipulated the arm, bringing the half-disk parallel with the ground. The evenly spaced yet jagged teeth glinted dully in the sunlight.

"Folks," Detweiller had produced a compact public address system from somewhere and was favoring the crowd with that *y'all come in and sit a spell* smile of his. "This is the Detweiller Mark-One Trax. It weighs slightly more than a good snow-blower, can maneuver into the tightest of corners and climb the steepest of hills, and won't devastate the landscape like those dinosaur-style timber machines of old. Okay, Phil, give the folks a look-see."

The teeth of the circular buzz saw suddenly blurred together as the machine popped to life with a high pitched whine that was much, much softer than everyone had anticipated. Reading their expressions, Detweiller lifted the electronic megaphone to his lips. "Sound baffles built right into the equipment to dampen the noise, folks."

Harry noticed the tree was adorned by a single red ribbon on a branch about six feet off the ground. That's how the men knew which one to cut, he assumed. The operator manipulated the control sticks in the cabin and the hydraulic arm extended, the saw suddenly biting into the tree. The spotters on either side slipped goggles over their eyes, although they stood well outside the volley of bark and wood chips.

This sound was much louder and several people in the crowd covered their ears. "That tree's at least thirty-five inches in diameter, folks, and Phil will zip through that sucker in less than—"

The whine stopped abruptly. The explosive *thwang!* of metal on metal reverberated around the clearing, followed by an eruption of wood and steel from the tree. The tractor snapped backward, one of the support legs buckling under the stress. The cabin's windshield suddenly spider-webbed.

The businessmen and college administrators stood, mouths agape. Harry grabbed Kate and fell to the ground behind a picnic table, taking the impact of the fall himself. He looked around madly and saw McMurdo align himself behind the wooden pillar he had been leaning against.

Christopher Detweiler scrambled over his picnic table as bits of shiny steel and rough bark arced through the air.

Takeshi Nakano was momentarily confused, his eyes darting around the clearing as the young translator groped for his hand and tried to pull him away. Lee Connar, L. Charles "Chuck" Eckersley and the other administrators scrambled out of the way. L.C. Noraine and Neil Keiter slammed into each other, each in an effort to find cover.

(Dodge swore aloud and scrambled over a stone and mortar barbecue pit.)

A thousand flat chunks of the disc saw fragmented in every direction like the Oriental throwing darts in bad kung fu films. Harry covered Kate's head with both his arms as shrapnel clattered on the ground beside them and embedded itself in the picnic table.

And just like that, the noise ceased. Birds chirped. Harry could vaguely make out a protest song coming from the main gate, about half a mile away.

Someone started crying. There was a shouted obscenity, followed by the low murmur that escapes any crowd as it comes out of the collective somnambulism of shock.

"Holy Mary Mother of God . . . " someone began chanting. Kate struggled out of Harry's grip and lifted herself to her hands and knees, straddling his prone body. "Are you all right?" she asked, her nose only inches from his.

"Yes," Harry replied. "You?"

"I'm okay. Do you know first aid?"

He shook his head as Kate climbed to her feet. "There're some buildings by the parking lot, Harry. Call nine-one-one, then find me a first aid kit."

CHAPTER FOURTEEN

The Clackamas County sheriff's deputies were quick and thorough. Detweiler Farms was cordoned off, a yellow strip of high-density ribbon strung across the blacktop driveway. The protestors were corralled in a Quonset hut used for housing the farm's heavy equipment, while a deputy took their names and statements. None of the environmentalists claimed to know what was going on.

One woman with stringy brown hair began haranguing the officers in charge, demanding to see a lawyer and shouting something about the ACLU. Harry, who sat on a barrel outside the Quonset hut, recognized her as the one who had confronted Kate.

Two LifeFlight helicopters had circled the picnic area a few moments earlier, eventually settling down in the parking lot. A fine film of dust from the birds' wash had settled on all the cars. All three of the farm hands in the tree-cutting demonstration had been seriously injured by flying debris. Two had been flown to Meridian Park Hospital in Tualatin. The Trax operator had been shipped to the crisis center at the Oregon Health Sciences University.

Most of the symposium people had suffered only minor wounds or were stable enough for the twenty minute ambulance ride or left to their own devices.

After calling nine-one-one, Harry had hurried back to help Kate, who had established a commendable triage area on the wooden picnic tables. Lee Connar and Neil Keiter, the union rep., were helping her tend to the wounded. Taddy McMurdo was nowhere to be seen.

Harry, who had served with the U.N. Peace-Keeping Forces in Korea, knew just enough first aid to stand by and give a hand with this tourniquet or cajole that screaming panicker. He had hurried over to the Trax tree-cutter – or what was left of it – and shook his head in amazement. Kate had used her leather jacket and the driver's shirt to stop most of the man's bleeding. He didn't know if the doctors would be able to save the driver's arm but guessed that Kate had improved their chances greatly.

Harry had done what he could, had gotten in the way a bit, and had hurried back to the main building, adjacent to the Quonset hut, in order to direct emergency personnel to the site. It was there, standing outside the wooden building beside the dilapidated Dads Root Beer sign and waving to the row of ambulances and fire department emergency vehicles, that he had blacked out.

Now, with the emergency passed, Harry sat on a barrel of liquid phenol, a plywood epoxy resin, and tried hard not to blink. A young intern shone a pen light in one eye then the other, clucking her tongue in a tone that could be good news, could be bad news.

"Well?" Lee Connar asked.

The intern slid the pen light into her breast pocket and held up one finger. "Follow, please," she snapped, letting her hand glide to the right. Harry turned his head the opposite direction. "Kidding," he assured her. "Thank you, ma'am, but I'm just fine."

"Is he?" Kate asked, peering over Lee's shoulder.

"Yes," the intern replied. "That's a nasty bump on the back of your head, mister. There's a gouge, so it bled a little, but it's not all that serious, I don't think. Now, I've disinfected it and dressed it, but I want you to go to Meridian Park or Tuality or Willamette Falls today. Right away. Tell them you'll need X-rays. Got it? For now, I don't think you'll need that stitched up."

Harry shrugged. "Suture self."

The intern sighed and walked away.

66

Lee hoisted himself up on an adjacent barrel. He held his head at a strange angle. Harry noticed the ear piece was missing from the dean's glasses.

"You gave us quite a fright," Lee said.

"Oh, Auntie Em, I was in the most wonderful place! You were there, and so were you, Auntie Kate."

Kate's adrenal rush was subsiding and she leaned both hands atop a barrel of acetone varnish, head hanging between her arms, chin to chest.

"You were magnificent," Harry said gently.

"Brava," Lee added.

Kate looked up and forced a smile. "Thanks. Harry, what in hell happened?"

Harry shifted his weight onto one buttock and dug a piece of iron out of his front trouser pocket. He handed it to Lee, who twisted it in his hand, looking at every facet.

"It's a railroad spike," Harry explained. "Or at least something similar to it. Some person or persons unknown slipped in here one night and drove it into that tree, canting it at an angle so that the chain saw would be sure to hit it. As soon as the blade made contact with the iron, and it became clear that the two objects had no intention of sharing the same space at the same time, then, as they say, all hell broke loose."

Lee handed back the bit of shrapnel. "Who'd do that?"

"Environmentalists," Kate replied. She rested both forearms atop the barrel, her torso parallel with the ground. "They've spiked trees in the old-growth timber areas before, to discourage loggers from cutting them down. It's environmental terrorism."

"Maybe," Harry interjected.

"You've got a better idea?" Kate cut in, shifting to Russian.

"One or two," he replied in kind.

"Don't play detective here, Harry. This isn't some dime novel."

"Excuse-way ee-may," Lee cut in. "English-way anguage-lay, lease-pay."

"Right. Sorry." Harry climbed gingerly off the barrel, feeling his head throb. Immediately following the explosion he hadn't

67

felt a thing – in fact, he had been invigorated. That was the shock, he told himself.

He carefully slid one arm into his ripped, dusty jacket, then the other. "We'd best get back to the city while we can. Have you looked to the west lately?"

Kate and Lee looked to the west. A bank of dark, roiling clouds were piling up over the Coast Range, looking low and fast. Classic summer thunder bumpers.

"Can you drive?" Harry asked, resting a hand on Kate's shoulder.

"Sure. I'm fine," She replied. She stood up straight and smiled at him, rubbing her hands together. They were sticky and greasy, and Kate looked at them carefully, studying the blood stains halfway to her elbow, the brown patches of dried blood between her fingers and under her nails. She remembered jamming her fist into the tractor driver's abdomen up to her wrist, stanching the blood flow.

A low, keening hum began to form in the back of her throat as the adrenal high abandoned her. Harry and Lee reached her simultaneously, just as the shakes set in.

CHAPTER FIFTEEN

The X-ray showed what Harry knew it would show – a wacking great lump on the back of his head. He was given a prescription for Tylenol 3 and sent on his way.

The low, kinetic cloud bank had circled Portland on three sides by the time he made it back to his Sellwood apartment. Niccolo took one look at the bedraggled human who walked into the apartment, then sniffed suspiciously and curled up in Harry's best chair. No matter what non-cat-owners may think, cats not only have little curiosity, they despise surprises.

Harry showered carefully, keeping the water pressure low so as not to enhance the already-throbbing head ache, then changed into his only other suit. Christopher Detweiler and L. Charles "Chuck" Eckersley had called an emergency meeting of the symposium parties for that evening at the Trafalgar. Harry had no real interest in the project – he found wood to be monumentally dull. But among his legion of bad habits was an interest in the macabre. He was convinced that today's fiasco had been more than just environmental terrorism. The buzz-saw blade didn't just disintegrate, the entire front end of the Detweiler Mark-One Trax exploded with it.

Harry took two Tylenol and gave Niccolo a scratch behind the ear. He poured a pile of Happy Cat onto a plate then opened a can of tuna fish and dribbled the fishy water over the kibbles. The cat cried at the lack of substance, pleading with Harry for just a small nibble of the fish. *Please sir . . . may I have some more?*

"Begging for more food is useless when you're so clearly tubby," Harry replied.

Niccolo staggered back, shocked by the accusation.

First stop was the political science faculty office on the Astor campus. Harry rapped on the door to the department head's office and received a curt "What? What? Yes, come in."

Harry opened the door and peaked into the office which was easily thrice as large as his own. Lyman Bledsoe Jr. sat behind the immaculate desk and peered through coke-bottle glasses at him. "Yes? Yes? Who? Henry! What are you doing here on a Saturday?"

Harry marveled. Lyman was making some calculations on a piece of paper. It was the only paper allowed on the spotless desk. "You used to pick up your toys after playing with them, didn't you?"

"What? Henry, what are you talking about? You're not supposed to be here on a Saturday. The department is only allowed to have faculty on campus for forty-five point five hours per week. Anything more than that is a violation of the faculty contract for tenured personnel. Good lord, Henry, are you trying to get me in trouble with the teachers' union?"

"Whoa. Cease and desist." Harry interjected, his headache beginning to return. "I needed to see you about that class mix up. Can we have it rectified by Monday?"

"*Monday!*" Lyman screeched. "Henry! Are you mad! The computers were down yesterday! Do you know what that means?"

"Armageddon? The second coming? The end of society as we know it? Sweeps Week? The contracting universe theory? The—"

"Henry! Talk sense!" The little man fairly quaked with intensity. Harry had a tendency to do that to Lyman. "I'll do what I can on Monday, Henry, but you must realize these things take time."

"Meanwhile, I'm to coach a basketball team? Lyman, dear, dear soul, does that make sense to you?"

Bledsoe sat back in his too-large chair, aghast. "I know you don't appreciate all my hard work, Henry. You've never appreciated the trials of this position. But I'll try to do what I can on Monday. It will be an incredibly busy day for me, what with the Faculty Senate meeting and all my other duties, but yes, I'll put that all aside to fix your problem." He sighed.

"Ah, gee," Harry replied. "You're the best mom on the block."

"There's also a last-minute administrators meeting set up for the lunch hour. We simply must have a communicable disease policy, what with you-know-what going around."

"What what?"

"HIV."

"Henry the Fourth?"

"No! HIV! AIDS! Henry, don't you ever pay attention?"

"I'm sorry. What was the question?" Harry waved and swung the door closed. Bledsoe piped up, "And another thing. That fellow from the Department of Interior was here asking about you. I hope you're not disrupting the president's symposium, Henry."

Harry peaked back into the room. "Interior?"

"Yes. McMurdo, or something like that. He showed me your note so I opened your office for him. In the future, please don't ask to let people into the offices after hours, Henry."

"Yes, dear." He closed the door gently.

(Dodge tapped the pen against the plastic tablecloth in a staccato beat, thinking about the explosion at Detweiler Farms and the reactions he had observed. Most folks had been concerned only with good old numero uno. That included most of the educational types and businessmen, who scrambled to cover their own butts. A handful had reacted slowly or illogically. There was considerable panic, and that was well worth keeping in mind.

(One or two people moved pretty well, though, and seemed to handle themselves well. Those are the ones you want to watch for, Dodge thought. They're the ones who can become X-factors. Flies in the ointment, whatever that meant.

(The waitress set down a cup of coffee and a sandwich with cole slaw and potato chips. Taking the paper napkin, Dodge jotted down two names: *Bishop* and *Fairbain*.)

On a whim, Harry dropped by the sports center. He wore his coat now, although the rain hadn't hit yet. He could feel the humidity rising with the barometric pressure and the arthritic throbbing in his knee eclipsed the lesser ache in his head.

Sure enough, once in the main hallway he could hear the rapid-fire screeching of rubber-soled shoes and that tell-tale thump of leather against wooden floor boards.

He peeked in and found fully half of "his" class taking advantage of the summer session's liberal open-facilities rule. A rough and catch-as-catch-can game was ensuing, with elbows swinging and muffled, out-of-breath expletives flying. Harry counted six players, including tow-headed Wes Kiley from Texas.

One lanky young man put up a twisting jump shot (and a wing and a prayer, it seemed) which miraculously bounced in. Much to Harry's chagrin, that same player got the ball again. When an opponent stole it away, Harry shifted position to watch them hurl downcourt. They did no such thing, choosing instead to shoot at the same basket.

Which, of course, confused Harry to no end.

"Hold it, hold it," one of the young men held up an arm, then plopped down on the floor and began retying his shoelace. Wes Kiley laid down the ball then sat on it, breathing hard. He was the first one to notice the professor standing by the double doors. Wes waved ruefully and Harry advanced all the way in.

"Going well?" Harry asked, then wondered what the hell that question meant.

"Yessir," Wes replied. "Just playing a little three-on-three."

"Yes, I've been watching you. The rules aren't . . . exactly as I remembered them."

Some of the boys snickered. Wes nodded. "It's called half-court, make-it-take-it and call-your-own-fouls. Also known as street ball or Brooklyn rules or a whole lot of other names, depending on whereabouts you're from."

"Ah. Listen, men, once again allow me to apologize for the mix-up. I've just spoken to the chairman of my department and it seems unlikely anyone will do anything about our . . . mutual predicament until early next week. In the meantime, I'm without my class and you're without your coach."

"Yeah, and there's a four-way tourney on Wednesday, to introduce the summer sessions at a lot of schools," the tallest kid plopped down on his butt in the center of the painted key.

"Ah," Harry replied. "Most of you seem experienced. You probably don't even need a coach."

Wes and the others exchanged glances. "That's real nice of you, professor," one replied, "but we don't get any team work. Keith and me are from Oregon but the others are from all over. We got some height and some speed. We could of been the team to beat at this tourney."

Harry's heart sank. *This is not your problem*, he reminded himself, using the exact same tone of mental-voice he had used before adopting half a dozen cats and offering dinner to a plethora of winos over the past few decades. *This really is not your problem.*

"Gentlemen, have any of you made plans for Monday morning?" They all shook their heads. "Then I have a brilliant idea that will solve everyone's problems," Harry lied.

CHAPTER SIXTEEN

Harry stopped at a gas station/convenience store to fill up the Datsun's tank and bought two packages of Hostess Ho-Ho's and a Styrofoam cup of coffee, with two packets of non-dairy creamer and two packets of imitation sugar. Mustn't go without lunch, he reminded himself.

He ate the Ho-Ho's and slurped the coffee as he fought the Macadam Avenue traffic into downtown Portland. Late morning on a Saturday, rush hour on a weekday, 3 a.m. Sunday morning – it never seemed to matter when he hit Macadam, the traffic was always bad.

The first fat rain drops splatted against the windshield soon after. Harry cranked up his window all the way. He felt tense and told himself it was the proton bombardment caused by the formation of ionized clouds; a precursor for lightning. Yeah, sure. That sounded plausible. He beat a tattoo on the steering wheel and gnawed on his thumbnail. An empty space opened up in the pit of his stomach.

Things were wrong, he told himself. Things were wrong.

Three blocks later he saw the aurora of blue and red lights erupting from the Park Blocks, opposite the Hotel Trafalgar.

Harry arrived before the ambulance, and only two police prowl cars had shown up. Uniformed officers kept the first few rubber-neckers away from the hotel, but more gawkers were hurrying their way.

A weird shape rested on the sidewalk that lined the park. It looked like a wrought iron sculpture some artist had left laying around. Harry glanced up and realized it was a railing from one of the Trafalgar's balconies.

Two police officers were kneeling in the street, around what obviously was a body. Harry couldn't tell who it was, but the limbs stuck out at odd, rag doll angles. One cop hauled a tarp over the body as the rain began to pick up in earnest.

In room 818, Maurine Pringle posted the Do Not Disturb sign on the door and yawned. She had come back early from the telemarking show at the Memorial Coliseum, thrilled to be away from the crowds of business men and women eager to catch a glimpse of everyone's latest line of products.

Pringle was a good department manager and preferred to stay in her building, back home in Tacoma, where she could run her people and their projects. But these trade shows were a necessary evil, she recognized.

Resignedly, Pringle slipped off the killer high heeled pumps, stepped into the bathroom and started drawing a nice, hot bath. The sudden change in weather depressed her a bit and she hoped to slide back into the Regency romance she was reading, forgetting about FAX machines and video phones for a few moments.

As the water ran, Pringle stretched the kinks out of her neck and shoulders and padded across the front room. She yanked on the window cord, drawing the curtains open.

The upside-down scarecrow grinned at her and Pringle staggered back, bile rising in her throat. Her mind blitzed out and her knees buckled.

The very dead body of Christopher Detweiler hung from the ninth-floor balcony above, swinging in the rain-sodden wind outside her room.

CHAPTER SEVENTEEN

Harry turned up his coat collar and jammed his golf cap firmly over his gray hair, watching the ambulances and extra police arrive. The dead body in the street had drawn quite a crowd before someone in the park screamed and pointed up.

The crowd began to gasp and mumble. Harry stepped out away from the building and followed their glances upward.

A second body dangled upside-down, hanging by one leg about eight or nine floors up. Harry couldn't tell who this one was, either. As he watched, a uniformed cop appeared on the balcony beside the dead man.

Cursing, Harry hurried out of the crowd and around the building to a side entrance. A burly, uniformed cop was guarding this entrance and warned him away.

Harry tried arguing but that got him nowhere. Resignedly, he stalked around to the front, where two more men were stationed. While he had been gawking at the site on Park Avenue, the police had mobilized.

Harry stepped up and quickly explained to one of the officers that he was the official Hotel Trafalgar rabbi, and there was no time to waste. The young cop tipped his cap and ushered Harry in, wondering how many rabbis had Scots accents.

There was a great commotion in the lobby and mezzanine-level bar. It appeared as if every hotel patron was mulling about and discussing the situation. There was a palpable air of excitement in the crowd, Harry thought morbidly. Extra, extra, read all about it.

76

He pushed his way to the elevator and punched the fourteenth floor button. There were three other people in the plush, mirror-lined box. "Did you see what happened?" he asked no one in particular.

"Someone fell off the roof," an elderly woman replied crisply, relishing the gossip.

"Hell, no," a younger man snapped. "I hear there's two of 'em."

"D'you know who it was?" Harry asked. The other three shook their heads.

There had to be hundreds of people in the Hotel Trafalgar that morning, he reminded himself. No reason on Earth why the person or persons involved had to be related to Astor or the symposium.

He was the last one off the elevator and hurried down the pastel-coloured corridor. Room 1405, two doors down from the Astor suite, was open. Harry grimaced and rapped on Room 1401's door. He heard mumbling on the other side. After a moment, Lee Connar answered, sighing deeply when he saw who was out there.

"Harry! Thank God. Have you heard?"

"Only vaguely. What happened? And where's Kate?" Harry stepped into Astor's hospitality room.

"Right here," Kate replied. She sat on the bed, telephone receiver against her ear, one hand cupped over the mouthpiece. From her body language, Harry guessed she was on hold.

"So what happened?" he demanded.

Lee took a long slug from a bottle of seltzer water before answering. His eyes were red and the hand holding the bottle was shaking. "The police just called from the lobby. There's been a hell of a tragedy, Harry. You know Christopher Detweiler? According to the police, he just fell from a balcony. He's dead."

Harry grabbed Lee's arm and squeezed. "Damn. Lee, old man, I'm truly sorry. Are you all right? I know you were close."

Lee waved absently, not noticing the seltzer water splash from the bottle neck. "My God, Harry. We were just talking, not forty-five minutes ago, in the bar. He was worried that today's explosion out at the farm would ruin the conference." Lee let out a laugh that was more like a bark, devoid of all mirth.

Harry threw one arm over the smaller man's shoulder, hugging him. "Sit down, man. You look all out." He glanced at Kate, who held a hand over one ear and spoke softly into the receiver. "Lee, there were two people involved."

Lee sat on the edge of the single bed and set the bottle by his feet. He rested elbows on knees and bent over, lacing his fingers behind his neck. "Yes. There was an ITEU rep. here," he spoke to the carpeting. "I can't even remember the guy's name. God, that's terrible."

"Keiter," Kate said, still blocking the receiver with her hand. "Neil Keiter, I think." She leaned across the bed and touched Lee's shoulder softly, then suddenly sat up straight. "Hello? Operator? This is the Astor College party in 1401, we're . . . involved in what's happening. Can you get us an outside line and hold it open? Excellent. Also, I'll need a typewriter. Great. Thank you so much."

"How'd it happen?" Harry asked.

Kate stood up and waved him toward the room's sliding glass door. She shoved it aside, letting in a gust of frigid air. They were on the leeward side of the building, protected from most of the rain. Kate stepped out onto the iron balcony, grabbing a hold of the railing and leaning over. Harry, who suffered from a mild bit of vertigo, stood a step back and leaned over tentatively.

He could see the crowd still gathering on the street. The twisted, metal sculpture lay crumpled on the far sidewalk. An ambulance was carting away the first body. Five floors below them, Kate and Harry could see cops and hotel employees mulling about on a balcony. The dangling body had been removed. One cop was taking notes, standing on a balcony one floor below them and about five feet over. As Harry looked more carefully, he could see the front-facing railing was missing.

"I spoke to the hotel manager," Kate said softly. "It looks like Detweiler and Keiter were standing on the balcony of his – Keiter's – room, when the railing gave out."

Harry took a quick step back away from the railing which Kate was leaning against. He pointed to the officer on the thirteenth floor. "Was that his room?"

"Yes, I think so," she replied with a grim smile. "It's ironic. Many hotels and office buildings won't designate a thirteenth floor."

"Damned unlucky."

They both hurried back inside. Lee was no longer on the bed. They found him bent over the bathroom sink, splashing cold water on his face, his black plastic, horn-rimmed glasses resting by his elbow.

Kate touched Harry's elbow and spoke softly. "When Detweiler was in the state Senate, Lee was his office manager and chief advisor. They've known each other forever."

"Have the police spoken to him yet?" Harry asked.

Kate frowned. "No. I don't really expect they will."

Harry turned to her, fatigue etched in his long, angular face. "After today's fun and excitement at the timber farm, d'you think the police will consider this an accident? And speaking of which, are you all right?"

Kate nodded absently. "Of course. Sorry for the outburst earlier. How's your head?"

"Much better, thanks."

Kate exhaled slowly, wearily. "Harry, you don't think the two things are connected, do you?"

Harry raised one eyebrow in response.

There was a knock at the door. Kate turned and answered it while Harry stepped gingerly back out onto the balcony. He could see down and to his right at the balcony with the missing railing. The wind shifted slightly and fat rain drops splattered against his coat.

"Harry," Kate brushed aside the diaphanous curtain. "That man from the State Department is here. He'd like to speak to you."

Harry's heart sank a few inches deeper into his lower intestinal tract. He re-entered the room and nodded gravely at McMurdo. Lee stepped out of the bathroom, still looking wan and unfocused.

"You're professor Henry Bishop?" Harry nodded in return. "Sir, my name's McMurdo. I wondered if I could speak to you a moment. In private."

"Certainly, sir," Harry replied, almost against his will. He nodded to Kate, who looked perplexed but knew better than to ask.

The two men stepped out into the hall and McMurdo closed the door firmly behind them. "And now for a wee nip," he nudged Harry with his elbow. "You're a whiskey drinker, if memory serves, Harry lad."

CHAPTER EIGHTEEN

Daniel Tadson McMurdo had a classically Irish face; lumpy and not at all bilateral. One eye seemed larger than the other and the nose, broken more than once, Harry remembered, was decidedly off center. His eyebrows were uneven and too bushy and his hairline had receded a bit. Harry noticed it held more silver than red these days.

McMurdo clicked his tongue and waggled his eyebrows at Harry. "What say? A quick pick-me-up?"

"I'll not drink with you," Harry replied, shocked to hear the rigidity of his own voice. He hadn't felt this bad, this out of balance, in many, many years. He tried to relax his muscles but they refused. He felt like he was wearing some one else's face and it didn't fit properly on his skull.

"Fine, then. There's an observation deck upstairs. Shall we?" McMurdo made a sweeping gesture toward the bank of elevators at the end of the hall. Harry stood ramrod stiff, unmoving. His heart finally ceded control of the muscles back to his brain. Harry started down the hall.

The shorter, somewhat pudgy man swept back his suit coat and stuck his forefingers and thumbs into the watch pockets of his button-down vest. McMurdo whistling a spritely tune. Harry felt faint.

The observation deck was on the thirty-first floor of the historic brick building. It had once been a penthouse apartment for very important people, but several years earlier had been transformed into a mini-bar and lounge, with glass walls and a glass ceiling, revealing, on nice days, a panoramic view of snow-encrusted Mount Hood, decapitated Mount St. Helens and the Washington mountains to the north.

This was not a nice day at all and they could only barely see the U.S. Bank Tower, three blocks away.

McMurdo gave a drawn-out cat call. "This is wicked weather you have here, Harry boy. Yes indeed."

Harry found a table hidden behind a rubber plant and sat down in the uncomfortable metal mesh chair. His bad knee and his head throbbed in unison. McMurdo appeared a moment later from the bar, a glass of sudsy draft beer in each hand. The Trafalgar provided thick glass steins with handles, so seldom seen today.

McMurdo set down both drinks and eased himself into the second chair. "You say you won't drink with an old friend, Harry boy, and that's just fine. Whiskey is a 'drink.' Beer is . . . the preferred beverage of negotiations. To your ever-lasting health." His voice was a bit high pitched and lyrical. The Irish accent was mostly real with a bit of affectation, Harry knew. McMurdo was born and raised in Boston.

Harry took a sip of the beer and grimaced. American. "McMurdo, wha—"

"Taddy!" McMurdo barked. "It's been Taddy and Harry for over two decades, boy. What's with this formality?"

Harry took a stronger pull from the stein. He loathed watery, American beers but suddenly needed the reinforcement. "It's a . . . surprise seeing you," he said.

"I've no doubt of that, Harry. Would'ja look at you? A college professor. Tenured, yet." McMurdo shook his head. "Ah, Harry, 'retirement' has been mighty good to you."

"Er. Yes. You told my friends downstairs that you were with the state department?"

"That I did." McMurdo drained almost a third of the beer in one gulp, then smacked his lips.

"You told my department head that you were with interior."

"Right again."

"Which is true?"

"Both. Or neither. Whichever is convenient at the time.

82

Harry, Harry. What's with the virginal act? You know the grand comedy. You know how it's staged."

Harry felt himself relax a bit, for the first time. "Then you're not retired."

"Me?" McMurdo laughed. "And just what pray tell would I do if I retired. God's blood, Harry. I'd be climbing the walls in a day and a half, and truer words were never spoken."

Harry sipped his beer and allowed himself to see the panoramic view of downtown Portland, with the tarpaper roofs and at least one heli-pad. McMurdo pulled a pipe and pouch out of his suit coat pocket and began loading the bowl with tobacco.

"We'd heard you were dead," Harry said at length.

"And so I was, but a little of that goes a long ways. We'd heard you were dead, too."

"Hmm. I'm going to loathe myself for asking this, but what do you want?"

"Short-or long-term?" McMurdo lighted a wooden match one-handed, scratching it against his thumb nail. Harry remembered a much younger Taddy McMurdo practicing the exact same affectation a thousand years earlier.

"Short term," Harry replied.

McMurdo concentrated on the pipe, puffing studiously until the tobacco glowed. The *No Smoking* sign hung directly over his head. "I want to see the United States achieve an important trade agreement with Japan."

"I see."

"This is very important stuff, Harry Bishop," the plump man continued, waving his pipe stem to make a point. "This deal must go through. That's the true word. I was sent out to this upholstered septic tank you call a city to see that everything went according to Hoyle."

Harry actually smiled, but the action took phenomenal control. "You don't like Portland?"

"It's lovely, boy. A fine little burgh. Like the Home Game Version of a real city. But back to Taddy's little problem. Y'understand, Harry, my job was to see that this little deal went through, that everyone concerned shook hands and signed on the dotted lines and went home happy. That was my task.

The simplest of things. When what should occur? Lo, there came unto the negotiations a jerry-rigged explosive, followed swiftly by that ever-popular standby, the broken railing. And now one of the prime movers of the deal has, and you should pardon the expression, hit the bricks, while a second man only slightly involved has taken the self-same plunge. Therein, encapsulated, as they say, is my problem."

McMurdo drained his glass and set it down with a bang. He leaned back in his chair and clamped his teeth over the pipe stem, appraising Harry carefully.

Harry kept his hands wrapped firmly around the stein handle so McMurdo could not see them shake.

"Where do I come in?"

McMurdo laughed, a gleeful, breathy laugh of genuine pleasure. "Harry! This is me! Your old Taddy! Don't be playing the absent minded professor with your old partner in crime. I've known the Mad Hatter, boyo. Don't forget that."

"That . . . person is no longer around," Harry replied quietly, his eyes watching condensation roll down his stein.

McMurdo leaned forward, his voice suddenly subdued. "Harry, old kit, the game's called 'Timber, Timber, Who's Got the Timber.' Some of the players have taken their bats and their balls and gone home, but that doesn't mean the game's over. There are still hands to be shaken and dotted lines to be scrawled atop. Are you with me?"

"No."

"Harry, I can still make a go of this brouhaha. It'll not be easy, but then you know old Taddy's gift of the gab. Still, what I need to make it all work is to hand the culprit over to the authorities, to show our erstwhile oriental friend that we're not all barbarians over here."

"Culprit? What do—"

"Harry, I need the person who murdered Detweiler and this Keiter fella. You've always been the A-number-one best man for that sort of detail, and it'll not surprise you to know we've been keeping up with your recent antics here in Portland. Harry, Takeshi Nakano and his entourage leaves by tomorrow or Monday at the latest. And before they do, you've got to figure

84

this business out for old Taddy."

Harry honestly thought he was in control. That's why he was so surprised to find himself leaning over the table, speaking through clenched teeth. "You listen to me, McMurdo. I'm not a detective and I'm not part of your world any longer. I'm a middle aged professor. I've got high blood pressure and too much cholesterol and a bad back and a bum knee. I don't sleep all that well and I haven't been 'regular' since Reagan's first inauguration. Now I'm asking you: Keep me out of this. Please!"

McMurdo just smiled a lopsided smile and wagged his head sadly. "Harry, Harry, Harry. In is in. You know that. All this blather about 'retirement' is just that. Blather. We need you, laddy. I need you. And truth be known, you don't really have any choice."

Harry sat back and rubbed his eyes, forcing his lungs to take in as much as air possible, hold it, then release. Again. "I don't want to have anything to do with this," he said at last.

"Harry, my son, the situation is this: I've got to have the trust of the Japanese, especially old man Nakano. And that means the government of the U.S. of A. has got to have a murderer – any murderer – behind bars. And fast. Now if you won't help, I'll just have to do it myself."

That feeling of vertigo was back. Harry gripped the table's edge and steeled himself. "I sense an implied threat."

"That's because you were always the bright one," McMurdo replied, sucking on the pipe. "Now this is just off the top of my head, mind you, but I'd say this Dean of Faculty fella, Lee Connar, would make a fine suspect."

Harry said nothing.

"From what little I know, Dean Connar has known Detweiler for a long time. And Connar certainly looked the worse for wear, just now. Yes, he'd be a fine suspect."

"Why would he kill Detweiler?" Harry wasn't even sure why he asked the question, since he knew the answer wouldn't mean anything.

"Well, let's see. Because . . . " McMurdo looked at the glass ceiling panes, his brow furrowed. "Because, Mrs. Connar –

there *is* a Mrs. Connar, I hope – was having an affair with Detweiler. How's that? Too hackneyed? Because Detweiler stole the notion for this whole symposium from the Dean and hogged all the credit. Because they were secretly homosexual lovers. Now *that's* got a ring to it. I'm just spit-balling, you understand."

Harry pressed his palms against the table and stood. He didn't know if his legs would support his mass and was a touch surprised when they did. "Where will you be?" he muttered.

"Room 718 of this fine establishment," McMurdo replied. "Won't you stay for another drink? It's your turn to buy."

Harry walked away from the table and caught the first elevator down to the ground floor. He walked out onto Broadway and around to the back, Park Blocks side. Harry stood for a while studied the yellow nylon ribbon that had been strung around the humanoid outline on the street and the twisted remains of the balcony railing, not consciously aware that the rain had stopped. He walked three times around the building, which took up an entire city block.

An hour later, Harry had a vague idea of what to do.

CHAPTER NINETEEN

Harry found a secluded phone booth in a nearby coffee house and dialed one of the few phone numbers he had memorized.

"Hello?"

"Martin? Harry here."

Harry could hear the obvious cheer in Martin Kady's voice. "Harry! How are you? What's up?"

"Martin, I'm in a bit of a jam," he replied. "It's imperative that I speak to Tucker. Straight away. His latest post card said he was in San Salvador. D'you have any idea how to contact him?"

"Well, I think so," Martin's voice came back hesitantly over the line. "It's not going to be easy. But I think it's just vaguely possible. Hold on a second, Harry."

Harry waited. He could still taste the weak after-flavor of the American beer and scrounged through in his pockets for some Tic Tacs.

"Hey, Harry?"

"Tucker!" Harry nearly dropped the phone. "Good God, man. Is that you?"

"Yeah. I just got in about an hour ago. Harry, the bastards kicked me out!" The younger man's voice was roiled in rage.

"The government kicked you out of El Salvador?"

"Hell no! My own goddammed newspaper kicked me out of El fucking Salvador! Pulled the whole team out, photographers and all. I'm gonna quit, Harry. I swear to God, I'm going to pack it in. Teach journalism at a community college somewhere.

Maybe finish that novel."

"You've started a novel?"

"Almost. Well, I meant to. One lousy note from the Right Wing Death Squads and the weasels fold their cards. God, I'm pissed! Anyway, I know this guy who does fake I.D.s. I'm going back to finish this story then—"

"No you're not," Harry heard Martin's voice in the background. The sound became muffled but he could make out a refrain of "Yes I am . . . No you're not . . . Yes I am . . . No you're not . . . ."

"Tucker? Tucker?" He tried to cut back in.

"What? Harry, can I call you ba—"

"There's been a double homicide downtown at the Trafalgar and I'm looking into it," Harry cut in quickly.

"What? Double homicide?"

"Yes. I've been . . . asked to look into it, Tucker, and I desperately need your help."

"No kidding? Hey Marty, things are looking up. Someone's been killed."

"Oh joy." Harry barely caught the muffled reply.

It was a few minutes past dusk when Tucker Nelligan found Harry seated at a booth in Hamburger Mary's, a downtown eatery famed for its bizarre collection of pre-War advertisements adorning the walls. Harry was hunched in a corner, his long legs sprawled beneath the table, a cup of coffee before him. He was concentrating on a much-abused paperback – He always kept one in his raincoat pocket.

"Knock, knock," Nelligan rapped a knuckle on the chipped formica table and slid into the booth opposite his old friend. Harry's haggard, angular face suddenly blossomed into a wide smile.

"Welcome home, sailor." Harry set down the novel and sat up straight.

The reporter suddenly flashed a grin across his handsome face and motioned toward the book. "You don't look like the type to enjoy William F. Buckley's fiction."

88

"Wasn't aware Buckley had ever written anything that wasn't fiction," Harry murmured.

Nelligan was famished and ordered the largest hamburger with fries available, with iced tea. He was dressed for the role of the Intrepid Reporter by way of Indiana Jones – baggy, khaki trousers, comfortable canvas tennis shoes, blue work shirt and a well-worn leather jacket that was devoid of all the ersatz military insignia which were so in fashion that season. The younger man's sandy hair was a little shaggier than usual – Nelligan was neurotically fastidious about his appearance – and he hadn't shaved that day. In all, Nelligan looked like Hollywood's Central Casting version of a reporter just back from El Salvador.

"Something about Right Wing Death Squads appeals to you, Tuck. You've never looked better."

Nelligan scowled. "The less said about that, the better. They let the geeks scare away the U.S. media and then wonder why the government's living fat while the villagers are starving to death." They waited while Nelligan's tea was served and Harry's cup refilled. Harry noted the waiter giving Nelligan the once-over, but Nelligan, a confirmed monogamist, missed the cue. He was too busy being amazed by Harry's coffee ritual, which included two packets of sweetener and two plastic mini-cartons of creamer, stirred into a nebulous glop.

"So what's new? How's the campus."

Harry fell back on that typical American form of politeness and gossiped for a few minutes, filling Nelligan in on the goings-on of Portland and Astor, ending with his own rather unfortunate contretemps with the Summer Sampler program.

Like Kate Fairbain before him, Tucker Nelligan nearly fell out of his chair laughing. "Jeez! Harry, the picture of *you* coaching a basketball team is . . . God, that's great." He wiped a tear away with his knuckle.

Harry was a touch surprised to find himself stiffening. "My dear Tucker. It's not my forte but then again it's not brain surgery, either. I *have* seen basketball games on the television. All seems rather straight forward, really. One tries to throw a ball of X circumference through a horizontal ring of metal

89

with a circumference of approximately 2X. That team which accomplishes this more often wins. Good lord, man, it's not like cricket or the really complicated games."

Tucker laid down across the booth seat and howled, drawing glances from throughout the restaurant.

Harry waited patiently for his friend's attack to end. When Nelligan eventually blew his nose on a napkin and made the time-out signal with his hands, Harry nodded.

"Tuck, I'll make my apologies to Martin later for stealing you away. This is exceedingly important and I really need your help." Harry spoke softly but his baritone voice, with its remnants of a Scots accent, tended to carry anyway.

Nelligan struggled down a new fit of laughter and nodded. "I have this vague recollection of another Harry Bishop sitting at the bar in the Deco Penguin and vowing on his immortal soul never to get involved in another murder. Whatever happened to that guy?"

"Believe me, Tucker, I wouldn't have anything to do with the situation if I could help it. I've been . . . asked to participate."

"By whom? Our bosom buddy Sergeant Wiley?"

"Only a writer would say 'whom.' No, 'fraid this is something of a federal matter. There's an agent of the . . . Justice Department, who asked me to look into things."

As concisely as possible, Harry explained the international timber conference and Astor's connection to it. He touched briefly on Christopher Detweiler's astounding suggestion of an all-encompassing exchange program with Japanese schools, then segued to the Trax explosion at Detweiler Farms.

He ended with a description of the twin deaths, with Keiter hitting the pavement and Detweiler's leg catching on a balcony five floors below his room.

Nelligan was jotting the notes in his ever-present memo pad, using his own brand of note-hand. "And you're sure this was murder and not just what it looks like – an accident?"

Harry nodded, then told Nelligan in full detail the situation at Detweiler Farms, complete with a description of the explosion and rain of shrapnel.

"Is Kate OK?" Nelligan interrupted.

90

"Yes, thank you. *We're* fine. But like you, I don't believe in coincidence. Let us assume the deaths of Detweiler and Keiter were tied to the explosion at the tree farm."

"So where do we start?"

Harry thought about it for a moment. "As far as I can tell, there are only a handful of pertinent people – peoples whose actions seem noteworthy. First, there's a timber magnate named Noraine. He and Detweiler were the two primary movers on the American side of the conference. Next would be Takeshi Nakano, the Japanese businessman who's an ad hoc ambassador."

"He'll be tough to get at, Harry."

"I believe I can take care of that." Harry averted his vision, a sure sign of trouble to those who knew him well.

Nelligan grinned. "Ah yes. Your federal angel. So who is this guy?"

"Not sure, Tuck. I wrote his name down somewhere."

Like a bloodhound on a scent, Nelligan suddenly perked up. "Uh huh. So how does this federal angel know about you? Is this someone who knew you from your deep, dark past? An associate of the Mad—"

"Tucker," Harry set down his cup and leaned slightly forward, vision locked on Nelligan's chocolate brown eyes. "Truly, my friend, I'm pleased you're home in one piece and I'm thrilled that you're willing to help me on this. But don't let's discuss that subject any more. Shall we?"

Nelligan held up both hands, palms forward. "Roger that. Sorry."

Harry dismissed it with a wave. "I should think Nakano's personal translator would be interesting to speak to, as well. She certainly would know the state of the negotiations."

Nelligan rattled his glass, shaking loose the ice cubes that had adhered to the side. "Anyone else?"

"Yes. There were environmentalist protestors at the Trafalgar last night, and again at Detweiler Farms this morning. A young couple – man and woman – seemed to be in charge."

"Okay. I'll take them," Nelligan nodded. "So who do the cops and the federal guy suspect?"

Harry replied honestly: "No one seriously, to the best of my knowledge. I'll attempt to speak to Nakano-san and Noraine, if you'll take the environmentalists."

Nelligan pocketed his pen as his food arrived. "Sounds like a plan, Harry. Damn, it's good to be back in the saddle."

Harry raised his cup in salute. "Yippie ki aye."

CHAPTER TWENTY

Sunday morning dawned bright and beautiful with a slight pink haze hovering behind Mount Hood, tinting the downtown Portland sky line.

Harry untangled himself and the cat from the bed spread, then showered and got dressed carefully, trying not to notice the dull throbbing in the back of his head. The doctor at Meridian Park had assured him there was no concussion but this morning he was none too sure.

Harry fixed himself the regular morning feast: a hearty bowl of Lucky Charms, two cups of his syrupy coffee, and two Pamprin for his head and the dull arthritic pain in his knee. (Harry had no idea why Pamprin helped his arthritis more than other pain killers, but it did. It always made him self-conscious buying the product in the store, just as he used to hate buying 'feminine products' for his late wife.)

His morning ablution out of the way, Harry was prepared to conquer the world.

He was surprised by the dawning realization that he had had nothing alcoholic to drink the night before. That was highly unusual on a weekday – unheard of on a Saturday. Harry had just been too tired after speaking to Tucker and swinging by the Astor campus to visit the library, which stayed open to one in the morning.

He had checked out every library book on the subject of the timber industry and spent three hours jotting down notes and making cross references.

Now, in the sobering light of dawn, Harry spread the notes across his kitchen alcove table and studied them, his academician's mind storing information in logical sequences.

By about nine that morning, Harry was into his fourth cup of coffee, Niccolo curled up on a pile of market statistics on one corner of the table. Harry had needed to peak at those stats for more than an hour but he knew how territorial Niccolo could get. Best to let him dominate a few pages, rather than risk a tantrum and having the research shredded.

Neither Harry nor Niccolo had any doubts as to who ran the household.

"My friend," Harry rubbed the cat's neck, "I cannot believe anyone would commit murder over the sale of lumber. This is, without a doubt, the most boring subject I have ever researched."

Harry stood, stretched, made a quick trip to the bathroom then picked up the telephone in the kitchen and dialed Tucker's number.

"Hello?"

"Martin? Harry here. Sorry to ring you up so early on a Sunday."

"No problem. I'm just going over some legal briefs. I'm sorry, but Tuck took off about forty-five minutes ago."

Harry hoisted himself up on the yellowing counter. "It's all right, Martin, I was hoping to speak to you."

Harry proceeded to explain his mission. The attorney's voice coming over the line became more and more suspicious as the conversation continued. Eventually Martin Kady interrupted. "Yes, yes. That's possible of course, Harry. And you know I'd love to help. But I'm not sure it's appropriate."

"Ah. Quite." Harry backed down quickly. "You're right, of course. Shouldn't've asked."

"No, no. I mean it when I say I'd love to help," Martin cut in. "It's just . . ."

"You did save him more than $3 million," Harry added.

"True. But . . ."

"And he did say he'd be pleased to return a favor to you."

"Well, yes, but . . ."

"But nothing, Martin! You're right as rain here. It was wrong of me to ask. I should probably trot along now. People to do and things to be."

"Wait a minute." Martin's voice sounded resigned across the wire. "Look, I'll call him up right away and see. Okay? No promises, Harry."

Harry grinned. "You're a prince, Martin Kady."

Detective Sergeant John Wiley held open the door to the interrogation room and stood aside as Daniel Tadson McMurdo stepped through.

Wiley was a small, black man with hair cut close to his scalp and gray beginning to form above both ears. He carried his own body self-consciously, moving with small, precise motions, his every gesture reminiscent of a tai chi exercise.

Wiley motioned to a chair on one side of the long table, then selected a chair for himself opposite McMurdo. The room was off-white with sound baffles lining the walls and one bad fluorescent light flickering above the table.

McMurdo wore a too-familiar smile across his doughy face and leaned back in the chair, tipping the front two legs off the carpeted floor. "Sergeant, I appreciate your time."

Wiley nodded and folded his hands together on the table like a good little boy awaiting his dinner.

"As you know, we're investigating the deaths at the Trafalgar yesterday."

"Yes," Wiley replied softly, his voice just more than a whisper. Although he smiled politely, his force field allowed neither friendliness nor hostility to peek through. "We're still not certain why the Secret Service is concerned with this situation."

McMurdo leaned forward and dropped his voice into a conspiratorial tone. "International ramifications, Sergeant. International ramifications."

"Ah," Wiley said.

"Furthermore, we're certainly planning on sharing any and all information that comes our way with our friends at the Portland Police Department, don't you know," McMurdo continued.

"There's some that think inter-agency rivalry is a good thing, but not Daniel Tadson McMurdo. No, Sir."

"Ah," Wiley said.

"We've also been fortunate enough to secure some outside assistance in this matter. A private citizen of your fair city – and may I say I've enjoyed my stay in Portland thoroughly? – has agreed to take a look-see around and, as they say, see what's to see."

"Ah," Wiley said.

"Perhaps you know the fella. Professor Henry Bishop, John Jacob Astor College."

Wiley nodded. It was the first movement he had made since sitting down. "That would not be considered . . . a viable situation," Wiley began. "I know the professor. He has been of assistance to us on a number of occasions. But it's the philosophy of this department that outside, amateur intervention does more harm than good. I'm afraid I must agree with that assessment. We'd prefer that the professor not be involved in the investigation."

McMurdo tipped his chair as far back as it would go then released his grip on the table edge. The chair wavered on its hind legs for a second before gravity pulled it forward again. The off-center smile never left his features. "That's your final word, Sergeant?"

"Yes, sir. I'm afraid so. I trust you understand."

"Oh, yes indeed." McMurdo tipped the chair back again and reached into his suit coat pocket, withdrawing a plain white envelope, unsealed. He set the envelope down and tapped it with his finger nail. It slid across the smooth surface, bumping against Wiley's hands.

Wiley carefully removed his reading glasses from his suit coat pocket, then opened the envelope and withdrew the single piece of paper. He unfolded it and laid it down flat on the table. Wiley silently scanned the single page once, then started at the top and read it all again. McMurdo continued toying with his chair's center of gravity.

"I see," Wiley said. He refolded the paper, returned it to the envelope and handed it back, then removed his glasses.

"Good!" McMurdo's chair settled noisily down on all four legs. "I knew we could count on you, Sergeant."

Wiley knew a pat hand when he saw one. "Please tell Professor Bishop he can have access to anything he wants."

The Sergeant stood and walked out of the room without any further comment. McMurdo's grin threatened to rupture his face.

CHAPTER TWENTY-ONE

Tucker Nelligan checked in with the City Editor and told her what he was doing. Dembrow blew up, shouting into the phone and demanding that Nelligan take the week off after his harrowing experience. Nelligan recommended she not tell too many people about the car bomb – at least, not until the publisher and editorial board could be convinced to let Nelligan go back to San Salvador and finish the damned story.

When Dembrow slammed down the phone, Nelligan took that as an 'Okay.'

Showered, shaved and dressed in a black and white plaid shirt, red knit tie and tweed jacket, Nelligan hurried out of the house he and Martin Kady had recently purchased in Lake Oswego's First Addition, jumped into the Jeep and hurried off to the Pogue residence. Saturday's rabbit-punch storm had passed well away, bringing back the sunshine and scrubbing much of the pollution out of the air.

The address in the phone book had put the Pogues in Milwaukie, in a low-income housing development near the railroad warehouses that parallelled the Willamette River. Nelligan went north on Macadam then cut across the Sellwood Bridge into Sellwood and Milwaukie, U2 blasting from the Jeep's speakers.

The development was a sterile grid of one-story houses, pre-fabricated and painted cheaply maybe five years earlier. All the houses – about thirty of them, all dull blue – showed bald spots where the paint was peeling away. Few lawns were mowed.

Nelligan checked his address again, then pulled up to a curb behind a dilapidated green Buick. It was a warm Sunday and the housing project was swarming with little kids. A drag race of grimy-faced children on Big Wheels forced Nelligan off the sidewalk halfway to the Pogues' residence.

There was no doorbell on the aluminum sided home and the threadbare, oatmeal colored drapes were pulled taut across the window. Nelligan rapped on the wooden door. Inside, a very large-sounding dog started barking madly. Nelligan could hear its claws pacing back and force across the linoleum floor.

Nelligan rapped again and the dog howled. One of the window curtains swayed gently and a faced peeked out. A moment later, the door was opened the length of a safety chain and a pair of large, feminine, brown eyes peered out. "Yes?"

"Ms. Pogue? My name's Tucker Nelligan. *Portland Post*."

Nelligan handed his business card toward the crack in the door. After a moment's pause, she reached out for the card. Her hand was calloused around the base of the fingers, Nelligan noticed, and the fingernails were clipped short and unvarnished.

"What do you want? We already subscribe to *The Oregonian*," Mrs. Pogue said.

Nelligan smiled his winningest smile. "I'm not circulation ma'am. I'm news. I'd like to talk to you about what happened out at Detweiler Farms and down at the Hotel Trafalgar yesterday. May I come in?"

Phoebe Pogue thought about it for a moment, mumbling something negative. Nelligan applied just a touch more smile. He was an exceedingly handsome man and knew how to play a good trump card.

With a nod, the door closed. The chain could be heard sliding back before the door swung open.

Phoebe Pogue was a tall woman, easily matching Nelligan's five feet, ten inches. She was anemically thin, all angles and corners, with straight brown hair pulled back and held with a rubber band at the nape of the neck.

Nelligan wondered why she had bothered chaining the door. Beside her stood a German shepherd that looked vaguely like his Jeep. It stood beside Mrs. Pogue, black eyes fixed on Nelligan, its face screaming 'Dinner's here!'

Nelligan hated big dogs and hoped it could smell that better than it could smell his fear.

"May I come in?" He said, pasting the smile more firmly in place.

"Sure. Axel, sit."

Axel? he thought. *This isn't a German shepherd, it's a Nazi shepherd.*

The dog sat obediently and Phoebe Pogue led Nelligan into a dismal front room. The carpeting was a hideous mix of greens and oranges which perfectly avoided matching any part of the furniture – a rag tag collection of items which spoke of garage sales and St. Vincent de Paul. The television was on. Nelligan was surprised to notice it was on C-SPAN and U.S. House Ways and Means Committee hearings were showing.

Phoebe Pogue turned down the volume and stole a chair away from the adjacent dining room – really an alcove between the front room and the kitchen. She placed it firmly in front of the couch before sitting down.

Nelligan took the couch which smelled of dust. "What can I tell you?" Mrs. Pogue asked.

Nelligan took his narrow notepad out of his jacket pocket and flipped it open. "First, can you spell your first and last name for me?"

A hint of doubt crossed Mrs. Pogue's gaunt face and she glanced sub rosa at the shepherd, still sitting in the entryway. She spelled the name carefully.

"Thank you, ma'am. Am I right in saying you were at the farm yesterday morning when the explosion occurred?"

"Yes," she replied. "But we didn't actually see it. When I say 'We,' I mean my husband and myself. His name's Joshua. Same last name."

"Thanks. So you didn't see this explosion I've heard about?"

"No." Phoebe Pogue was a protestor. That meant she was more than willing to discuss her cause, as Nelligan had known she would be. "You see, Detweiler is . . . or I guess, *was* . . . involved in the destruction of Oregon's Old Growth timber, and

100

he was trying to put together a deal that would have tripled the destruction. Several of us were out there protesting. Of course, the farm is private property so we couldn't go inside. We were out on the road, just outside their property."

"How many of you?"

She thought about it for a moment. "Oh, fifteen, I'd say. I was in charge of making the phone calls to get everybody. Anyway, we heard a chain saw start up, then we heard this big crack or bang. We didn't know what it was, so we just kept protesting. You know, we'd called *The Post* and *The Oregonian* and all the TV stations about our protest and no one showed up. Not even the Wilsonville paper."

Nelligan dredged up a look of surprise. "I'll have to tell my city editor this. She won't be pleased that we missed the protest," he lied. "So then what happened?"

Phoebe Pogue was enthralled in telling the tale now. She leaned forward, bony elbows on her knees. "We just went back to protesting. We feel that Oregon's Old Growth timber is being destroyed at a fantastic pace. By the turn of the century, only two percent of the original forests primeval will still be standing in the Northwest unless people wake up and see what we're doing to the countryside. And that's not even mentioning the run off from the land that can't handle the rain without the significant floral coverage provided by—"

"Yes," Nelligan frowned and leaned forward in a mime of her own body language. "Absolutely right. We've seen it coming for some time, but trying telling that to the big corporations."

Mrs. Pogue nodded vigorously. "God, do we know! Anyway, about five or ten minutes later, I guess, ambulances and police cars started showing up. Then a helicopter flew over and it had 'LifeFlight' written on the side of it. So then we knew there'd been an accident."

"Well, I'd say that put the old kibosh on this Kuroshio Group deal," Nelligan added, leaning back and adding a crooked, knowing smile. "That and the accident at the hotel. You've heard, I suppose?"

"Oh, yeah," she replied, leaning back in her chair. Nelligan barely sensed a shift in Phoebe Pogue's demeanor but the shepherd clearly picked up the rising tension. The dog let loose a low growl and shifted its forepaws in a little dance. "Yeah. Mr. Detweiler's dead. We heard about it on the radio this afternoon. I can't say I'm glad, though. I mean, no one wanted him dead or anything." She was studying Nelligan carefully, tip-toeing her way through a minefield. Nelligan hadn't anticipated the woman being that savvy.

"Hell, no," he agreed. "That goes without saying, of course. I hear someone else took a dive, too. A union guy."

Phoebe Pogue nodded but didn't say anything.

"Ms. Pogue, were you protesting at the Trafalgar today?"

There was a pause. The shepherd looked from its mistress to the stranger and back again, a small whine escaping its black lips. "No," she said at last. "The sheriff's deputies wanted to talk to us after the thing out at the Wilsonville farm. We didn't get away from their office in Oregon City until about 3:30. Anyway, there was going to be a show about Greenpeace on the local PBS affiliate, KOAP. It's that "Focal Point" show. Anyway, I got there about . . . four-thirty or five, I'd guess. From what I heard, Mr. Detweiler was already dead."

"Let me make sure I got that right, ma'am. You said, 'I got there between four-thirty and five.' Right?"

"Uh huh."

"So that means Mr. Pogue arrived later, I take it?"

Phoebe sat for a moment, jaw open, about to answer. She studied the reporter passively.

Nelligan had a number of philosophies in life. One was: when all else fails, fall back on honesty. "Ms. Pogue, I've got to tell you – the deaths at the Trafalgar may not have been accidents."

Phoebe Pogue didn't move. Her big, brown eyes bore into Nelligan.

"There's some reason to believe that Detweiler and the other guy, Neil Keiter, were murdered. Have you heard anything along those lines?"

"Get out," Pogue said softly. She sat perfectly still, her skinny body ramrod straight, her arms at her sides, hands grasping the sides of the chair's seat.

"Beg your pardon?"

"Get out."

"Ms. Pogue, please, don't for a moment think I'm accusing anyone of anything! I just thought—"

"Axel, one."

Axel suddenly roared to his feet, letting loose with a cannon's volley of barks and growls. An invisible tether kept the dog in place, but Axel strained against his training, eyes focussed on the journalist de jure.

"Hey! Whoa!" Nelligan stayed seated but raised both hands in an I-give-up motion. "You want me out of here, I'm out of here. No problem."

"Thank you," Phoebe Pogue replied. "Axel, sit."

Axel did so, clearly dissatisfied with the direction this conversation was taking.

"I'll just be on my way," Nelligan hesitantly stood. When he wasn't instantly transformed into kibbles and bits, he managed to make his feet move towards the door.

CHAPTER TWENTY-TWO

Harry arrived at the hotel around ten o'clock that morning and was told at the front desk that the Kuroshio Group party was leaving within the hour. He thought about Taddy McMurdo's threat to indict someone else – anyone else – and decided to act quickly.

On the thirteenth floor, Harry searched the corridors until he found what he was looking for – the two Secret Service agents who had been on duty at the Friday celebration. They were flanked by two uniformed police officers, all four standing in a semi-circle around Room 1314, glowering at each other.

" 'Scuse me," Harry smiled politely. "I was wondering if—".

"This area is off limits, sir," one of the cops cut in.

"There's a federal investigation here," the agent beside him added. Harry could see the row of hallway lights reflecting in his Foster Grants.

"Actually, it's a police matter," the second cop entered the fray. "Move along please."

"This was fed turf before you yokels stumbled in," the second agent responded.

"Yeah? Listen, pal, you're in Portland, Oregon. Here, the PPD is in charge. Go find your federal charter and your decoder ring and see if that ain't so."

"Watch your step, little man," the first agent applied in his finest Clint Eastwood through-gritted-teeth voice.

"Back off, James Bond," the other cop nudged between them, hiking his gunbelt up over his not inconsiderable paunch.

"Back off, mister," said an agent.

"Take a hike, fella," said a cop.

"Oh, a tough guy," said an agent.

"Pardon me," said Harry and entered the hotel room.

"This is our town," said a cop.

Inside the room, Detective Sergeant John Wiley looked over his shoulder, sighed, and nodded. "Hello, professor. You didn't happen to see two uniformed officers and two federal agents in the hall, did you?"

"Not that I recall."

"Ah. Then please sit down."

Wiley himself was seated in a chair identical to the one Lee Connar had in his room. The Japanese delegation's quarters were much larger than Astor's – a suite with full kitchen, two bedrooms and a living room. Harry had lived in much smaller apartments during his government and graduate school days.

Takeshi Nakano and his interpreter, Kimiko Sheppard, sat on either end of the Earth-tone couch, opposite the glass and bronze coffee table from Wiley. The cop turned his attention back to the Japanese and motioned toward Harry. "Mr. Nakano, this is Professor Henry Bishop. He's . . . been the police department's liaison with the college on a few occasions. He'll be sitting in on this. Do you mind?" Wiley spoke in his soft, melodic voice, his dark brown eyes focussed on the wizened gentleman.

Nakano muttered something in Japanese and nodded. Even in the quiet room, Harry couldn't make out individual words. "That's quite all right," Ms. Sheppard replied, turning to Harry and smiling politely. "You're welcome. Mr. Nakano is sorry that he cannot stay longer and be of more service to the policemen."

Harry took a bar stool situated well to the rear of Wiley. He wanted to intrude as little as possible.

"Thank you, Sir." Wiley continued to treat the petite interpreter as a non-person. Harry could tell it was making Wiley (normally the most considerate and non-sexist of persons) uncomfortable. "When will you be leaving?"

"Our plane leaves Portland International in about four hours," Ms. Sheppard replied. "We'll be flying to Chicago then on to

105

London for the EEC conference. We'll spend twelve days in London and Bonn, flying back and forth several times, I suspect, then on home to Hokkaido."

Wiley nodded. He took no notes, but Harry knew from personal experience that no detail went unnoticed. "Mr. Nakano, sir, if the deaths of Mr. Detweiler and Mr. Keiter aren't cleared up, we—"

The elderly Japanese man nodded and spoke quickly, his hands gesturing in synch with his words.

"Yes, of course," Ms. Sheppard seemed flustered by Nakano's interruption. "Um, Mr. Nakano wishes to express his dismay at this most unfortunate incident, and also wishes to add that he does not hold the City of Portland or Astor college in any way responsible."

"Oh." Wiley nodded. "Thank you very much. Now, if we can't clear up this situation with alacrity, it may be most inconvenient for us if you leave."

Sheppard spoke softly, leaning toward her employer who nodded occasionally. As he replied, his eyes stayed on Wiley. To Harry, the aged man's reply seemed long and a bit heated.

Ms. Sheppard just nodded and waited for him to finish before translating. "Mr. Nakano regrets any inconvenience stemming from this situation and will, of course, obey any commands from the police. If you will not allow us to go, then of course we will stay."

Wiley nodded sagely. "There will be no question of detaining you, sir. The proper U.S. authorities already have made that point . . . crystal clear." He turned slightly in his chair and glanced at Harry, who blushed. *Taddy*, he thought.

Sheppard passed along the message, then noted the reply. "Thank you, Sergeant. Please feel free to contact Mr. Nakano before we leave, if we can be of any help."

Wiley stood and the elderly gentleman followed suit. Harry and Sheppard, both momentarily sitting, caught each other's eye.

Nakano apparently believed in the When in Rome adage. He reached across the coffee table and shook Wiley's hand.

Harry stood also. "Sergeant, um, I was wondering—"

"My associate, Professor Bishop, would like to have a word with you. Would that be all right?" Wiley cut in gracefully.

"Yes," Sheppard replied after consulting with her employer. "What can we do for you?"

"Er, a bit wobbly here. I apologize for intruding. Would you mind, terribly, telling me where, that is, where you both were at, say, 4:30 to 5 p.m. yesterday afternoon? If it's not a problem, I mean."

Wiley turned to him and rolled his eyes to the ceiling.

"Yes sir," the interpreter rose also, since everyone else was standing. "We both returned here about four o'clock or a little later. I typed some letters for Mr. Nakano and faxed them to Japan and London, then answered Mr. Nakano's E-Mail, sorted—"

"Er, pardon. 'E-mail'?"

Ms. Sheppard smiled. "Sorry. I don't usually fall into jargon. Electronic mail: In-house correspondence from the headquarters. The hotel was gracious enough to allow us access to the switchboard. We have a modem connecting the switchboard to my lap-top computer." She gestured to the folding computer that looked slightly smaller than an attaché case. "It allows us to communicate with the home office from my room, Mr. Nakano's room – in fact, from anyone's room. The modem was designed by a subsidiary of the Kuroshio Group."

Sheppard blushed, realizing she was hard-selling. "Anyway, I took care of some office things then showered and looked at your local newspaper. During that time, Mr. Nakano had a nap and studied. He has a great deal of – how do you say? – homework, to do before we travel to London. We were here until approximately 5:45, when we went downstairs for dinner. We heard the commotion outside but I'm afraid we didn't investigate. The police came up to our table and asked to speak to us. That's when we first heard of the tragedy."

"I see. Thanks. Sorry to pop in like this and root about. Appreciate your help. I'll just, um . . ." he motioned toward the door.

"Thank you again," Wiley cut in. He touched Harry gently on the elbow and guided him toward the door.

As Harry stepped outside, the cops and agents rang out "Hey!" in chorus.

"Ah, did everyone sleep well?" Wiley smiled at the four taller men. "Excuse us."

He led the way down the hall. Wiley's short legs moved mechanically, metronomically, while Harry's much longer legs strode at his side. "You don't do a great many interrogations, I take it."

Harry blushed again. "Damned uncomfortable, Sergeant. Felt like a Penny Dreadful detective in there. I take it you spoke to Mr. McMurdo?"

Wiley nodded. "I'm to give you any and all assistance in this matter. You're officially assisting the police in our investigation." He spoke to the carpet.

"Yes. About that. May I tell you something in confidence?"

Wiley stopped before the bank of elevators and hit the arrow-shaped down button. "Of course."

"McMurdo laid down the law to you, right? Told you there are no options in this situation and you're to do as you're told?"

Wiley didn't reply.

"Well, he told me the exact same thing, the perisher. I've no more interest in poking around this mess than you have in my being under foot."

Wiley appraised Harry, his head tilted, the hall lights glinting off his thick lenses. "Oh," he said at last. "I should have realized that. I'm sorry. I take it your . . . unusual abilities are known to the Secret Service, then."

Harry considered commenting on McMurdo's "Secret Service" status but voted against it. For now. "If you mean the popular myth of my talents, I'm afraid so, Sergeant. Am I right in saying the balcony collapsed at about five yesterday afternoon?"

"Yes, professor. Almost at five on the nose. And no, we can't prove Mr. Nakano was in his room at that time. We've only his interpreter's word for that and, frankly, I can't imagine her saying anything to indict him."

"Nor I," Harry replied.

"On the other hand, we know they were in the dining room at round 5:45. This hotel has a somewhat sophisticated system for allowing waiters to ring a customer's order into a cash register computer, where it's transmitted back to the kitchen. That cuts down on running back and forth to the kitchen and it also give us a receipt saying exactly when they ordered dinner."

"Ah." Harry scrounged through his pockets for a pen and something to write on but came up empty. "I see."

"We also know a few other things." The elevator arrived and the door opened but Wiley kept talking and it eventually closed. "Christopher Detweiler called the hotel's maid service around 4:35 yesterday to complain that he hadn't received fresh sheets and towels. According to the chief day-shift maid, she and another woman hurried up and took care of the problem. They left Detweiler's room at about 4:45, give or take."

"All right," Harry said, making mental notes of the time.

"Neil Keiter called room service and asked for dinner around 4:50. The food arrived at approximately 5:10, but no one answered when the waiter knocked. We know of course that Mr. Keiter was already gone."

"Yes, most gone. Tell me, did he order dinner for one or two?"

"One," Wiley replied.

"Which means that Detweiler came down to Keiter's room after he, Keiter, called for dinner? And that the two men went out to the balcony to talk and the railing gave way?"

Wiley nodded.

"Aw. Well, thanks for sharing that."

"We haven't spoken to other guests on that floor, yet. I hope to have someone on that by tomorrow," Wiley continued. He noticed a bit of lint on the sleeve of his navy blue suit and frowned, carefully removing it. "We should have had statements already but I'm understaffed this year. Portland's reputation as the methamphetamine capital of North America has drained a lot of personnel into the narcotics division."

"I can well imagine," Harry replied.

109

"One other thing, sir." The detective sergeant fished into his suit coat pocket and pulled out two Zip-Lock plastic bags. In the first rested three one-inch screws, each one the color of soft clay. "We finally found these three on the street."

Harry looked at the screws carefully. "Rusted completely through."

"Yes, sir. This accident may have been that. An accident. But here's something else."

Wiley held up the second bag, which contained a wild mass of shiny string. "It's fishing line," he explained. "We found it wadded up in Mr. Detweiler's pants pocket. Does twenty feet of fishing line indicate anything to you?"

"Slow room service? Detweiler decided to catch his own dinner?" Harry ventured. Wiley didn't smile. "No. Thought not."

The elevator opened again and a couple stepped out. Wiley stepped aboard. "Professor, I understand your situation, vis a vis Agent McMurdo. But please, sir, you'll let us do our jobs?"

"Oh, absolutely. Scout's honor."

The doors slid closed, obscuring Wiley's look of doubt.

CHAPTER TWENTY-THREE

Tucker thanked Phoebe Pogue for her help and exited the dilapidated house, smiled nicely at Axel the Wonder Dog and hoping against hope that the old adage about smelling fear was apocryphal.

Outside the weather was surprisingly wonderful, especially when compared with Saturday. The sky was criss-crossed with slowly disintegrating contrails made by zoomies from the nearby Civil Air Patrol wing. Nelligan had flown in everything from a Goose to a 'Herky-bird' to a Hewey helicopter to an F-14 Tomcat, and he knew the heart-stopping wonder of flying on a crystal clear day. He envied the pilots their fun.

It was nearing noon and Nelligan hoisted himself up on the Jeep's hood, shoes resting on the wheel well cover, cab radio turned on to KINK. He was obscured from Phoebe Pogue's front room window and so long as she didn't step outside, she would have no idea he was here.

It was a gamble, he realized. Joshua Pogue could have worked Sundays, or could have been out of town visiting relatives or could have been golfing.

But he wasn't.

Twenty minutes later, Nelligan saw the man matching Harry's description come walking along thirty-second, brown grocery bag nestled in one arm, chin resting against his clavicle, studying the ground beneath his work boots.

"Mr. Pogue?" Nelligan waited until the bearded man was abreast of the Jeep. Shocked out of his reverie, Pogue looked up quickly, smiling. The smile faded as he faced the stranger in front of his house.

Nelligan read the man's face correctly. "No, sir. I'm not a bill collector or anything. My name's Nelligan. I'm a writer with the *Post*. I was hoping to ask you a few things about your environmental protests."

He handed Joshua his laminated card. The man studied it for a moment then handed it back. "Sure. I guess so. Come on in."

"No, thanks." Nelligan smiled politely. "I've got a bad allergy to dog hair. I spoke to your wife for a moment and ended up sneezing like crazy. Too bad, that's a pretty dog you've got in there."

"Thanks." Pogue shrugged and set the groceries down on the sidewalk. He rested his butt against the Jeep's fender, arms folded across his chest. He was a pleasant-faced, trim man with a bald spot forming on the crown of his skull and a beard decidedly more red than the rest of his hair. "What did Phoebe tell you?"

"Pretty much the thrust of your group," Nelligan replied, pulling forth the ever-present note pad. "Personally, I couldn't agree with you guys more. Just between you and me, sir – and I do mean 'just between you and me.' We've got to look completely neutral on these things or they don't let us write about them. You know?"

Joshua nodded. "Right. Did Phoebe show you any of the stats we've put together?"

"Not really. Didn't get a chance before my eyes started watering up."

"Well, the numbers are just staggering, man." Joshua shook his head sadly, kicking absently at a tuft of crab grass growing through a crack in the cement. The Big Wheel derby careened madly past the Jeep again. "In a twelve-state Western region this year, lumber producers are raking in about 480 million board feet per week. Per *week*, man. In 1988 – that's the last year I've got statistics for – in 1988 they chewed up and spilt out something like twenty-one billion board feet. That's 'billion' with a B. Can you believe that?"

112

Nelligan whistled as if shocked by the numbers. "Is that an average year?"

"Hell, yes. They're stripping the hills all over Oregon, Washington, Idaho and Montana. And now they're taking lumber from the Bull Run aquifer, which feeds all the drinking water for the metropolitan Portland area. Without the ground cover, the aquifer will become polluted inside five years. There's just no future-thinking in the industry, man. It's all bottom line, quarterly income and profit margins."

"I hear you," Nelligan nodded. He dutifully took notes, then remembered that Marty had asked for bread and mayonnaise from the store. He jotted that down, too. "Listen, are you guys getting anywhere? I mean, are you making a dent?"

Joshua looked west at the evergreen-covered hills of Dunthorpe and Lake Oswego and sighed. It wasn't a melodramatic gesture, just the effects of fatigue and disappointment. "Off the record?"

Nelligan tossed the notepad down onto the car's hood. "Shoot."

"No," Joshua replied softly, turning his gaze onto his clapboard house, visualizing his wife within. "Phoebe thinks so. She's a true believer."

How true? Nelligan wondered.

"But no. I don't think anyone gives a shit. You know? It's just not making any difference."

"You ever think of calling it quits?"

There was a longer pause. Joshua scratched his beard and continued to kick at the crab grass. "Yeah. Sometimes. Phoebe doesn't know that, though."

"Does the death of Christopher Detweiler help?" Nelligan asked softly.

Joshua arched his back and pulled away from the Jeep, suddenly jamming his hands into his pockets. "No. That's got nothing to do with us, Mr. Nelligan. Nothing whatsoever."

"Where were you at five yesterday afternoon?" Nelligan kept his voice soft, kept the note pad out of his hand. When Joshua suddenly shifted his vision up to Nelligan, the reporter smiled politely as if he had asked about the weather or the Mets.

Joshua thought about the question for a moment. "I went to the KOAP studio, down on Macadam. They were shooting an episode of 'Focal Point' on Greenpeace. I wanted to attend."

"Your wife said you showed up late," Nelligan cut in quickly but kept his voice light.

Joshua whirled and marched toward his front door, cutting across the weedy lawn.

"I'd really like to know where you were at five, Mr. Pogue," Nelligan called after him.

The front room window curtain was pulled back slightly. Nelligan gathered his note pad and slid off the hood, onto the ground.

"I went to get a drink with some guys!" Joshua spun around and shouted back. "Anyway, it's none of your business!"

The busted screen door flew open, hinges screaming, and Nelligan threw open his car door. He was in and the door closed before Axel was halfway across the lawn. In a one-on-one wrestling match, the Jeep had points for weight but Axel had speed, meanness and good old fashioned ugliness.

Nelligan decided not to press his luck and hit the ignition.

CHAPTER TWENTY-FOUR

Harry rapped on the door to Room 544 and waited a while, then rapped again. L.C. Noraine didn't answer.

Harry considered what he knew about the timber magnate and took the elevator down to the mezzanine level bar, but no luck. Resignedly, he reversed his trip back up to the thirty-first floor and the Sky View Room, where he and Taddy McMurdo had shared watery American beers the day before.

Sure enough, he found the rotund man sitting by himself at a four-person table near the southern windows, staring out at the gently curving Willamette River and uninhabited Ross Island. Mount Hood glistened, not too far away.

"Mr. Noraine?" Harry stepped up to the table. "My name's Henry Bishop. I'm with Astor College. May I speak to you for a moment?"

L.C. snapped out of his reverie and grinned up at the lanky professor. "Hell, yes. Siddown, Mr. Bischoff. Siddown."

"Thank you. Er, Bishop. Like the chess piece."

"Gotcha. Hey! Waitress! How's about some beers here?"

There was an empty, handled flagon already in front of L.C. As the waitress approached, Harry waved her off. "None for me, thank you. Busy day yet."

"Yeah? Well, I guess I'd better wet my whistle anyhow. One more, honey." L.C. winked at the waitress. Harry's mouth dried out. A visiting dignitary from the Department of Education had once referred to the political science department secretary as "sweetheart" and promptly received a blistering, three-minute tirade from Harry on the propriety of such comments. Now was not the time for such diatribes, he reminded himself.

"What can I do for you?" L.C. was dressed once again like a dime store cowboy. He leaned forward on one forearm, his breath an unsettling mixture of beer and tobacco. Harry leaned back appropriately. "To be honest, sir, I've been asked by . . . the police to ask around a bit on yesterday's tragedy. I have a special relationship with the authorities." *A very special relationship. Usually I'm a victim*, he almost added.

L.C. clucked his tongue and wagged his head theatrically. "I tell you, professor, Chris Detweiler was a man's man. Hell of a guy. This is just a crying shame, to see him go like that."

"You were close?"

"Oh, hell yes. Like brothers. Y'see, the real timber tycoons of yesteryear are a damned rare breed these days. Too many huge, Eastern, corporations own too much of the land, not to mention the damned federal government, which owns the rest."

He shook his head sadly, *tsking* for emphasis.

"Me and Chris were one of a kind. Hate to see him go. Anyway, what can I do you for?"

"Primarily, I was wondering if you were injured in yesterday's explosion at Detweiler Farms," Harry replied, knowing that egotistical people enjoy nothing so much as discussing themselves.

"Nah, not so's you'd notice," L.C. waved his hands dismissingly. Harry thought instantly of Danny Kaye as Walter Mitty: *No problem, sir. I set the bone myself.*

"Mainly I got bumped around when some asshole fell on me, trying to get out of the way. That wasn't you, was it? Ha ha! Just kidding, Bishop. Just pulling your leg."

L.C. grinned like the village idiot and put away a third of the beer in a gulp. Harry thought he was handling this mourning business rather well.

"Did you go to the hospital?"

"Nope. No need to. 'Course, when you've been ranching and working the timber market as long as I have, well, hell, you just end up getting thick skinned and thick skulled. Nah, I just gave Chris a piece – that is, poor old Chris a piece of my

116

mind for letting those damned crazy environmentalist faggots on his property. Now over in Montana and Idaho where I've got the lion's share of my land, we just keep a shotgun loaded with rock salt in our pick-ups, and when they come sniffing around, preaching and telling us how to run our businesses, why we just give'em the business end of an over-under barrel. Ha! That's the answer."

Another third of the beer disappeared. Harry couldn't remember disliking anyone this quickly before. "So then came you back to the hotel?"

"Yeah. I don't know anyone much in Portland. Seattle, I know, and Tacoma. But Portland's virgin territory. And hey! Don't think that very thought didn't pass through my mind more'n once, huh?"

L.C. actually leaned forward and winked. The man was trying so hard to look like a 'good ol'boy' that Harry began to feel sorry for him.

"Er, sorry to ask and all, but d'you recall when you got back here?"

The dimwit cowhand persona retreated slightly. "Sort of."

Harry smiled. "Afraid I really must ask these things. Embarrassing, truth to tell. Er, when did you find your way back here?"

This time L.C. took a small, dignified sip of the remaining beer. "I'd guess it was around 3:30, give or take."

"Ah. And, um, did you . . ."

L.C. grinned, crossing his arms over his not insubstantial girth. "You think Chris and that union boy were murdered, don't you?"

Harry considered how best to answer that and opted for the truth. "Yes, sir. That seems a distinct possibility. Certainly by no means a probability, but at least possible."

"Well, it'll please you to know the local cops already came around here. Some colored fellow name of Wiley. He asked and I told him and now I'm telling you. I went down to the bar on the second floor and I had myself a drink or two. I talked with some folks, then I ordered a steak and all the trimmings, which ended up looking like something that'd sit on your back porch fence and screech all night, I don't mind saying, and then I had myself maybe another drink or two and I paid my bill with cash, as I always do and my daddy did before me, and I took my leave."

"Ah. And that was– "

"Six o'clock, almost dead on. Is that what you were hoping to hear, fella?"

"Actually, yes." Harry stood and smiled politely. "Sorry if these questions seemed rude."

Now the beer disappeared in one fell gulp. "Only rude if they meant anything like an accusation. If not, then no hard feelings. If so, then watch your step. We got lawyers where I come from, you know."

"Quite. Thank you again." Harry made his leave before L.C. demanded to arm wrestle.

Halfway down the elevator, Harry pushed the stop button and felt the car shudder to a halt. He folded one arm across his chest, leaned back against the mirrored wall and rubbed his temple with the other hand, trying to drown out the Muzak with his concentration.

He pictured Detweiler Farms and the eery uniformity of the trees. He pictured the rough, redwood picnic tables beneath the covered picnic area, and the electronic megaphone Christopher Detweiler spoke through. He envisioned the material of Kate's jacket and the color of her low-heeled shoes. He saw the Detweiler Mark-One Trax and the red ribbon on the tree.

Harry pictured the people. L.C.Noraine had been to his – Harry's – left, at about four o'clock. As far from the exploding tractor as one could get.

Harry relaxed and released the stop button, suddenly glowering at his own reflection across the elevator car.

Taddy McMurdo had been over in that direction, too, with a wooden pillar directly between himself and the line of fire.

118

CHAPTER TWENTY-FIVE

Tucker slid into a red plastic booth at the Willamette Diner and asked the waitress for a cup of Stash tea. She was dressed in a poodle skirt and bobby socks. *Jailhouse Rock* throbbed from the ceiling speakers.

Martin Kady set down his *U.S. News* and slid his reading glasses atop his balding head. "Howdy, stranger."

"Hey, counselor."

"So what fool's errand has our friend Harry sent you on this time? During your time off from the paper, I may add."

Tucker accepted his tea and ordered a bacon burger with fries. Marty sighed the sigh of a true martyr and ordered a tossed salad, no dressing. He was a thin, narrow waisted man who, at forty, still had no paunch. As long as Tucker had known him, Marty had been dieting. He never did know why.

Tucker leaned across the formica table and spoke softly, explaining to his lover of seven years that the deaths at the Hotel Trafalgar might have been murders, and that Harry had been asked by some federal official to look into the situation.

Marty arced his eyebrows. "Someone who knew of Harry in his 'Mad Hatter', CIA days, maybe?"

"Maybe," Nelligan sipped his tea. "'Knew' or 'knows.' Harry's as good a friend as I've ever had – present company excluded – but I've never truly believed he's as retired as he claims to be. Anyway, if he's right it's a hell of a story, so I'm helping with the leg work."

He told Martin about his conversation with Phoebe Pogue,

who seemed careful and sly, and Joshua Pogue, who seemed nervous and on edge. And about his through-the-windshield conversation with Axel, who seemed hungry.

"What's next?" Marty asked, staring forlornly at his naked salad.

"Now, I swing by the PBS station and see if I can make any confirmations. What's your Sunday been like?"

"Fine. Harry called me, too, you know. I've got a super-secret special assignment, too. Nya nya." Marty then proceeded to tell Tucker about his own conversation with Harry and Harry's unusual request.

Nelligan grinned. "You think it'll work?"

"Maybe. I did save him several million dollars in that suit. And he did say he owed me one. I'm talking to someone in about an hour. We'll see how it goes."

Nelligan leaned back in his booth and laughed. "God. This sounds like Harry. Well, here's to him." They raised their cups in salute.

Harry ordered a Scotch on the rocks from the waiter, a small, chunky man with fierce gray hair cut like a Brillo pad. He was in his mid-fifties, Harry thought, and looked like an ex-boxer. Quick, small, tough, with a doughy nose that had been broken at least once.

The mezzanine bar in the Trafalgar was warm and dark, with a real wooden bar and a massive, gilt-framed mirror behind it. Racks holding scores of liquor bottles flanked the mirror and the beer taps were old style – long dowels of dark wood, intricately carved.

Harry waited until the bartender had served his other customers and was drying glasses before waving him over. The man tossed his towel over one shoulder and walked the length of the bar toward Harry, moving at his own pace, swaying with a sailor's gait. "Yes sir?"

"Wonder if I might ask you a few questions," Harry began. The barkeep selected a toothpick out of a small, ceramic container and stuck it ceremoniously at the corner of his mouth. He didn't respond.

120

"I'm somewhat involved in the deaths of those two gentlemen, yesterday."

"Yes sir?" the man replied. His eyes were a light gray and they never wavered far from Harry.

"Yes. This is a bit . . . dicey, actually. But one of the . . . er, suspects, I guess you'd say, claims he was in your establishment when Messrs. Detweiler and Keiter fell."

"Yes sir?" The bartender affected a look of absolute boredom, as if Harry were regaling him with the tales of a shoe salesman's harrowing day. It was a bit unnerving.

"Quite. The point being, I'd like to confirm that, one way or t'other."

The bartender said nothing.

"It's L.C. Noraine. Fellow about our age, pudgy, loud. Dresses like a cowboy, or p'raps the way one might expect a cowboy to dress, had one never seen an actual cowboy. D'you follow me? Sort of Tom Mix meets Lou Costello."

The bartender chewed on the tooth pick and nodded solemnly. At the end of the bar a man motioned toward his empty glass. "Excuse me, sir." Harry waited for the bartender to tend his bar, then watched the man amble back toward his end.

"So anyway, was he here?" Harry finally asked.

"Yes, sir. If we're talking about the same guy. Can I freshen that for you?"

"Er. Yes, thank you."

The barkeep did so, providing a fresh napkin with the new drink. "Anything else I can get you?"

"Yes. Do you recall when this fellow was here?"

"No," the barkeep replied promptly. "I don't keep track of people's comings and goings."

"Ah. Thank you," Harry replied.

That information, of course, confirmed absolutely nothing.

CHAPTER TWENTY-SIX

There were a few bars around Portland where journalists generally could count on finding fellow pen-pushers. Portland isn't that large a town, and after a while most members of the industry meet each other.

Nelligan had shared a few drinks and a few ribald stories with the news producer at the local PBS station, a frenetic woman named Nora Leipzig who, now in her late forties, had mastered the art of perspective. Nelligan had seen her cover an exhibition of miniature roses with the same intensity and organizational skills she had used while covering a major radiation leak at the Hanford nuclear facility.

Leipzig poured Nelligan a cup of decaf and gave him a thumb-nail description of "Focal Point," the weekly news program that featured two or more panelists and an audience of anywhere from fifty to four hundred, set up like "Donahue" but in the round, with the moderator and panelists surrounded by audience members who asked questions and made comments.

She confirmed that Saturday's live tape had focussed on the Greenpeace movement and that the audience had numbered about eighty. And yes, recording cartridges were kept for later viewing. Leipzig also asked about Martin's health – some time earlier, someone hoping to hurt Tucker Nelligan missed and hit Marty instead. The attorney remained in therapy and walked with twin, metal crutches.

Finally, small talk out of the way, she refilled Nelligan's cup and led him to a booth where a techie loaded up the "Focal Point" cart.

They showed Nelligan how to run the equipment then left him alone in the small, cube-shaped room with cheap plastic panelling and one wide, glass wall.

Nelligan punched the fast-forward button and whizzed through a pre-taped presentation that included the "Focal Point" logo and theme song, plus the moderator's brief description of the Greenpeace movement, complete with footage of the bludgeoning to death of baby seals and shots of small boats criss-crossing the path of Japanese whaling ships.

When the cameras shifted to the studio, Nelligan hit the play button and leaned back, feet up on the panel, fingers laced behind his head. It was an hour show, and almost forty-five minutes passed before he leaned forward and hit the pause button.

There, five rows back and to the moderator's left, sat Phoebe Pogue. He kept watching. At the fifty-one minute mark, only about five minutes away from the wrap-up, the camera swung toward the crowd. Joshua Pogue was there now, seated beside his wife. They were bent toward each other, Phoebe whispering in his ear.

Nelligan jotted the time down in his note pad then hit the rewind button. When the cart returned to the beginning, he started it all over again.

Nelligan was nothing if not patient. He watched the exact same show again, this time mentally keying himself to the space behind the moderator.

Sure enough, the camera showed that space at four minutes into the show. No Phoebe Pogue. At the nine minute mark and again at twelve and a half minutes: No Phoebe Pogue.

Nelligan kept his eye on the time-monitor. Seventeen minutes, eighteen, twenty three, twenty nine, thirty seven. Zip.

The first time he saw her was close to the forty-five minute mark.

Phoebe Pogue hadn't arrived at the studio until 5:45, fully three-quarters of an hour after Christopher Detweiler and Neil Keiter hit the pavement of Broadway.

Harry trudged down the corridor to the Astor hospitality room and rapped on the door. He tried collating what information he had learned and realized there was precious little of it. His head had begun to throb and his arthritic knee picked this opportunity to flare up.

Kate Fairbain answered the door and waved him in. "You look terrible."

"Well, I eat right, take care of myself, and root around in other people's tragedies every morning. The Henry Bishop Quick-Fix Diet Plan. How's Lee?"

"I sent him home with Penny," Kate replied, settling down in one of the two chairs. The table before her was strewn with research papers and text books. The television set was chained to one end of the table so she just stacked files atop the set. Kate was "dressed down" by her standards – black denim slacks, flats, and an emerald green sweater, the puffy sleeves shoved up to her elbows. Her reading glasses were nestled in her black and silver hair.

"You've been working on the timber program all day?" Harry asked. "Come along, I'll buy you some dinner."

"I can't," Kate replied. "Lee thinks there's still time to save this program, somehow."

"P'raps, but not tonight. The Japanese should be leaving right about now and there's not much we can do about it. Believe me: I've tried. Come on, we can grab a nosh."

She turned to him, smiling. "Nosh? My, aren't we becoming the Yank."

"Nosh. From the Yiddish *nosherai*, meaning 'tidbit.' From the Old High German *nascon*, meaning 'to gnaw or nibble.' Shall we gnaw or nibble something?"

Kate stretched her neck one way, then the other, feeling the muscles protest. "You're right, Harry. All right: Where to?"

Harry Bishop's parents had been the most frugal of Scots.

It was a character trait their son never got the hang of.

Thus, while Kate stayed in the car, Harry extracted the last one hundred and sixty dollars out of his checking account, via an Automatic Teller Machine nestled into a corner of the nearby 7-Eleven between the Slurpee dispenser and a comic book spinner rack.

Back in the car, he thanked Kate for waiting and directed her to Buttertoe's, a converted Victorian house on Belmont, in a less than reputable neighborhood on the east side of the river.

Kate parked the silver Saab apprehensively, engaging the security alarm, then followed him up the stairs to the old house. Any misgivings evaporated as they entered.

The house had been converted into a tiny restaurant with just two rooms and about ten tables. The walls, still adorned in the traditional beveled wooden moldings, were covered in period bric-a-brac and paintings.

The food matched the decor perfectly, a combination of European classics with American twists. Their meal, especially the all-chocolate dessert, was rich and sensuous.

Harry and Kate doddled over their food and the incredible dessert, which contained approximately seventeen trillion calories. They finished it off with coffee for Harry and tea for Kate.

Kate not only enjoyed every bite of the meal, she also noticed that Harry ordered a single glass of red wine – not two or three double Scotches, as he so often did when they were out together. She chose not to say anything but applauded mentally.

And, Kate being Kate and Harry being Harry, they soon shifted from small talk to politics, with Kate launching a lengthy and able defense of ten years of Reagan/Bush policy on Central America; adding that, while she didn't condone military responses to all situations, one would have to admit that the people of Grenada were happier now than they had been before the American rescue operation.

Harry countered by pointing out that the invasion had been an almost total brouhaha, with American troops sweltering in winter gear, no military maps, and an astounding lack of intelligence (the "rescue" team liberated one medical school campus, only to learn that there were two more campuses and most of the American students were elsewhere). He also relayed the story of the Army commander who had to use his AT&T calling card to call the Pentagon, since he was unable to get proper intelligence from the Naval vessels off the Grenadine coast. And finally, of then-Secretary of Defense Caspar Weinberger going on national television, three days after the invasion, to announce that the American students had been saved. Almost a third of the U.S. medical students were still in downtown St. George's, Grenada, watching the broadcast live via cable and wondering what the hell old Cap was talking about.

Kate argued vociferously, spouting figures and statistics on communist aggression in the Western Hemisphere. Harry didn't bother to wonder about the stats accuracy – Kate Fairbain was a walking Cray Computer, with an endless array of data stored accurately in her brain.

Forty-five minutes into the argument, Harry realized they had both slipped subconsciously into Russian. They were drawing very strange glances from the rest of the patrons.

Kate agreed that that was a good cue to leave.

The Saab purred up to the curb, three houses down from Harry's. "Come on," Kate said, slipping off her shoulder harness, "I'll walk you to the door."

The fine weather had decided to linger and the evening smelled sweet and dry. There was no hint of rain in the air and they could hear a solo blues guitar coming from somewhere nearby. Harry took a chance and let his hand slip over Kate's. She squeezed gently.

"Thanks for a lovely evening. It was good to get away from the hotel," she said.

"Thanks, also. We should do this more often."

"No," Kate smiled. "Don't be fooled. Tonight was wonderful but for the most part we drive each other crazy."

Harry sighed and fished through his pockets for his keys. "True. Come in for a wee dram?"

Kate thought about it for a moment, then shook her head. There was a three-quarter moon and the silver that had come to dominate her hair glistened. "I've got to get some sleep."

"Ah, well. That's all right. My basketball team has a rehearsal in the morning."

"Practice. And you still think you can coach a team, Harry?" Kate's eyes glittered like quicksilver when she tried not to laugh.

"Yes, actually. How difficult can it be? I've been reading up on it a bit and following the sports page in back issues of the *Post*. I've decided we should emulate the Celtics. They seem awfully good."

Kate almost lost control but reined in a guffaw. "SSSSeltics, Harry. You pronounce it with an 's'."

"Really? Ah," Harry replied. "Well then. Thanks again. Good night."

"Good night, Harry."

He leaned forward and kissed her politely on the cheek.

She leaned forward and kissed him on the lips, one ice-cold hand resting on his cheek. She held the tension a moment, then pulled back, smiled, and started back to her car.

It took Harry almost a minute to remember his keys, sift through them for the house key, and unlock the door. Kate tapped the car horn once as she passed.

Harry closed the door behind him and leaned against it, almost delirious. *I'm too old to be giddy*, he chastised himself.

"And if it isn't the Prodigal Son." Taddy McMurdo stepped out of the kitchen with a bottle of Scotch and two tumblers. "So tell me about your day?"

Harry loosened his tie, tossed his suit coat over an arm of the couch, and took one of the tumblers from Taddy.

The men settled down, Harry on the lumpy couch, Taddy in the over-stuffed rocking chair with thread-bare arm rests. The room echoed Harry's life. One entire wall was dominated by book shelves, with the texts on politics, history and economics filling one half, his fiction paperbacks the other. Harry was methodically collecting the comic strips of Milton Caniff, Will Eisner, Noel Sickles, Winsor McCay, Peter O'Donnell and Alex Raymond, and these hard- and soft-backs lined a lower shelf. There was a television with a VCR his daughter and son-in-law had purchased for him three years earlier. Harry had never figured out how to use it. Instead of paintings or prints, the few wall decorations were one-sheet movie posters for "Duck Soup," "Animal Crackers" and "A Day at the Races."

Taddy sipped his drinks and slipped off his scuffed, brown shoes, canting sideways in the chair and hoisting his stockinged feet up on a convenient book shelf. "That's a pretty, pretty lady, Boyo. You've been doing good for yourself these days. It'd be a crying shame to see her go to trial for the murders of Detweiler and Keiter, now, wouldn't it?"

Harry cocked one eyebrow. "I thought you were framing Lee Connar for this one?"

"Hmm? Oh. That's right. Sorry. Start over: My, that's a fine friend you've got there in Dean Connar. It'd be a crying shame to see him go to trial for the murders of Detweiler and Keiter, now, wouldn't it?"

Harry sipped his drink, feeling the fatigue wash over him. He hadn't wanted this confrontation – had actually fooled himself for years into believing it would never come about. He closed his eyes and reopened them. Taddy was still there, twirling his glass and listening to the ice cubes clink.

"And so our good friends the Japanese sail off into the sunset, Harry? Is that the end of this tale?"

Harry lifted his legs up onto the couch and laid back, the drink resting on his chest, ankles crossed. "I don't know, Taddy. This is your game. You write the rules."

"Too true," Taddy nodded. "But one can't always get the principles to play their parts as they should, and by my watch Mr. Nakano will fly the friendly skies right out of here in about fourteen hours. And the timber deal will be relegated to the ash heap of history."

Harry grinned and lifted his head off the couch's arm to take a healthy swig out of his Scotch. "Taddy, you're a liar."

"Moi?"

"Vous."

"Granted." The hefty man stood and retrieved the bottle, refilling both glasses before sitting again. "And what brings you to this conclusion?"

"Because I cannot imagine you giving a tinker's damn over this or any timber deal. The sale of lumber is, by its very nature, pedestrian. Mundane. Boring, even. And that, Taddy, t'ain't you."

McMurdo laughed. "I doubt there's a soul on Earth knows me better than the Mad Hatter."

Harry gulped a third of his drink. "The Mad Hatter and the March Hare. We were a pair, weren't we?"

"That we were, Harry. And now look at you! Skulking around this two-bit town!"

"This is where I live," Harry murmured. "I'm retired."

This brought another burst of laughter from Taddy. "Please! You may have the locals believing it's as easy as all that. Do your twenty years then retire with a pension and a gold watch. But don't try'n sell that Vaudeville routine to me, boyo. I knew you when! Hell, I'm Caroline's godfather."

Harry sipped his drink quietly. McMurdo again refilled their glasses.

"You've never told her I exist, I'll bet," McMurdo said softly. Harry didn't reply.

"And your bosom buddies here in Portland? Do they know about your . . . colorful past?"

"Some," Harry almost whispered. "Very little, but too much. By design, Taddy. I don't talk about the past."

Taddy chuckled, swirling his glass and watching the amber liquid whirl around the ice. "Let me guess. They think you were on the side of the angels?"

"Taddy. Please."

"Fine, fine. 'Nuff said. All of which brings us back to the Japanese," he said, propping his feet back up on the book shelf. "You may not be interested in trans-Pacific trade, buckaroo, but some folks are – the trade deficit being what it is. And I can't have the ambassador leaving here without a deal."

"Then don't let him leave," Harry suggested.

"These things are best done gently and subtly, as well you know, Harry. Any other suggestions?"

"Yes." Harry finished off the drink in a gulp and carefully set the glass down on the carpet. He threw one arm over his forehead, shielding his eyes. "Meet Mr. Nakano at the hotel tomorrow morning, before they check out, and inform him that you're sorry the deal fell through, especially since the first, small shipment of logs from Detweiler's land just arrived at a Port of Portland holding facility. Still, a buyer in South Korea has expressed interest, so the sale isn't lost. Then bid Mr. Nakano a *bon voyage*."

Taddy's eyes narrowed as he considered Harry's prone form. "And then?"

"And then Nakano's major domo – doma? – will inform the front desk that they're not leaving yet. Not until they do you the courtesy of at least examining the logs and letting the Kuroshio Group administrators know of this last-ditch, good-faith effort by their valued American friends."

Taddy grinned. "And what in hell are you up to, boyo? What's this about?"

Harry's forearm still covered his eyes. "Just do it, Taddy. Trust me."

McMurdo slipped into his shoes and stood. "Harry, do you know who killed Detweiler and Keiter?"

"No."

"Are you lying to me?"

"Possibly."

Taddy nodded, then knelt and refilled Harry's glass. "Right then. Good night, sweet Prince. See you in the morning."

130

CHAPTER TWENTY-SEVEN

Harry awoke at about eight the next morning and realized he was still on the couch. His lower back hurt and his legs were cramped and the head throbbed dully with a hangover. Niccolo had curled up in the space between his bent knees and the back of the couch.

Harry stood gingerly, waited for the vertigo to pass, then hauled himself into the bathroom for a long, hot shower and a shave.

Twenty minutes later, as the coffee machine gurgled to life, Harry called the front desk of the Hotel Trafalgar and asked to be switched through to Room 1314.

"I'm sorry sir," a cheerful voice replied. "The Nakano number is on do-not-disturb."

With Nakano and his translator still in town, the principals would all stay in place, Harry wagered. He poured a cup of the thick, oily coffee, slid two frosted strawberry Pop Tarts into the toaster oven and dialed Tucker and Martin's number.

"Hi, you've reached the Kady/Nelligan residence," Martin Kady's mellifluous courtroom voice sounded. "We're not home right now but at the sound of the beep, please leave your name, number and the time of day you called and we'll get back to you. If this is Sidney, the answer is yes, prima facie. If this is Harry, my associates and I will meet you at Astor around noon. *Beeeep.*"

Nelligan pulled into the two-car wide driveway of Detweiler Farms and let the Jeep drift to a halt. The metal gate hung akimbo from the fence, almost inviting him in. Why be rude? Nelligan thought, jamming the stick shift into first and gunning the engine.

He'd come dressed for the occasion, eschewing the tweed jacket and woolen sweater for blue jeans, thick-soled workboots and a Portland State University sweatshirt, ripped ragged around the collar. He swung along the cliff edge overlooking the Willamette River toward the Quonset hut and outbuildings adjacent to the oldest and tallest stand of planted timber.

Several buzz saws whined in the distance, as did the more basso rumblings of heavy machinery inside the tall hut, its metal skin rounded and glowing dully in the sunshine. As Nelligan stepped out of the Jeep, a thick-necked man in an unbuttoned leather vest and yellow hard hat stepped out of the building and hoisted a can of Dr. Pepper.

"Help you?" the man queried as Nelligan approached.

"Yeah, who's union shop steward?"

"Pete Rosenthal," the man answered. "You with the union?"

"It's about Neil Keiter." Nelligan blithely side-stepped the question and strode purposefully past the worker and around the Quonset hut. He found one corrugated metal shed and checked inside. It housed a tangled pile of hoes, shovels, coiled garden hoses and long, steel stakes. Inside the next, larger shed was a Caterpillar tractor and two backhoes.

As he approached the third shed, another man stood up from tying his boot laces and asked Nelligan what he was doing. "I dunno. Ask Pete Rosenthal," Nelligan shrugged.

The worker shrugged as well and went back to tying his laces.

Nelligan finally found the Detweiler Mark-One Trax – or what was left of it. It had been jacked up and towed to a corner behind the third shack and covered with an oily tarp. Nelligan hauled the material away, exposing the carcass to the sun. The Trax had been bright yellow and shiny, washed especially for the crowd of dignitaries. The butt end was still shiny, while the gnarled stump of the extensor arm and most of the single-seat cabin were

132

chipped and scarred by the rain of shrapnel. Exposed wires stuck out of the yellow arm and a jagged pattern of so-called safety glass rimmed the metal windshield sill. Nelligan had seen a great deal of blood in his day and could still detect the chocolate brown stains across the plastic seat and bathing the walls and floors of the cabin.

Harry had said the driver survived, though Nelligan couldn't figure out how. The guy must have lost more than half his blood supply.

Fifteen minutes later, Nelligan found what he was looking for. He had done a three-part feature story a few years earlier on the Portland Police Department's bomb squad, and had picked up some esoteric but interesting information on the nature of demolition. Inside the cracked stump of the extensor arm, some of the insulation had melted away from the wires, leaving the copper to glint in the sunlight. Nelligan tore off a thin wedge of iron that was all but disconnected to begin with. He rubbed the edge of a fifty-cent piece against the inside of the metal. Greasy soot came away.

Harry had said that someone spiked a tree, the way some environmentalists had done in other parts of the state, hoping some buzz saw would come along and disintegrate against the iron spike. That clearly happened here, Nelligan thought. But to make sure the effect worked, the disc saw and extensor arm had been rigged to blow up.

Nelligan pocketed the wedge of metal and a coil of wires from inside the stumped arm. Harry would know a chemistry professor or grad student up at Astor who could figure out what blew up inside the machine.

CHAPTER TWENTY-EIGHT

Harry circled the Trafalgar three times before spying a fifteen-minute parking slot on the Park Avenue side. Parallel parking wasn't his forte and that took another five minutes.

Being a Monday, downtown traffic was heavier than it had been the day before, although Park Avenue – with its stop signs at every block – remained fairly quiet. Harry left his obligatory rain coat draped over the passenger's seat and stepped out of the Datsun, walking halfway down the block to the remains of Neil Keiter's outline. The parking space where Keiter landed was empty, he noticed, due to a leather bag over the parking meter. Four more meters were likewise bagged, and on inspection, Harry realized why. Detweiler Farms had reserved almost half the block for the stretch limousine and the company.

The Portland police had taken to using athletic tape rather than chalk, Harry noticed. The human outline lay almost exactly inside a parking space on the Trafalgar side of the street. Yellow plastic warning ribbon staked out the area to keep away galkers but Harry stepped over the tape and studied the outline, leaning his shoulder against the Detweiler Farms van parked in the next space.

Several pedestrians, all dressed for the office, stared at Harry as they passed, wondering why anyone would step inside a cordoned-off zone.

"Good morning." The greeting snapped Harry out of his reverie. Detective Sergeant John Wiley stood on the other side of the tape barrier, hands clasped behind his back, his conservative suit and tie neat as a pin.

"Hullo," Harry offered a hand and Wiley shook. "You're up early."

Wiley almost smiled. "It's nearly nine, professor. I take it you're not a morning person."

"True." Harry stepped back over the warning tape and the two men started down the street toward one of the Trafalgar's side doors.

"By the way, Mr. Nakano didn't leave this morning after all. He's still here."

"Really?" Harry murmured. "How odd."

"Can we do anything for you today?" Wiley asked, his high pitched voice almost lost behind the din of the traffic.

"I think so," Harry replied. "I wondered what you'd found."

Wiley stopped in the shade of the hotel's deep, brick inlaid alcove, not reaching for the glass doors that led to the lobby. "The autopsy and investigation showed just what we thought, professor. Mr. Detweiler and Mr. Keiter must have been in Keiter's room, 1322. They were standing on the balcony, probably one or both leaning against the railing farthest from the wall. The railing gave away because of badly rusted screws. Mr. Keiter fell all the way to the ground, landing right where you saw him. He died instantly, of course. Mr. Detweiler fell closer to the building. He bounced off at least one other railing before catching his leg on a ninth-floor balcony. It was a woman on the eighth floor who discovered him dangling outside her window."

Harry winced.

"He also died instantly," Wiley continued, his voice soft and a bit harmonic. "He fractured his skull somewhere along the fall. Also snapped his spine when his leg caught on the ninth floor balcony."

Harry rubbed at the hang-over headache behind his forehead. "Horrible."

"Yes."

"But there's more?" Harry pushed. "Something bothering you – I mean, other than the violence and death?"

Wiley smiled. "Yes, sir. First, the hotel manager is almost a lunatic about being sued over this fiasco. He began checking every other balcony in the building. I don't have any people to spare, but his employees seemed to do a thorough job. They haven't found a single screw on any balcony as badly rusted as the ones from Mr. Keiter's room."

"Coincidence?" Harry asked, but there was a trace of sarcasm in his voice and Wiley didn't reply directly.

"Second, we found a notepad in Mr. Detweiler's suit coat pocket. One note said something about meeting with 'Dodge.' Do you know anyone named Dodge, sir?"

Harry shook his head.

"Neither do we, as of last night when I left the office. I haven't checked yet this morning. There was a second reference to 'Dodge': This time it was the name – or the *word*, I should say – scrawled heavily in Mr. Detweiler's notepad. Underlined twice, three exclamation marks."

"Ah ha," said Harry, since that seemed like a cue for a real detective to say 'Ah ha.'

"Third and finally, and I'm sorry to be graphic about this, but Mr. Keiter didn't . . . bounce."

Harry's hangover tumbled out of his head and down into his stomach. "Beg pardon?"

"Concrete is notoriously inelastic, professor, while the human body is made up mostly of water, and—"

"— and water doesn't compress," Harry finished.

"Yes sir. Meaning some people – not all, mind you, but many – bounce when they hit the sidewalk or street. Mr. Keiter didn't. He landed solidly."

"I need a pick-me-up in a way I can't even describe," Harry replied, feeling more than a bit nauseous. "Could you join me?"

"Thank you, sir. No. I've got some business to take care of. Was there anything else?"

The much taller man looked down on Wiley and gave him a wry, crooked smile. "You're taking my interference with more magnanimity than I would have expected, Sergeant. Why is that?"

"Because it's been brought to my attention by your friend in the Secret Service that I have no real choice in the matter. My job is awfully hectic, professor. I learned years ago not to worry about those things I cannot affect."

"I see. P'raps you're not completely without options, though."

A hint of interest twinkled in Wiley's eyes. "No?"

Harry opened the door to the lobby and stood aside for the cop to enter first. "I would think that 'my friend in the Secret Service,' quote unquote, would be anxious to avoid the media while in town. It'd be a pity if the photo dogs sniffed out his presence, wouldn't it?"

Wiley smiled broadly. It was the first reflexive display of genuine emotion Harry had ever noticed from the otherwise contained man.

"Have a nice day, professor." Wiley said.

CHAPTER TWENTY-NINE

"Business Journal. Can we help you?"

"Editorial, please."

"One moment."

Pause.

"Editorial."

"Hi. Is Dawn in?"

"Yeah. Hold it."

Shorter pause.

"This is Dawn."

"This is Tucker."

"Tuck! How're you doing? Is Marty feeling better?"

"He's great. He's bitching about the lack of bran in my diet, which is a good sign."

"So what's up?"

"Dawn, you're covering the Kuroshio Group venture with Detweiler and Astor College, aren't you?"

"Yeah, sure, but that deal is dead in the water, you should pardon the expression. Haven't you heard?"

"Sure. But now it's cop-shop, and that's my beat. Listen, let me ask you something: You know that explosion out at Detweiler Farms on Saturday?"

"Yeah?"

"Were you there?"

"No. No media knew they were going out to Wilsonville, at least no one on the international commerce beat seemed to know anything about it. Detweiler served in the State

Legislature for a couple terms, back in the seventies, and I don't think he likes . . . liked the press much. Anyway, we were told diddly about this whole affair. Right from the start it was hush-hush."

"So, as far as you know, the tour of the tree farm was top secret."

"Far as I know, Tuck."

"Thanks, Dawn. You're a pal. Give my love to Steve."

"The hell I will."

Click.

The two police officers had been removed from the Nakano suite but the two agents remained, both standing. Someone had brought two comfortable chairs out to them but both agents eschewed the comfort. They were tough as nails and proud of it. Only wimps and commie sympathizers use chairs.

"Is Miss Sheppard in?" Harry asked. The two men exchanged glances through their polarized shades, trying to decide where national interests lie.

"No sir," Agent Johnson said at length. "She left about fifteen minutes ago."

"Yes sir," Agent Jensen concurred. "She said she wanted some fresh air."

Harry sauntered back to the bank of elevators. Fresh air meant Kimiko Sheppard either went for a walk around Portland, or was still somewhere in or near the hotel. Considering how dependent the old man seemed on her translation skills, Harry figured the latter more likely than the former. When the elevator came, he hit the button for the thirty-first floor.

Sure enough, he found Sheppard sitting by herself at a round table on the observation deck, dressed this morning in a pleated skirt and a cream colored blouse with ruffles at the sleeves and high neck. The lightness of the material contrasted with her jet black hair, which she wore in a wedge. Her ever-present lap top computer sat on the table beside a china coffee cup and a scone.

"Pardon me, Ms. Sheppard. May I join you?"

Sheppard looked up from the flip-open monitor screen, frowning. Once she registered who it was, the frown melted. "Professor . . . Bishop, wasn't it? Please sit down. How are you this morning?"

Harry took the opposite seat and Sheppard put the machine on sleep mode. "That's a wondrous instrument you have there," Harry said, then ordered coffee with cream and sugar from the passing waiter.

"Thank you. The Kuroshio Group designed and markets this computer, you know," Ms. Sheppard replied, blushing slightly. A corporate mentality makes bragging about one's merchandise second nature, Harry realized, but some people are more comfortable with it than others. "Believe it or not, I was just writing a memo to a clerical worker at the headquarters in Hokkaido, reminding him to forward some contracts to our London office. This technology means Mr. Nakano can be at the office even when he's on the other side of the planet from his office."

"Wondrous, indeed," Harry replied. His indifference to computers was monumental, but why be rude? "Ms. Sheppard, may I ask you a few questions?"

She sat up a fraction straighter, like a school girl called upon by the teacher. "Of course, professor. But there are some matters I honestly cannot discuss without permission of Mr. Nakano."

"Of course. Perfectly reasonable. Please let me know when I overstep that boundary."

She smiled politely and folded the lap top's screen down over the keyboard, directing her entire attention upon Harry. She had absolutely spellbinding eyes, Harry noticed. Chocolate brown and brimming with intelligence and wit. They reminded him somewhat of Neil Keiter's eyes.

"How long has the Kuroshio Group been doing business with Detweiler Farms?"

"Several years, I believe. At least since 1982. But of course, the corporation has never worked as closely with the late Mr. Detweiler as we would have if the trade negotiations had come to fruition. This was Mr. Nakano's most fervent

140

dream. He's something of an Americanophile, if you'll excuse that terrible bastardization." Sheppard smiled shyly.

"Of course. 'Though he doesn't speak any English?"

"Japanese people of my generation study English for six years, in what you call high school. My father is an American Naval officer, so I spoke English even before my mother's Japanese. But Mr. Nakano was about fifteen when the war ended and the bombs were dropped. In this time, people were . . . discouraged from learning too much English. He also has an old-fashioned belief that he's too old to learn, although I disagree."

Harry nodded. "I'm not so sure, Ms. Sheppard. I tried to pick up some French about seven years ago for a trip I was taking and had a terrible time with it. P'raps some things are best taught to children."

"Perhaps," she replied.

"Let me ask you another question. Why didn't you and Mr. Nakano leave this morning?"

Sheppard frowned, vertical creases appearing in her forehead. "I'm . . . not positive, sir. An American official called this morning to wish us bon voyage. He also said a shipment of timber had arrived from Mr. Detweiler's company. When I mentioned it to Mr. Nakano, he insisted I change our reservations. We went down to the docks at dawn this morning to inspect the shipment."

She seemed genuinely concerned by the change in plans, Harry noted. "And what did you see?"

Sheppard shrugged slightly. "Forgive me, sir. My degree is in business administration. I'm not very good with understanding lumber products. To be honest, it looked like several truckloads of logs. I couldn't even tell you what sort of trees they were."

So Taddy actually dredged up some real lumber to go along with the fib. Despite himself, Harry was impressed. "The logs pleased Mr. Nakano?"

"Y-yes. *Pleased* is a good term," she nodded slowly.

"One last question. Has the Kuroshio Group had good working relations with the American labor unions?"

"I hesitate to answer that, professor. We've had almost no relations with them, I believe."

"But you had met Neil Keiter before?"

"Yes. He came to Japan last year. I remember seeing him in a board conference at our headquarters."

"Thank you, ma'am." Harry left money beside his coffee cup and stood. "I appreciate your help."

"Not at all, professor." She replied politely. But there was a hint of doubt and concern in her voice now. Something Harry asked had triggered a memory.

CHAPTER THIRTY

Nelligan waited for the receptionist to finish her telephone conversation, then smiled his warmest smile and flashed his *Portland Post* identification. "Hi. I'm Tucker Nelligan with the *Post*. Can I talk to you for a moment?"

The bubble-gum chewing receptionist was dressed in Spandex and wore her ice blonde hair clipped close around her ears. It was this month's "in" look for a certain "in" crowd, Nelligan assumed. The wall sign behind her chair read *Welcome! Let Elliot's "Show-fur" Service Show You the Town!*

"Yeah?" the receptionist continued to frown, the vertical stripes of red, pink and amber in her eye-shadow blending together.

"I understand one of your drivers was hired this weekend by Detweiler Farms. I need to speak to him or her, please."

The reception chewed the gum more vigorously. "I don't know. We're probably not supposed to give out that information."

" 'Probably' not?" Nelligan smiled again.

"Well, no one's ever asked that before. But I just figured."

"Ma'am, my newspaper has reason to believe that the driver of that limo saw something that could crack open an international conspiracy!" As Nelligan leaned forward to whisper, the receptionist's eyes expanded. "Listen, this is just between you and me, right?"

"Yeah," the receptionist breathed.

"Ma'am – um, I didn't get your name."

"D'arci. That's with an apostrophe after the D and ends with an i."

"Ah. Got it. I'm Tucker. D'arci, the *Post* would truly appreciate any help you could give us on this one. We're talking one of the major stories of the year, here. Once my story's broken, the big TV crews will be scouring all over this place. But there may not be a story unless I can speak to that chauffeur. Huh? What do you say?" He smeared the sincere Mr. Nice Guy smile on even thicker.

"We-e-e-elll," D'arci wavered. "This is an *international* conspiracy?"

"Yes, ma'am. And your help would be greatly appreciated, D'arci."

"I dunno. *All* the big TV networks will be here? Doing interviews and stuff?"

"Bet on it. Dan Rather himself is in on this one. '60 Minutes,' too."

"Wow. Ok, the guy you want is in today. Hold on and I'll get him." D'arci picked up the old Princess style telephone and punched three digits. Nelligan hadn't realized how long it had been since he'd seen a regulation AT&T telephone. These days almost every business had plastic Japanese models with a thousand bells and whistles.

D'arci told the person on the other line that a reporter was here and wanted to ask him a few questions. Nelligan was surprised that she didn't relay the information about Dan Rather and the international conspiracy. As she hung up, D'arci blew a quick, pink bubble and smiled at Nelligan. "He'll be right out."

"Thanks, D'arci." Nelligan winked at her.

"And Mr. Nelligan, sir?"

"Yes?"

"I've got a masters in telecommunications and a minor in psychology. You might mention that to Dan Rather, next time the two of you get together for an international conspiracy."

Nelligan's Mr. Nice Guy smile faded, replaced by the real thing. "Damn. Right. Sorry about that."

D'arci returned to her telephones as a man stepped out from behind the counter. "You looking for me?"

Nelligan offered a hand and decided to eschew the bullshit – at least in front of the receptionist. "I'm Tucker Nelligan with the *Post* and I'm looking for you if you drove the limo for the Japanese trade delegation at the Trafalgar."

The man shook his hand. "Yeah, that was me. Ernest deSidrio. Sit down. What can I do for you?"

The men sat in matching, uncomfortable dining room chairs – the only comforts afforded to the lobby. "Were you out in Wilsonville Saturday, when that explosion occurred?" Nelligan asked, flipping open the palm-sized note pad.

"Yeah, but I didn't see anything," deSidrio replied. "You see, I'm just the wheels. They don't invite us drivers to take part in stuff, once we get where we're going. That's just one of the basic rules of the chauffeuring game, y'understand." DeSidrio was a hefty man wearing bright red suspenders over a red plaid work shirt. Like most overweight people, sitting was uncomfortable and deSidrio squirmed in the hard-backed chair, seeking a good position.

"You were in the car when the explosion occurred?" Nelligan asked.

"Yessir. Like I say."

"Did anyone leave the exhibition early?"

"Nope. And I got to tell you, the cops already asked me these things. But of course, ask away. Anything you want."

Nelligan was well aware that some people loath being interviewed while others thrive on it. "Were you hired by Christopher Detweiler?"

"Well, sort of. A secretary from his office called and set up the gig. But I talked to Mr. Detweiler both on Friday and Saturday. He's the one who told me where we were heading each time. He gave me the word and I hauled that Chinese or Japanese couple wherever I was supposed to. That's one of the rules of the chauffeuring game, y'understand: You go where you're told. Like in the Army."

"Uh huh. Mr. deSidrio, when were you told to head out to the farm in Wilsonville?"

"When?"

"Yes sir."

145

DeSidrio shifted his ample rear in the seat again and hoisted one beefy ankle up to rest on his opposite knee, then quickly shifted out of that position. How this man stayed seated behind the limo wheel long enough to drive was a mystery to Nelligan.

"I guess I got the word, or D'arci here did, on Friday afternoon. We were told early so I could have the old bus gassed up and ready to roll. One of the rules in chaufferring is never, and I mean *never*, stop for gas while you got a customer in the back. That's like a *golden* rule."

"I see. One last question. Did you tell anyone where you were heading on Saturday?"

"No sir. Not a soul," deSidrio replied, nodding once for emphasis. "I didn't tell anyone."

"You told your brother-in-law and your wife," D'arci cut in, not looking up from her massive, green Selectric.

"Huh? Well, sure. I tell Darlene everything! We've got that kind of relationship, Mr. Nelligan. Real close. And I told Roy but so what, right? D'arci, you wanna pay attention to that desk and let me talk to the man, please? All right?"

D'arci carefully slid a rectangle of correction tape behind the typewriter's hammer and blotted out an error, not looking up. "And you told some guy in the bar across the road. The guy you were playing darts with, remember? I was in having a drink and—"

"All right!" deSidrio roared at the receptionist, who remained absolutely unflustered by his bluster. "Jesus H. Christ on a bicycle, D'arci! I'm talking to the man, here. Can't you see?"

"You told someone in a bar about driving out to Detweiler Farms?" Nelligan cut in softly.

DeSidrio blanched and shifted in the chair. "Yeah. Some guy. It was no big deal."

"Anyone you know?"

"No. Like I say. It was a guy."

Nelligan took pains to write "a guy" in the note pad. "Can you describe him? Is he a regular of this bar? I'd like to talk to him."

"No, I never seen him before. Like I say, it was no big deal."

"But you *can* describe him?"

146

"Sure I can. I got a memory like a steel trap. I remember my locker combination from high school, still. This guy was a Negro. Now, some folks wouldn't have a drink with one of them, let alone play darts. But not Me. I'm not like that. The Negroes are just fine, I always say. Anyway, like I'm saying, this guy was big, about six-two or so, and he wore jeans and and a Levi jacket."

"And he had eyes to die for," D'arci added.

DeSidrio bristled. "Anyway, he didn't say his name and I don't think I said mine. It was just a game of darts, y'understand."

"Yes sir," Nelligan replied, mentally comparing and contrasting this desciption with Harry's description of Neil Keiter.

CHAPTER THIRTY-ONE

The hotel day-manager was a twitchy little man with dark brown hair turned white over both ears. The effect was so bilaterally perfect that it looked like an amateur actor's attempt to "age-up" a character using white dye. The manager jangled his key ring nervously as Harry glanced around Room 818.

"Nothing even remotely like this has ever happened at the Trafalgar before," the manager said for the sixth time.

" 'Course not," Harry soothed, stepped out onto the balcony and inhaling the fresh air. The Trafalgar's bulky, cubist shadow had settled over Park Avenue, just touching the base of the Oregon Art Institute and the Masonic Temple on the far side of the narrow, wooded strip. Harry turned and peered up. There was no sign on the iron balcony above him that a former state senator's carcass had recently dangled there. The fine-tooth investigation by the homicide squad and the hotel's panicky clean-up had eliminated all evidence of the tragedy.

"I understand this isn't the first murder to be associated with that college up on the hill," the manager sniffed. Detective Sergeant Wiley had provided Harry's bone fides, and the manager naturally assumed he was talking to another police investigator.

"So I hear," Harry replied dryly. "One thing about the Astor faculty, you can generally tell where they've been by watching the obituaries. And the woman who was staying here?"

"Left," the day-manager replied, blanching a bit more. "She didn't even pack. We had to send her clothes to her. At our expense, of course."

"Of course. Thank you, sir. I s'ppose that's all I really wanted to see."

They stepped back out into the hall and the manager locked the door behind them. Harry shook his hand, then found the elevator and rode up to the fourteenth floor, hoping to fine Kate or Lee in the Astor hospitality suite.

The door was wide open and Lee Connar was sitting on the window sill, talking on the telephone. Harry waved from the door and Lee lifted a can of V-8 juice in salute.

He said "Yes" three times, "Fine" once and "Thanks. Bye," then hung up. "Harry, it looks like Takeshi Nakano didn't leave this morning."

"So I hear. What's the plan now?"

Lee rubbed his eyes. From the red circles under his eyes and his pallor, Harry guessed Lee hadn't slept a wink that night. "You look like death on a soda cracker, Lee."

"You're not exactly Douglas Fairbanks Jr."

Harry sat on the edge of the bed. "So now what?"

"I don't know. Except that I guess Astor is now hosting this whole damned thing, instead of . . . poor old Christopher."

Harry rested his elbows on his knees and steepled his fingers under his chin. He had a vague notion of what was going on – vaguer than vague, actually – and he needed some time. "Were I you, heaven forbid, I'd give Nakano-san a tour of Astor, with an emphasis on the International Affairs department. After what happened this weekend, he may not want anything to do with Northwest timber, ever again, but that's no reason to assume he's uninterested in the cultural exchange projects."

Lee drained his vegetable juice and mulled the notion. "Makes sense, Harry. I hear he wants to fly out to Europe tomorrow. No sense wasting today."

Lee picked up the phone again and began making plans. Harry checked his battered old Timex and realized he was going to be late for his appointment with Martin Kady's client. He waved to Lee and headed back to the elevator, punched

149

the bottom button, and leaned back against the mirrored walls, rubbing his temples in a futile gesture. The hangover was persistent.

He began playing the moves through in his head, trying to get the principals to play their roles again: Christopher Detweiler and Neil Keiter return from the Wilsonville tree farm and head to the irrespective rooms. Detweiler later goes over to Keiter's room, where the two of them step out onto a balcony. The balcony gives way. Keiter falls all the way to the street, while Detweiler slams against at least two of the lower balconies.

His headache hung on tenaciously and Harry decided he was hungry. That usually helped him get past the truly obnoxious hangovers.

Why was Detweiler in Keiter's room, he wondered. What did the timber magnate and the union rep. talk about? Why were they on the balcony?

What's Kate Fairbain doing for dinner tonight?

Harry scrounged through his pockets and found a capless pen and a month-old late-book notice from the library. Holding the paper against the mirror, he made a note to ask Sergeant Wiley if any liquor glasses were found in Keiter's room or smashed on the street.

The elevator door hissed open and Harry stepped out, stopping suddenly when he realized he was lost. He faced a long cement wall, unadorned by wallpaper. The floor was cement and light bulbs in metal cages hung from the ceiling. To his left was a massive spider web of steam pipes and boiler plating, and to his left was a tall, shallow metal box, similar in size and mass to a row of lockers in a high school. The box, Trafalgar's switchboard, hummed and clicked as Harry stood there. A narrow, aluminum attaché case sat beside the switchboard, attached by two coaxial cables. The logo on the side read Kuroshio.

Wonderful, he thought. *I'm in the basement.* Harry turned and tapped the only elevator button – an up button.

"Can I help you?" a heavy set black woman with a rolling laundry basket came around the corner and eyed Harry critically. "Guests aren't allowed down here, you know."

"Quite. Sorry. Seemed to have lost track of the elevator," he replied.

The door slid open and both Harry and the maid stepped aboard, Harry sandwiched in one corner to make room for the laundry hamper.

"Hold it!" Someone called and whisked into the elevator just as the doors began to close. His body broke the electric beam and the doors bounced fully open again before closing.

Harry reached over the laundry basket and hit the Lobby button. The maid hit six. The newcomer hit thirteen.

"Hey, Josh," the maid smiled at him. "How you doing?"

Harry glanced at the man and recognized him as the bearded protestor he had seen both outside the Trafalgar and at the tree farm in Wilsonville.

"Pardon me," Harry snagged the man's attention. "You're one of the environmentalists, aren't you?"

The blood drained quickly from the man's face. He said nothing. The elevator shuddered to a stop on the lobby and the doors opened.

"I'm Henry Bishop, Astor College. You are?"

The man glanced around the tiny cubicle and realized there was no way out of politeness. "Joshua Pogue," he mumbled.

"Your floor, sir," the maid said to Harry.

"That's OK. I think I'll head up. Actually, Mr. Pogue, I wondered if I could talk to you."

Joshua bolted quickly through the door and out into the plush carpeted lobby. Harry tried to squeeze past the hamper but the doors hissed closed. "Damn."

"Mister, what floor *do* you want?" the maid asked, exasperation dripping off her voice.

"The thirty-second," he replied dryly.

"This building's only got thirty-one."

"Then I'm in the wrong building. Sorry to have bothered you. D'you know that fella?"

"Josh? Yeah, sure," she replied as the elevator coasted to a stop on the sixth floor. "He used to be a custodian here, up to about a month ago."

CHAPTER THIRTY-TWO

Daniel Tadson McMurdo awoke around nine that morning and dialed the Trafalgar's room service, ordering eggs, sausage, home fried potatoes, wheat toast with jam and as much black coffee as they could provide. By the time he had showered, the breakfast had arrived, along with a copy of *The Oregonian*.

Taddy frowned at the paper. He ate quickly, browsing through the sports section (with special attention to the box scores), the business and financial listings, the comics, the opinion columns and Doonesbury, and finally the A section of national and international news.

His stomach was sated but his mind wasn't. Taddy threw down the paper in disgust. Small towns all had horrible newspapers, he firmly believed. Utter trash. Now the *Boston Globe* – there was a newspaper.

Sighing the sign of the historically put-upon, Taddy slipped into his shoes, pulled a handful of coins out of the pockets of his other slacks and headed down to the lobby, to find a copy of the *Globe, The New York Times* or, at very least, *The Wall Street Journal*.

What he got instead was even more of *The Oregonian* – courtesy of a reporter and photographer accompanied by writers and shooters from *The Post* and *Willamette Week*, three journalists from radio stations with their tape recorders slung over their shoulders and microphones held high, and techies from all four local TV news programs, their on-camera talent standing back, waiting to ask a few questions.

The barrage hit him in the lobby: A million questions about the Secret Service's interest in the deaths of Christopher Detweiler and Neil Keiter.

Steaming, Taddy tried to wave off the pack with "no comment" comments. It took him almost fifteen minutes to sidle back to the bank of elevators and escape the Fourth Estate.

Taddy stood in the center of the elevator, fists clenched at his side, and sizzled as he rode up. This had all the trappings of The Mad Hatter.

Portland can feel like some forested Magical Mystery Tour. Harry's beat-up Datsun jostled through the stop-and-start traffic of downtown for a good fifteen minutes before reaching the southern tip of the West Hills. The street changed in a flicker from urban commercial to turn-of-the-century homes, wide, sloping lawns, verandas and wild ivy on trellises. He had entered the realm of the rose gardens for which Portland is rightly famous, and thorny, irridescent rose bushes festooned almost every home for a few blocks.

Then suddenly the road took another turn and Harry might as well have been driving through a national forest, miles from civilization. Great conifers towered over the road on either side and underbrush dropped lateral visibility down to a few yards. Harry had a fleeting glimpse of a deer behind a Douglas fir to his left, but after a decade in Portland the site hardly surprised him anymore. Harry remembered when he first moved to the city and heard people in West Linn talk about the damned deer coming down off the hills to eat their flowers.

That had been a major factor in Harry's decision to stay.

Now the road looped to the right and the sprawling campus of John Jacob Astor came into view, the ultra-modern library and massive brick physics building, known as the Keep, towering over the lower campus.

Harry was late and parked in a fire lane, knowing the odds were against getting towed. It did happen on campus but not all that often. With his rain coat over his arm and his worn, leather doctor's bag in the other hand, Harry hurried across the campus, cutting through the Western Lawn and down the wide, flat-stone steps to the Student Union Building.

He stopped first in the cafeteria to pick up two maple bars and a Styrofoam cup of coffee, along with two packets of non-dairy creamer and two packets of non-Earth originating sweetener. Harry carefully wrapped the maple bars in three paper napkins and stored them in his doctor's bag.

That took care of lunch – provided he found time to eat. Next stop was his campus mail box, which contained three warning notices from the administration, regarding clerical forms he was supposed to have turned in weeks earlier. Harry couldn't remember ever having heard of the forms before, so he tossed the notes away (as he had their predecessors, weeks earlier).

"Hi, professor."

Harry looked up from the garbage can to find a Japanese-American student in a Red Sox cap, working behind the post office window. "Mr. Takimura? How's your summer fairing?"

Makoto Takimura grinned at him and shoved aside the Sports Illustrated he had been reading. "Pretty good, so far. I'm not taking any classes. Hey, have you heard from Sandi?"

"Your old editor is burning up Los Angeles, I understand. She sent me a post card last week; said she's enjoying the internship quite a bit. How about you? I assume the college newspaper is shut down for the term?"

"Yeah," Makoto replied glumly. "I haven't taken hardly any photos all months. It's pretty boring."

Harry thought about that for a moment, resting his coffee cup on the post office window sill. "Well, there's to be a bit of excitement on campus this afternoon. Maybe you could take a few photos."

"Great!" Makoto's smile threatened to bisect his face. "When and where?"

Lyman Bledsoe Jr., chairman of the college's political science department, skidded around the corner, his pudgy arms waving at his side. The department secretary sighed heavily and wondered what new crisis awaited her.

God bless Monday mornings, she thought.

"Barbara!" Lyman squeaked. "My God, where's Henry?"

"Professor Bishop is . . ." she stretched away from her PC terminal and thumbed through the notes held by a magnet to her in-basket. ". . . over in the sports complex until about noon."

"Sports! Sports?" Lyman's tubby body all but quivered and his thick glasses slid down his nose. "My God, we've got a major problem here! What's he doing in the sports complex?"

Barbara sipped her herbal tea and coaxed a smile to her face. "I don't know, Lyman. If you'll watch the phones, I'll walk over and see."

Lyman blanched and backed away from the beige, plastic master telephone module that looked like a primary monitor board at Cape Canaveral. "No, no. We'll go find him. Thank you."

As he stormed out, Barbara shifted in her chair to see who "we" were. Behind the diminutive Lyman Bledsoe Jr. trooped a dozen young and bewildered students and a man in sweats with a whistle hanging from a loop around his neck.

"Oh dear," Barbara sighed again, suddenly understanding that Harry's errant Summer Sampler class had been unearthed.

Nelligan brought the Jeep to a halt outside the college's information booth and honked once. The work-study student inside slipped open the window.

"One second," Martin Kady said to the passenger in the back seat, then rolled down the passenger-side window and smiled at the student.

"Yes sir?"

"Hi. We need a parking permit for the sports complex, please."

She consulted a clipboard. "Is this college business, sir?"

Nelligan leaned to his right, away from the steering wheel and into the student's line of sight. "Right. We're proctors with the A.D.B.L. conference. President Eckersley asked us to help out. Hell of a situation you folks have here."

The student scanned her clipboard, shrugged, and made out

a parking pass for the Jeep. She glanced at the passenger in the back seat, her eyes locking on his face, recognition dawning.

"Thank you," Martin took the notes and rolled up the window. "A.D.B.L., Tuck?"

"Any Damn Bunch of Letters. It's a big campus, counselor. No one knows everything that's happening here."

As he accelerated the work-study student's jaw dropping open.

"Ohmygoddd . . ." she breathed.

Harry found three of "his" players in the long, tiled corridor that abutted the gymnasium, dressed in jeans and letterman jackets, Nike athletic bags tucked under their bench. One of the boys, Wes Kiley, lifted his Dr. Pepper can in salute. "Morning, sir."

"Hullo, Mr. Kiley. Gentlemen. Has practice not started? You're not in costume."

"Uniform," one of the boys correctly politely.

"Quite right. Uniform." Harry was breathing heavily and plopped down on the bench beside them. "Am I early?"

The three boys smiled at each other, but without much mirth. "No, sir," the tall, black kid in red canvas hightop sneakers replied. "Um, we're heading out."

"Leaving?"

"Yes sir," Wes nodded. "One of the deans is in the locker room, telling the other guys about what's happened."

"Ah. I see. What *has* happened?"

Wes leaned forward, elbows on knees. "No offense, professor, but this was supposed to be a summer basketball camp. I mean, the twelve of us can play hoops all day long, but we're not really learning anything. We sort of need a coach."

"But you have a coach," Harry replied, a touch of angst in his voice. "Come now, things have been a bit . . . spotty, I'll admit. Not to worry. I have a plan."

The three boys exchanged glances. Their countenances did not glow with renewed faith, Harry noted.

Dean of Students Jocelyn Stuyvesant, a decidedly monumental woman with a bouffant hair do, stepped out of the locker room with the other nine boys in tow. They looked as dejected as their team mates.

"Professor Bishop?" Dean Stuyvesant scowled at him. Harry had known her for years and honestly couldn't remember ever seeing any other expression. "I understand there's been a terrible mix-up about this Summer Sampler course."

"One might say that, yes," Harry smiled politely.

"Which you made no effort to correct through my office." Dean Stuyvesant peered down her bulbous nose at him. She was widely regarded as the most by-the-book member of a by-the-book administration. Harry's inability to handle this situation accordingly had set her afire.

"I contacted my department chairperson and let him handle it," Harry replied. "Proper channels."

"My office handles all Summer Sampler programs, professor. Surely you were aware of that?"

The boys looked sheepishly at Harry. They didn't like seeing anyone balled out.

"Henry!"

"Oh, dear," Harry sighed. Lyman Bledsoe Jr., a tall man in sweats and a dozen young men and women burst into the corridor from outside. Lyman's chubby cheeks were almost eggplant purple. "This is a terrible situation, Henry! Terrible! Do you realize you didn't attend your own Summer Sampler class indoctrination period, last Friday? Henry, that's completely against regulations!"

"You didn't attend your own class's indoctrination program?" Dean Stuyvesant arched her painted eyebrows.

"Lyman, my dear fellow, as I told you, I wasn't assigned any political science students. Rather, I was given these twelve young men and a basketball camp."

"*You're* my round-ball team?" the man in sweats piped up.

"Coach Baldwin? Did Professor Bishop have your students?" Dean Stuyvesant asked. Her voice snapped dully like flint against coal.

"My God, people," Harry finally stood. "Let's not invoke that Mann Act, shall we? I'm not a white slaver, whisking whole basketball teams off to be sold to the European leagues. Coach

157

Baldwin, I assume you have my students and I had yours. No harm's been done, I'd say."

"No harm?" Stuyvesant almost hissed. "We are an accredited school, professor. Accredited with the State Department of Higher Education and the United States Department of Education. That means the faculties offering our classes are qualified. Neither you nor Coach Baldwin are qualified to run the courses you've been running. I'm afraid there will have to be an investigation."

"Investigation!" Lyman squawked. "Henry! How could you get me into this situation."

"You understand any of this?" Coach Baldwin asked Harry.

"'Fraid not."

"Me either. Here are your students. Sorry about the screw up."

"I'm afraid we'll have to reconsider the political science and sports departments' participation in further Summer Sampler programs," the dean pronounced heavily, pursing her lips as if the punishment, while vile, hurt her more than it did the irresponsible faculty members. Lyman began bleating, explaining that nothing like this had ever happened before.

"It was only one day and a weekend," Coach Baldwin cut in. Lyman and the Dean glared at him, aghast at his simplistic appraisal.

"Sorry for the bother," Harry said as an aside to the coach. His twelve students and the twelve basketball players had begun mingling, hoping to stay out of the firefight.

"No sweat," the coach replied. "I didn't have much to say to 'em. I didn't even know what the hell political science was."

"Ah well," Harry replied. "I also was less than the ideal basketball coach. Still, I made some plans for today. I called in the cavalry."

"Yeah? Me too," he replied. "My brother-in-law is in town. We don't get along all that great but the guy knows his stuff and he's been on TV a lot. Anyway, he's visiting and I asked him to come speak to the kids today. I hope that's cool with you."

"Absolutely. I also acquired an assistant to, er, run some drills, as they say." The outer door swung open as Nelligan and his two passengers entered. "Here he is, now," Harry waved.

Martin Kady rested his weight on one metal crutch and waved with the other hand. The third man, towering over Nelligan and Kady, nodded shyly at the crowd inside.

"My God," Dean Stuyvesant hissed.

"Jesus, Joseph and Mary," Coach Baldwin whispered.

The two dozen students began bubbling as if ready to explode.

Coach Baldwin blanched and turned to Harry. "That's Larry Bird!"

"Ah, you know each other, then?" Harry smiled. "My friend Martin here is an attorney. He represented Mr. Bird once. How d'you do, Mr. Bird. I'm Henry Bishop."

The Celtic shook his hand.

The students suddenly encircled the towering man, a thousand compliments and questions ringing through the halls. Harry began to realize they all had heard of Mr. Bird. He suspected Bird would be an adequate assistant coach for today's practice.

"This is . . . Geez . . ." Baldwin shook his head. "I owe you, professor."

"Tosh," Harry replied. "By the way, who d'you get for my class?"

"My brother-in-law. My wife says he's a real pistol. You might have heard of him: John Galbraith?"

Harry almost fainted. Lyman and Dean Stuyvesant stopped nattering at each other, their jaws dropping.

"John *Kenneth* Galbraith is your brother-in-law?" Harry whispered.

"Yeah. He's in town visiting. It's all right, isn't it?"

"John *Kenneth* Galbraith is on campus?"

"Yeah. I told him to meet me in the faculty lounge in about fifteen minutes. Hey, that's OK, isn't it? I don't want to step on any toes or anything."

"No, no," Harry's eyes shimmered. "He's, ah, quite sufficient."

Baldwin shook his head and stared at the Celtic. "Geez! Larry Bird!"

"Yes," Harry drawled, shaking his head in bewilderment. "He's not Galbraith, mind you, but he's not bad."

CHAPTER THIRTY-THREE

The students in Baldwin's basketball camp followed their real coach and the Portland Trail Blazers into the locker room, their eyes as large as doughnuts.

The students in Harry's poli.sci.course followed Lyman Bledsoe Jr. to a vacant lecture hall, while Dean Stuyvesant waddled off toward the faculty lounge to locate John Kenneth Galbraith, one of the greatest economists, historians and political scientists in America.

Harry whined and moaned and threatened to pout, but Martin and Tucker convinced him that a council of war was required. It had been Kate Fairbain's idea, and she was awaiting them at her office in the economics department faculty building.

"But I'm missing John Kenneth Galbraith!" Harry wailed.

"Yes, yes," Martin soothed him. "Don't worry, I'll record him for you."

Nelligan shot him a questioning glance. "You're going with the class? We might need you."

"Are you nuts?" Martin replied. "This is *Galbraith*."

Harry began to plead, but Nelligan took him by the arm and lead him toward the economics department.

Kate kept a wicker basket of Stash tea bags and a Pyrex coffee pot filled with water on a heating element behind her desk. As Harry and Tucker settled down on either end of the gray and copper couch, she poured tea for all three of them.

"But it's *John Kenneth Galbraith!*" Harry implored, certain he would find a kindred spirit here.

Kate sniffed. "Over rated. I've read everything he's ever written. He's good, of course. No Jeane Kirkpatrick, but—"

"Aaaargh!" Harry buried his face in her throw pillow.

Nelligan accepted the tea with thanks. Kate's office – at least three times as large as Harry's cluttered cubbyhole – looked like the plush waiting room of a $500-an-hour attorney. Two lovely Monet prints dominated the walls, while a lush ivy climbed along the edge of her window, peach colored mini-blinds turned just so to keep out the direct sun light but let in a little of its brilliance. Some classical symphonic piece was playing softly on the radio behind her desk, the sound issuing from two small but very expensive speakers on either side of the room.

Kate folded her lime green skirt around her legs and sat in the chair that matched the couch. "Tucker, we really can't thank you enough for helping on this thing. It was devastating when Christopher Detweiler and Neil Keiter died at the hotel. This whole affair may have been Detweiler's to begin with, but I can't help but feel it's Astor's now. Dean Connar feels the same way. Anything you can do to help us will be greatly appreciated."

She reached toward him. Nelligan matched the motion and squeezed her hand in his. "Anytime, Kate. You gotta know this whole thing will make one hell of a story for the paper."

"Galbraith," Harry mumbled into the pillow.

"Harry, do you think you could join us for a moment?" Kate asked politely. Harry sighed melodramatically and tossed the pillow aside, frowning and hunched down low.

"Sit up straight," Kate said.

Harry did so.

"Thank you. What do we know so far?"

"That it was no accident," Harry replied, the usual timbre returning to his voice. "Much as we might want to think otherwise, I'm afraid Messrs. Detweiler and Keiter were murdered. According to the police, no other balcony in the entire hotel shows the slightest signs of rusting. I cannot believe that this was coincidence."

"I disagree," Nelligan cut in, his ever-present notepad resting on his knee, pen behind his ear. "I'd rather say this is *probably* murder. I'm about ninety or ninety-five percent sure. But on the other hand, you've got two full-grown men standing on the balcony together. Those iron balconies aren't all that big, and according to the official police report – which I picked up this morning – Keiter was six-two and really put together."

"Point well made," Harry acquiesced. "Let us not slam the door altogether on an accident. But certainly we're all agreed that this was most likely murder."

Nelligan and Kate nodded.

"Good. Question Number One: Were they both the target of murder? Highly unlikely, on the face of it. Or was one person the target and the other an innocent bystander. And if so, who was whom?"

Kate shrugged out of her suit coat and slung it over the back of her chair. From her leather portfolio she drew forth a legal pad with powder blue paper and her reading glasses. "I spent part of last night and this morning in the college library, digging up everything I could on Christopher Detweiler. Tucker, you'd have been proud of me."

"Already am."

"What I found doesn't lead anyone to think of murder," she continued. "Detweiler served in the Navy during the Korean War but didn't see any combat. He got his masters in business administration from Harvard in 1960. Graduated with honors. He returned to Oregon and started Detweiler Farms from scratch, beginning in the Christmas tree industry, which as you know is one of Oregon's most lucrative crops."

"Right behind marijuana," Nelligan cut in dryly. "Technically, it's the state's number one cash crop."

Kate glanced over the rims of her glasses at the reporter. "True, and ironic you should mention 'grass.' By the late 1960s he had shifted much of his wealth away from Christmas trees and into grass. And no, not *that* grass. He was growing blue grass and several other strains at about six farms around the Willamette Valley. Made of lot of money doing it, too.

"Detweiler's first foray into politics came in 1966, when he ran successfully for the Wilsonville City Council. He stayed on

162

for one term, then in 1970 ran as a Republican for the State House of Representatives. He won and stayed there until 1976, when he ran for the State Senate. His legislative assistant was a young Lee Connar, a history professor on sabbatical from the University of Oregon."

Kate flipped a page in the legal pad. "Let's see . . . Detweiler ran for re-election in '80 and lost by only four-point-three percent. Lee had already left his staff in 1978 to take a position at Astor. Detweiler returned to his business, which had grown considerably. By that time, Detweiler Farms had most of its resources tied up in timber. He arranged his first trans-Pacific trade agreement with the Japanese – in fact, with Nakano's Kuroshio Group Limited – in 1982, and within two years was a multi-million dollar operation. By the way, he still owns . . . owned, Christmas trees and grass."

"All of which, as you say, hardly leads one to envision murder," Harry finished his tea. "Tuck?"

"Well, I was following in Kate the Great's footsteps, doing what research I could on Keiter," he replied. "And I don't know how to tell you guys this, but there isn't murder written in this guy's biography either. Keiter was born in San Diego but moved around a lot, including a few years in Europe and one in Hong Kong. His old man was a Naval officer. Keiter eventually ended up back in California and got into San Diego State on a baseball scholarship. Apparently he didn't do so well in school and dropped out a year later, to take a job driving trucks with a logging company in Montana. Like everyone else, he joined the union, which seemed to turn his life around."

Nelligan stood and walked behind the desk, helping himself to more hot water and relating the story from memory. "In 1971, while only twenty-one, he transferred to a lumber job outside Banff, in the province of Alberta, pretty close to Lake Louise. Either of you ever been there?"

Both Harry and Kate said no.

"Beautiful country. Marty and I spent our anniversary up there two years ago. Anyway, while in Canada, Keiter did well in the union, moving from on-site jobs to office work. He left the timber industry in 1974 to attend McGill University. Lo and behold, whatever was wrong at San Diego State had corrected itself and he graduated in four years with a B.A. and two years later with a masters in biz, like Detweiler. He returned to the union in 1980 as a junior contract negotiator. The ITEU liked what they saw and sent him to the Northwestern School of Law of Lewis and Clark, right here in Portland."

Kate nodded. "LC has one of the nation's top programs in environmental law. Makes sense."

"Right," Nelligan continued. "Since then, he's been a gun-slinger for the union, going where ever they needed a bit of polish and muscle in a contract negotiation. From what I can see, he had a gangbuster reputation. Even the timber company owners respected him because he knew when to kick ass and when not to." Nelligan flipped closed his pad.

"And that's about it, except that on Friday, a man matching Keiter's description tricked the driver of Nakano's limo into revealing the trip to Detweiler Farms. If that was Keiter, then he knew where Detweiler was taking everybody."

"And he had the technical know-how to sabotage the chain saw device," Harry added. "Had Keiter negotiated for Detweiler Farms' employees?"

"Nope. Never directly, anyway. As far as I can tell, he'd never met Detweiler."

Kate turned to Harry. "And what have you discovered?"

"That John Kenneth Galbraith is on campus and I'm missing him."

"Harry!" Kate and Tucker said in tandem.

"Oh, all right. What I found is far less than either of you. First, there's an environmentalist couple named Joshua and Phoebe Pogue."

Kate didn't recognize the name and Nelligan filled her in on the Pogues and his interviews with them.

"Ah, I remember her from the lobby of the hotel," Kate replied.

"Right," Harry cut in. "What I discovered is that Joshua Pogue worked at the Trafalgar up until a few months ago and still has access to the employees' entrance. I saw him this morning in the basement."

"Which makes him a hell of a suspect," Nelligan said. "I reviewed the tapes from the PBS talk show and I'm sure neither of the Pogues were in the audience until the very end. Meaning they both lied to me and have almost an hour of unaccounted time on their hands."

"Speaking of time," Kate interjected. "Do we know the whereabouts of Detweiler and Keiter?"

"Yes," Harry replied. "Keiter returned from that debacle at the tree farm—"

Kate shuddered, remembering the Trax driver's blood soaking into her blouse sleeve.

"—and went to their respective rooms. Mr. Detweiler apparently showered, then discovered the bed hadn't been made nor clean sheets provided. According to Sergeant Wiley, Detweiler was feeling quite peckish about it. Called housekeeping and read them the riot act. He apparently waited there, half dressed, while the chief domestic and two of her maids hurried up to set things aright. Meanwhile, Mr. Keiter went to his room and ordered dinner. Which I find most odd."

Kate and Tucker exchanged glances. "You lost me," she said.

"Following that unhappy occurrence at the tree farm, I was bruised, aching and covered in dust. The first order of business was a shower. If I remember, Kate, Neil Keiter was helping you establish triage and first aid."

"Yes," she replied, her skin tone blanched white at the memories.

"Well, no offense, m'dear, but by the end of that ordeal you looked like something the cat would refuse to drag in. I can't help but feel Keiter was a bit mussed up by the time he returned. Yet according to the dear Sergeant, he didn't shower, just ordered food."

"I dunno, Harry," Nelligan shook his head. "When I'm in an adrenalin-rush, I get hungry. That's not all that uncommon. Suppose he just scrubbed his face and hands and ordered food? I'd buy into that theory."

Harry thought about it for a moment, then nodded. "I concede the point. I don't say his lack of showering is a damning indictment, just an interesting aside. Anyway, no one seems to know why Mr. Detweiler went down to Mr. Keiter's room, and the hotel switchboard isn't the type that records room-to-room phone calls. They may or may not have rung each other up first. The next thing anyone knows, the two of them are out on Mr. Keiter's balcony, the balcony railing slips and they tumble to their doom. And that, as they say, is that."

The three friends sat silently for a moment. The sounds of daily college life drifted in through Kate's window.

"All right," Nelligan stood. "I guess our best suspects are the Pogues. Harry, how about a little of the old divide-and-conquor. You take one Pogue, I'll take the other, we'll rattle their cages and see what happens."

"Sounds logical. But rattle gently, Tucker," Harry replied, standing also. "Whoever killed Detweiler and Keiter isn't above using violence to achieve his or her goals."

"Gotcha," the reporter replied. "If I've got time, I think I'll swing out to Wilsonville again to see if the local cops have anything on the explosion. How about you, Kate?"

"I'll do what I can to help Lee keep the Japanese here and happy, while you boys snoop around," she replied.

Harry, of course, had another theory entirely. But it sounded ludicrous, even to himself, and he opted to test it before saying something that would make him look foolish.

"Right then," Harry pushed back his sleeve. "Let's circumcise our watches."

166

CHAPTER THIRTY-FOUR

Nelligan drove Martin Kady back downtown to Kady's law firm office, all the while listening to his lover ooh and aah over the Galbraith lecture. True to his word, Martin had recorded the speech for Harry, and he gave Nelligan the tape to pass along.

Nelligan used Kady's office phone to call his editor at the *Post*, to see if he was still on "leave of absence." She assured him the situation with El Salvador was almost cleared up. At best, the newspaper's team could return to San Salvador by the middle of the week to finish their report on the Arena party's effect on the poor, agricultural centers.

At worst, the story was spiked and the reporters and photographers on special assignment would return to their regular beats Wednesday morning.

One way or another, he had about thirty hours left to help Harry.

Nelligan knew one tried and true method for inciting action from lovers and spouses. He didn't particularly like this schtick, since it could be considered mean-spirited, cruel and unethical.

What the hell, he thought, jamming the Jeep into gear.

Harry never did get to see John Kenneth Galbraith. But he and Coach Baldwin thanked the Trail Blazers for their help. The Blazers said they were only too happy to lend their attorney, Martin Kady, a hand.

167

Harry bade "his" team adieu and handed them over to their rightful coach.

Carefully avoiding contact with Lyman Bledsoe Jr. and Dean Stuyvesant, Harry checked in at the administration building and discovered that Dean Connar was due to lead a tour of the campus for visiting international dignitaries, beginning around four p.m. That gave Harry almost three hours to see what he could see.

He returned to his Datsun and scrounged a much bedraggled map out of the glove box. All during his tenure with the U.N. Peace Keeping Forces in Korea and his ill-remembered stint with the Central Intelligence Agency, people had tried to teach Harry Bishop the fine art and skill of refolding maps. He never did grasp the concept, and his Portland metro map was more wadded than folded.

Nelligan had said that Joshua Pogue worked and lived in Milwaukie, which is on the east side of the Willamette River. Everything east of the monumentally tacky McLoughlin Boulevard was *terra incognita* to Harry. Still, he doggedly perused the map, found a logical path that led him thither, and scribbled the street names and right- or left-hand turn instructions on a convenient Dunkin Donuts napkin.

Harry then carefully rewadded the map and set off for a rendezvous with destiny.

It took him ten minutes to get hopelessly lost.

Before they left Kate's office, Harry and Tucker had flipped a coin to see who got which Pogue. Nelligan got Phoebe.

It didn't take him long to find out that Phoebe Pogue worked three days a week as a volunteer for KPCH Radio, a left-of-center pastiche of news programming, drama, poetry readings and all the music every other station wouldn't pick up. He tuned the Jeep's radio to the station at the low end of the FM dial and caught the tail end of a Zydeco gig as he parked a block from the station. The amateur disc jockey told him to stay tuned for Celtic fiddle music.

The station was in a disreputable section of town, surrounded to its left and right by abandoned buildings that were constantly being raided by Portland's Finest, as either crack houses or shooting galleries for addicts. Two anemic hookers patrolled the sidewalks on either side of the street. The radio station occupied a narrow storefront office and Nelligan could see the disc jockey he had just been listening to, seated at his monitor board and facing the storefront window adorned with three conical bullet holes.

Three small bells over the entrance jingled as he pushed open the door. The office inside was musty and dusty, the walls completely covered in promo posters from record companies. A battle scarred wooden desk dominated the small room, with two mismatched, hard back dining room chairs facing it. Behind the desk sat Phoebe Pogue, telephone cradled against her ear, methodically thumbing through a thick pile of forms, date-stamping each, and separating them into three lesser piles.

Nelligan chose to stand rather than risk either rickety dining room chair. Pogue sat like Quasimodo, one shoulder pressing the receiver against her ear, as she stamped the forms and transferred them to their appropriate stack. She worked with metronomic precision, pressing the stamp to the over-inked ink pad between each two forms.

Wump Wump Squish. Wump Wump Squish.

The dates on each form were far too smudged to ever read.

Pogue finished reciting the Saturday air schedule – from memory – and twitched her shoulder. As the phone slid down, she caught it with one hand and returned it to its cradle, never looking at it directly. Like many receptionists, she had honed her job down to robot motions.

"Can I help you?" she asked, not looking up.

"Yes, Ms. Pogue," Nelligan replied, smiling gently.

She peered over the tops of her wide, round glasses, trying to place him. It took her a second, then her metronome stopped.

Wump Wump Squish. Wump . . .

"You're that reporter," she said dryly.

"Yes, ma'am. May I ask you a few questions?"

"No." She turned back to her task, the precision of her wumping and squishing would have made Henry Ford proud.

"It's about the murder Saturday night," Nelligan persisted.

Wump Wump Squish. Wump Wump Squish.

"And about the taping of the 'Focal Point' show."

Wump Wump Squish. Wump Wump Squish.

Nelligan thought about the tape he'd watched twice over at the PBS studio. Phoebe Pogue hadn't shown up until the last fifteen minutes of the hour-long show. Her husband showed up a few moments before the moderator signed off.

"We're pretty sure your husband didn't attend that taping," Nelligan said.

Wump Wump Tonk.

Pogue hit the edge of the ink pad with the stamp. The shallow, tin tray flipped up like tiddlywinks, landing ink pad down on a stack of forms she had completed. "Shit!" she cried, shoving back her chair and leaping to her feet.

"Oops," Nelligan said. "Need a hand there?"

An ink slick was spreading across the forms. Pogue grabbed the ink pad and tossed it toward the waste can, missing by a good two feet. A perfect rectangle of black ink appeared on a Motherlode poster.

"Get out," Pogue hissed.

"I want to know where your husband was," Nelligan replied firmly. He stood with the most unthreatening attitude possible – hands shoved in his trouser pockets, shoulder against the door frame, one foot hooked back behind the other. He smiled politely.

"Get out or I'll call the cops." Pogue bunched her fists at her side.

"In this neighborhood? Ms. Pogue, I'm not trying to fry anyone. I just want to know where your husband was when Detweiler and Keiter were killed."

"*He has nothing to do with that!*" she shouted. "*Leave us alone!*"

Two doors opened in the narrow corridor to Nelligan's left and heads poked out. "Phoebe?" someone called hesitantly.

"He has access to the Trafalgar," Nelligan went fishing.

Pogue blanched and her knees almost gave away. His accusation suddenly struck her full force.

With considerable mental effort, Pogue bucked up, squared her jaw, and pointed at the door. "Get the hell out."

"Right," Nelligan said, since the scene had begun to draw a crowd. "I'll be in touch."

CHAPTER THIRTY-FIVE

Milwaukie prospered during the era of the railroads. The very purpose for Portland's southern suburb was as a terminus for the endless flow of goods from the east.

But the endless flow ended. A noose of interstate trucking – I-5 to the west and I-205 to the east – began choking the rail town in the early 1960s. The decay continued into the 1990s, leaving Milwaukie dilapidated and bedraggled, struggling to retain what little economy remained.

Harry asked directions from two gas station attendants and eventually found his way to the Top-Notch Green Beans factory, a massive, cube-shaped building hunkered down next to a railroad spur line. Once, flatbeds and box cars had formed queues five miles long, waiting to take on goods. Today, the spur line was little used. Sturdy yellow weeds grew between the tracks and a family of ducks were squabbling over a mud puddle adjacent to the line.

Harry parked the Datsun in a row of pick-ups. Not locating anything like an office entrance, he circled the building, stepped across the badly rusting tracks and entered through the massive airplane-hangar style doors.

Inside, business was booming, belying the town's general economy. Fork-lift tractors hauled flats of canned green beans from one end to the other, a conveyor belt jerked unsteadily toward the door, boxes of beans jostling against each other to get to the waiting box car parked on the spur line outside.

Harry said "Pardon me" to three people before someone

172

acknowledged him. He had to shout above the din. The man nodded and pointed to a far corner of the warehouse.

Carefully avoiding the fork lifts and foot traffic, Harry weaved his way to Joshua Pogue, who was counting cans and sealing boxes, along with three other men. The noise was lessened a bit in this corner and Harry spoke in his natural voice; a deep timbered, resonating British accent that carried well over the din.

"Mr. Pogue?"

"Yes?" Pogue turned and smiled – the smile fading behind his beard as he recognized Harry.

"Might I speak with you a moment?"

Pogue thought about it for a second, then set down his clip board, slipped into a light windbreaker, and jerked his head toward an auxiliary door.

He led the way, Harry in pursuit. With his hands jammed into the jacket's vertical-slit pockets, Pogue shouldered open the door and stepped out, on the far side of the warehouse from the parking lot.

After the noise of the warehouse, the open space behind the building was unnaturally quiet, even though they stood less than one hundred feet from the buzzing Milwaukie Expressway. There was nobody about, Harry noticed. All the better.

"What can I do for you?" Pogue asked, his voice soft. He didn't meet Harry's gaze but stared at the steel toe caps of his work boots.

"I'd like to talk to you about the deaths at the Trafalgar Hotel. By the way, I'm Professor Bishop from Astor College."

"Hi." Pogue looked up and offered his hand, which Harry shook. "What's this got to do with you?"

"Ah, as to that," Harry replied, blushing a bit. "I've been asked to look about a bit. Nothing formal, of course. I assure you I have the permission of the police."

"Oh." That tidbit of news didn't seem to thrill Pogue.

"We're quite convinced the two men were murdered, Mr. Pogue. And to be honest, I thought perhaps there was something you could tell me about the affair."

"Nope," he replied quickly, watching his own boot kick at the dry, compacted earth, clumps of soil popping free. "I don't know anything about that."

"Forgive me, sir," Harry persisted, "but you weren't exactly happy about the proposed timber sale. And I saw for myself that you have access to the Trafalgar through the basement. You're a former employee, I believe?"

Pogue said nothing.

"Now, I'm not accusing you of anything, Mr. Pogue, but I have a feeling you possess some bit of knowledge regarding this affair. And I really do need to know as much as possible."

"The two guys were killed Saturday evening," Pogue replied, watching his boot kick the earth. "My wife and I went to a live taping of this PBS show, over on Macadam Avenue. We were there for more than an hour, just about the time those two guys died. All I know about this mess is what I saw on TV Sunday."

"Ah," Harry replied. "Mr. Pogue, forgive me, but a compatriot of mine viewed the videotape from the 'Focal Point' show." Pogue's head snapped up, his light gray eyes locking onto Harry. "Neither you nor your wife were in the audience until the last ten or fifteen minutes of the program, sir. Again, I'm accusing no one of wrong-doing, but it's my experience that one does not fabricate an alibi unless one wants to obscure some fact. And I ask you again—"

Pogue's left hand came out of the windbreaker pocket, carrying an Exacto-Knife. A fresh razor blade protruded from the steel rod.

The quiet man stepped forward, his right fist clenching around Harry's jacket lapel. Pogue braced his legs and shoved, sending Harry hurtling against the cinder block wall of the warehouse.

A serpentine line of cars zoomed by on the Expressway, thirty yards away. Harry could smell their exhaust but couldn't see any drivers, thanks to the mass of the warehouse.

"Now you listen to me," Pogue hissed, the flat side of the cool, steel razor blade suddenly pressing against Harry's carotid artery. "Phoebe and I were watching that taping, do you understand?"

"Yes. Oh yes," Harry replied quickly. He could feel his heart palpitating, feel the artery thumping against the razor blade.

174

"We don't know shit about Detweiler or the black guy, do you understand?"

"Yes."

"You leave us the hell out of this, do you understand?"

"Yes."

"Mister, this isn't a bluff," Pogue added, speaking softly. There was flame in his eyes but not in his voice, which hinted only at pain, not anger. "Don't call me on this, okay? Don't you do that. Am I understood?"

"Yes, indeed."

Pogue released his lapel, the razor disappearing back into the jacket. He stepped away and disappeared into the building, hauling the door closed behind him.

Harry knelt on his haunches and waited about two minutes for the panic to subside. He had to pee and he had to faint and he wanted to scream, but eventually all he did was stand, dust himself off, and circle the warehouse back to his Datsun.

CHAPTER THIRTY-SIX

Before stopping at the Wilsonville Police Department, Nelligan turned off the main road and drove down to Detweiler Farms.

He cruised past the high arch and gate that led into the tree farm without slowing down. Unlike his Sunday visit, this time the property was guarded. A Dodge pickup was parked just inside the perimeter and two men lounged against the closed gate. Peeking discretely through his rear view mirror, Nelligan noticed the Dodge's gun racks weren't just for show.

He parked the red and black Jeep a quarter of a mile further on, then reached under the passenger seat for a zip-lock plastic food bag that contained half a dozen government-issue maps for the entire Standard Metropolitan Services Area. Unfolding the Clackamas County map, he ran a finger along the boundaries of Detweiler Farms. The road he was on bordered the property on the south. To the north ran the Willamette River, leading to the Canby Ferry, five miles east. Nelligan thought about his last visit to the farm. Hadn't he seen a cliff to the north, overlooking the river? And hadn't there been a road at the bottom of the cliff, along the river?

Sure enough, the map showed a small service road following the winding river all the way to Oregon City. Nelligan traced it to the nearest intersection, then plotted his course and shoved the Jeep into gear.

There was no reason on Earth why Nelligan couldn't drive up to the front gate, flash his press ID, and ask to speak to someone in charge. But there's something about being sneaky that gets into a person's system.

It took him less than half an hour to circumnavigate the farm. Nelligan threw the Jeep's four-wheel drive into action as he hit the service road that abutted the Willamette River. The road was really not much more than twin ruts, with clumps of tall grass brushing against his axles as he drove along.

It was nearly three o'clock by the time he reached the twin outbuildings – the roofs of which he had seen from above on Sunday. As is so common along the Willamette, the cliff rose straight up, seemingly almost man-made. It had been carved by the Bretz Floods, thousands of years earlier; massive walls of water, thirty stories high and moving at sixty miles an hour, smashing their way from the Montana glaciers, forming the Mars-like scablands of Washington, rerouting the Willamette into different terrains. Now, the north side of the river rose into gently sloping woods. The south side was this impassable clay cliff. Between plate techtonics and the great floods, the land of the Northwest often resembled a geologic crazy quilt.

Nelligan parked the Jeep and stepped out, his aviator shades in place. There was a short wooden dock reaching out into the river, with a flat barge tied to it. Across the river was a fine forest, which no doubt belonged to Detweiler.

Or to Detweiler's estate.

There were two buildings ahead of him: a big, aluminium structure the size of a three-car garage that probably housed a boat or other equipment, with a small wooden tool shed beside it. Nelligan had hoped there was a back route onto the farm, and sure enough, on the far side of the corrugated aluminium outbuilding the path began to rise sharply around the curving cliff. In less than a mile, he estimated, the path would lead to the tree farm above. He climbed back into the Jeep and began to turn the key when something caught his eyes. There was a massive shape huddled behind the metal shed. It was covered with a black tarp.

Nelligan thought he recognized it as the Mark One Trax he had examined earlier. Someone must have hauled it down the steep and narrow path toward the river.

Why, he wondered.

Nelligan stepped out of the Jeep again and crossed to the shed, hoping to confirm it was what he thought it was. He reached the tarp and pulled it aside, peering beneath it.

It was the Trax all right, the blackened stump of its chain-saw arm protruding from its belly, the brown stain of blood still decorating the cab.

Nelligan pulled the tarp back as he had found it, then leaned against the wooden shed and thought about the situation. There were a criss-cross weave of tank-tread marks around the wreck. Nelligan assumed one of the timber machines – similar to the Trax itself – had been used to haul the derelict to its hiding spot.

The trail leading up to the Detweiler farm was winding, narrow and steep. Seemed like a hell of a lot of work, just to move the Trax out of the way. Nelligan mulled it over for a while, then shrugged and began trudging back to the Jeep.

He was halfway there when the glint of gold caught his attention. There was something ten feet to his right, lying in a wild spray of weeds at the cliff base. Nelligan moved over to the weeds, feeling the ground become more solid under his tread. He was standing on the remains of an ancient building foundation, all but invisible until he was on top of it. The foundation had crumbled into isolated pockets of concrete separated by a sea of weeds. Over to one side he now saw the outline of a brick fireplace. Only the bottom bricks remained.

He knelt, and shoved a handful of the waxy stalks aside.

A Rolex watch lay in the dirt, the metal accordion-style band snapped in two, the crystal cracked. Nelligan picked it up and turned it over. No inscription.

The gold was shiny and no mud clung to it. Since it hadn't rained since Saturday – and that was only a cloud burst – Nelligan surmised the watch had been lost on Sunday or today. Possibly by whoever hauled the Trax down the hill.

He pocketed the watch. Nelligan had never worked in a lumber camp but suspected there were damn few Rolexes among the workers.

Out of instinct (Nelligan loved grubbing around for clues more than most anything in life) he shoved away some more weeds, looking for anything else of interest.

It took him about three minutes of kneeling and sorting around the weeds and crumbling concrete to find the tooth and a greasy, pulpy mass about the size of a silver dollar. The mass certainly looked like blood and a wedge of skin.

Nelligan was beginning to enjoy this case more and more.

CHAPTER THIRTY-SEVEN

Harry drove slowly and uncertainly back on the campus. Joshua Pogue had succeeded in scaring the hell out of him. Harry was certain, beyond any shadow cast by the slimmest of doubts, that Pogue would have cut him to stop the questioning.

And yet, Harry realized, Pogue hadn't reacted violently until he, Harry, had mentioned the video tape at the PBS station. Which showed that both Joshua and Phoebe Pogue had made up their alibis.

Harry began to doubt Mr. Pogue had had anything to do with the deaths of Christopher Detweiler and Neil Keiter. He was not so sure about Mrs. Pogue.

He arrived on campus and parked in a fire lane. To hell with campus security. Harry hoped against hope he could make it to his office without seeing anyone. His hands were shaking and his knees felt like tapioca and he was in no mood for twenty questions.

Luck was with him and he sneaked in as the department secretary turned toward her filing cabinet. Harry quietly unlocked the door to his cubby hole office, stepped inside and relocked the door.

"And will you look at what the cat dragged in!" Taddy McMurdo sang out, rocking back as far as Harry's chair would let him.

Harry cleared the only other chair of New Republic back issues and slumped down. The intruder had rifled his desk and found the bottle of Passport scotch. Taddy located Harry's coffee cup and poured in three fingers of the amber liquid, then lifted the bottle to his own lips and took a swig.

"Ah, God, Harry. You used to drink better stuff than this."

Harry drained half his coffee mug, loosening his tie and undoing the top button of his shirt. "A man threatened to kill me with a razor blade today, Taddy."

"You don't say. Jealous husband? Co-ed who didn't like her grade?"

Harry finished the rest of the drink and Taddy poured again.

"The reason I got into academia was so that people would not threaten to kill me with razor blades, Taddy. That was the primary purpose behind getting my master's degree and my doctorate. No more razor blades. I don't like this."

"I don't seem to recall anyone ever threatening you with a razor blade back in the good old days."

"No, and I survived without that experience quite well, thank you. As I say, I do not like this."

"And I don't like the press learning that I'm about," Taddy cut in, his voice like dry ice. "That was a nasty surprise awaiting me this morning, Harry son. Had to change hotels and everything."

Harry sipped his drink and slid further down in the chair. "I didn't call the press," he said honestly.

"Hmm. That's as may be. As you've no doubt noticed, boyo, our Japanese friend stayed in town today."

Harry sipped his drink.

"But he's not buying a condo here, Harry. Time's running short. Do you have someone the local yokels can arrest?"

"No."

"No one?"

Harry thought about the Pogues, then finished his drink. "No. No one."

Taddy leaned forward in Harry's chair. "Boyo, I don't know if you're following me here. I don't necessarily want the right bad guy locked away – although that'd be fine, if you can do it. It'd be a hell of a hat-trick, but then they don't call you the Mad Hatter for nothing."

"They don't call me that at all," Harry reminded him.

181

"Whatever. The point is, we need to keep this trade agreement alive, Harry. Which means we have to show old man Nakano that this isn't the wild, wild west. We need to arrest someone. Right away. Now, you know me, pal. You know I never bluff."

Harry sat up straight and rebuttoned his collar, staring Taddy square in the eye.

Taddy returned the gaze. "Get me someone – anyone – to arrest. Or I'll take in one of your friends. Do you follow me, Harry?"

Harry tightened his tie, squared his shoulders, stood, and opened the door. He turned back to McMurdo before exiting. "Stay and finish your drink. I've work to do."

Taddy grinned from ear to ear and propped his feet up on the desk. He hoisted the almost-empty bottle in toast. "That I can do, Harry boy."

Harry closed the door softly then walked down the hall to the main office. "Barbara?"

The secretary turned from her filing.

"There's a Daniel T. McMurdo in my office. He's with the CIA and wants to talk to President Eckersley about establishing a spy school on campus. Please call the president's office and the Public Information Office and alert them."

Barbara peered over the tops of her half-glasses at him. "You're kidding, of course."

"Yes, but L. Charles 'Chuck' won't know that."

Grinning, Barbara picked up the telephone.

Lee Connar and the Japanese delegation arrived at John Jacob Astor College around four that afternoon. The only true "dignitary" in the group was Takeshi Nakano, but you wouldn't know that from watching the motorcade. Lee led the way in his station wagon, followed by Nakano and Kimiko Sheppard in the limousine (driven still by Ernest deSidrio), then Johnson and Jensen in an unmarked, four-door sedan that screamed *surveillance vehicle*. A rented Cadillac came next, carrying L.C. Noraine. Finally, a Portland Police Department prowl car brought up the rear. Detective Sergeant Wiley had said it might be a good idea to have officers on hand, since Astor was quickly gaining a reputation as a place where weirdness happened.

Especially, Wiley warned the officers, when Professor Bishop was afoot.

The motorcade crawled to a halt around the circular driveway in front of the Alice Joan Weymouth Hyde Memorial Administration Building, a nineteenth century manor house with matching gargoyles lurking above the cobbled front walkway. The tour participants left their cars and gathered before the impressive stone building.

Lee quickly relayed some of the building's history, including its stint as the county seat during a flood season around the turn of the century, as well as a young Ulysses S. Grant's stay in the building as postmaster general for the territory, prior to the war.

As he spoke, Kimiko Sheppard translated for Nakano, keeping her voice a discreet whisper that only he could hear. Nakano walked about the lower foyer with its stone walls and great Persian rug like a potentate, smiling broadly and admiring the suit of armor in one corner and the breathtaking view through the back window, which offered a panorama beginning with the gently sloping lawns, the reflecting pool, the wood-covered hills, downtown Portland and finally Mount St. Helens in the distance. It was such a clear day that Washington State's Mount Adams was barely visible over St. Helens' shoulder.

"Wow," Noraine said in a hushed whisper. "This is prettier than shit."

"Er. Yes," Lee agreed.

Kate Fairbain, who had seen the motorcade pull onto the campus from her office, now joined the tour. Lee nodded to her, thankful for a friendly face.

The tour reached the president's office, where his receptionist, secretary and file clerk all smiled brightly. All were young, absolutely beautiful and leggy. They were easily the three worst classified employees on the campus, but L. Charles "Chuck" Eckersley did so like his window dressing.

"I'm sorry," the receptionist smiled dazzlingly. "President Eckersley isn't in right now. There's an official from the CIA on

183

campus. The president, er, ran out about five minutes ago. He called a general meeting of the administration, Dean Connar." There was a touch of reproach in her voice.

"Oh?" Lee frowned. "Well, never mind. Mr. Nakano, allow me to show you our new library facility. It's one of the state's finest."

The group trudged out, the cops feeling out of place, Johnson, and Jensen pivoting their heads to take in the full view, keeping their backs to the walls in the gunfighter position. Jensen peeked into the suit of armor to make sure there were no terrorist squads lurking within.

They crossed the Western Lawn, keeping to the cobblestone paths. One of the English professors had moved his Summer Sampler class outside and had propped a portable chalkboard against a great oak tree, the students sitting or sprawling in the grass before him.

Lee and Kate led the Japanese and Noraine into the library through the main entrance. The Secret Service agents and cops edged around the anti-book theft device, figuring their guns might set it off.

As Lee began to relate the history of the old library that had occupied the same site, Harry Bishop appeared from behind a card catalogue file. Nakano nodded and mumbled something unintelligible. Ms. Sheppard nodded as well. "Greetings, professor. You have a splendid campus here."

"Thank you. I decorated it myself, you know."

Lee continued to smile as he nudged the professor with his elbow. "Ixnay, Harry."

"It is good to see you," Ms. Sheppard bowed slightly to Harry.

"Enjoying your tour?" Harry asked.

Rather than answer, Sheppard translated, then waited for her employer to reply. "Yes, indeed. It is a most beautiful campus. Are you teaching today?"

"Me? No, no. Just a bit of research," Harry lied elegantly. "Don't let me keep you."

Lee motioned toward the Native American exhibition on display through the summer in the history text room, leading the group along, Sheppard's translation in syncopation with his words. Harry followed along.

Makoto Takimura, photo editor for the student newspaper, entered the building in the tour party's wake, holding his canvas camera bag and equipment over his head like a man crossing a river. He had no idea whether or not the magnetic field of the anti-theft devices could fog his undeveloped film, but why take chances?

He asked one of the librarians which way the Dean's party headed, then followed in hot pursuit.

CHAPTER THIRTY-EIGHT

As Lee led the tour into the library's history room, Nelligan rounded the corner and entered the college, tires squealing. He couldn't wait to tell Harry that there was a new corpse on the scene.

Things were looking up.

Taddy McMurdo stepped out of the lavatory and into the main office of the political science department. He was instantly greeted by a sea of navy blue suit coats, dotted with gold tie clasps.

President L. Charles "Chuck" Eckersley presented himself, flanked by the college's coterie of vice presidents, assistant vice presidents, deans, assistant deans, provosts, administrative aides and other assorted persons whose jobs no one quite understood but who nonetheless were vital to the on-going health of the institution.

"Agent McMurdo?" the president proffered a tanned hand with a firm grip and favored Taddy with an irridescent smile. "I'm L. Charles 'Chuck' Eckersley, president of this fine institution. And just let me say that it's both a privilege, a pleasure and an honor to have you on our campus today. Now, I know that relations between your people in, quote, 'the company,' if I may use that bit of tradecraft jargon, and the hallowed halls of academia have been, shall we say, strained of late, but that sort of leftist thinking finds no haven among the administrators of John Jacob Astor College, most of whom you now see standing before you, with a few exceptions who otherwise were engaged – not, as you might suspect, with anything more urgent than the business at hand, to wit, but rather with obligations which they could not, in good faith, back out on at this date. But then I don't have to tell you about that!"

L. Charles "Chuck" stopped for breath and Taddy tried to reset his emotional gyroscope. "Pardon me, but—"

"Now then," L. Charles "Chuck" slapped Taddy on the shoulder, "tell us about this so-called spy school you've proposed, at least in a roughed-out, first draft, tentative sort of proposal."

Taddy was nothing if not resilient. He also smiled and returned the back slap, part of his mind shifting into overdrive, trying to find an out. The rest of his mind was busy planning pay-backs for Harry.

CHAPTER THIRTY-NINE

Nelligan checked with the poli. sci. department secretary and was told Harry could be found with Dean Connar's tour group, in the library.

By the time Nelligan caught up with them, the tour had moved on to the library's vast literature department. While Lee and the head librarian showed off the facilities, Nelligan tapped Harry on the shoulder. Harry turned and tapped Kate on the shoulder and the three conspirators moved off together behind a microfiche machine.

"What's up, Doc?" Nelligan asked.

"Shhh," Harry replied. "We'w hunting wabbits. Heh heh heh heh."

Kate slapped him on the arm. "Would you two knock it off! What are we going to do?"

Harry peeked over the massive microfiche projector and made sure the tour was commencing. "First things first, fellow musketeers. I'd very much like to speak to Nakano-san. Something's not kosher with that fellow."

"That can wait," Nelligan cut in. "I've got some news of my own. It looks like we've got another dead body." He almost burst with the news and quickly relayed to Harry and Kate the blood, tooth and watch he had found at the bottom of the cliff at Detweiler Farms, adding that he had replaced the watch where he found it, this time burying it behind some weeds so no one else would see it glinting in the sunlight. "I haven't called the cops yet. Figured I'd check in with you, first."

Harry pulled a plastic stool away from the microfiche machine and sat down heavily, his fingers tugging at his lower lip, his gaze a thousand miles away.

"Uh oh," Kate said, noticing his vacant stare. "Harry's either going to be brilliant or stupid again."

"I've got five bucks says brilliant," Nelligan nudged her.

"You're on."

Belatedly, Nelligan remembered Harry's 409th rule of law: Never bet with economics professors. They know the odds.

McMurdo was famous within the circles of espionage for his ability to think fast and lie with utter believability. They didn't call him the March Hare for nothing.

Shocked by the procession of college administrators who accosted him in the poli. sci. office, he nonetheless adjusted to the problem in the blink of an eye.

It was clear that the school's president, L. Charles "Chuck" Eckersley, was excited about any arrangement between the federal government and Astor. Taddy used that as a leverage – telling the man and his toadies that the CIA was very interested in Astor. Not as a *spy* school, but as the site for a think tank institution for foreign policy, specifically as it relates to the Pacific Rim, ANZUS and SEATO relations.

As he suspected, the gaggle of administrators cooed over the idea. Visions of federal grants danced in their heads.

Taddy didn't know any CIA operatives on the west coast and didn't even know if there was a Portland field office, so he fabricated as he went. "I'm not authorized to approve anything, you understand," he told the administrators, voice pitched low for secrecy. They nodded in unison. "However, I'm to report back to the Special Cell Unit for Academic Research Institutions at Langley. Field Directors Bolger, Lahr and Haley will have the last say, of course, but confidentially, ladies and gentlemen, I have their fullest confidence. Perhaps we could set up some meetings with the Prime Directorate for later in summer?"

L. Charles "Chuck" Eckersley shook his hand vigorously and favored Taddy with a gleaming smile. "It would be both an

189

honor, a pleasure and a privilege, Agent McMurdo. We here at Astor—"

"Good, good," Taddy patted him on the back and made a show of checking his pocket watch. "Ah, tempus fugit, ladies and gentlemen. Can't tell you how excited I am about the positive feedback I'm getting from Astor. Must run. Talk to you all soon. And remember: this is hush-hush."

The administrators all vowed their silence. Taddy reminded himself to look at Tuesday's newspapers, to see how they would leak the story.

Now: to business. Find Harry.

"Another dead body?" Harry repeated.

"Looks like it," Nelligan replied. "Leaving us with the sixty-four-thousand dollar question: whose is it?"

Harry frowned and tugged at his ear lobe, his brain racing. "I just don't know. Dodge, possibly?"

"Who?" Kate asked.

"Dodge. I've no idea who that is, but Sergeant Wiley said he found references to someone named Dodge in Christopher Detweiler's appointement book. Detweiler apparently met this Dodge person recently – here in Portland – and was none too pleased about it."

"Or maybe the blood belongs to someone who works at Detweiler Farms," Kate cut in. "Maybe someone out there knows something about the tree spike that made that tractor-thing blow up."

"I'll buy into that one," Nelligan replied. "Makes some sense, anyway."

Harry rested his elbows on his knees and buried his face in his hands. Nelligan and Kate could almost see steam pouring from his ears.

"Something's wrong," he said into his hands. "What are we missing? What?"

"Ahem." Taddy McMurdo stepped up to the trio, smiling broadly. "Hello, Professor Fairbain. Fine day, isn't it? Oh, Professor Bishop, might I have a word with you?"

Harry nodded sourly and stood. "Of course. Oh, Taddy, this is Tucker Nelligan. Tucker, Daniel Tadson McMurdo, thief, scoundrel and liar. Once my dearest friend. Taddy, come with me, please. I've need of your help."

He turned and walked toward the tour group, Taddy in tow. Nelligan and Kate hesitated, then followed.

"I'm going to get you for that little stunt," Taddy whispered so only Harry could hear.

By the time Harry and company caught up the tour, Lee Connar had led the visitors downstairs to the Macintosh and Apple computer laboratory, where students could use the PC's and rent time on the college's mainframe computer. As the dean proudly pointed to the vast assortment of software, disks and computer accessories, Nakano waved one frail arm around the room and spoke at length. Kimiko Sheppard listened to him, smiled, then turned to their host. "Mr. Nakano is very impressed that American students have so much access to so many wonderful machines, but he notes that very few of them were made by The Kuroshio Group, Limited. Mr. Nakano suggests the college was swindled by some fast-talking American computer makers, like in the American movie, 'The Music Man.'"

The comment got a laugh from everyone but Johnson and Jensen, who were prohibited from laughing on several articles and sections of the Secret Service code. One of the twin automatons moved constantly ahead of the tour, checking out each room with an utter lack of discretion. The other man – and like Rosencrantz and Guildenstern no one present could tell who was whom – brought up the rear, his obelisk-like vision taking in everything.

At the bottom of the stairs, Harry halted and nodded to his left. "We'll cut through the archives and meet them in audio-visual," he explained, suddenly moving off away from the tour.

With Kate, Nelligan and Taddy following, Harry circled around the computer lab, through the cool, dry recesses of the campus archives.

He and Kate waved to the Werewolf, the perpetual work-study student who had been running the archives as long as any faculty

191

members could remember.

On the far side of the archives was the audio-visual lab, a bare-floored room with rows and rows of metal shelves stacked to the ceiling with televisions, video cassette recorders, overhead projectors, film projectors, slide film carrousel projectors, Camcorders, microphones, speakers, compact disc players and even a half-dozen laser disc players which the college had purchased with grant money a month earlier. A half-dozen work-study students and an equal number of college employees were tagging audio-visual equipment or tearing machines apart for repairs or cleaning, working at long, belt-high, benches with phosphorescent lights above. The facility looked like a high-tech version of Santa's workshop.

Nelligan stopped in his tracks and uttered a two-tone whistle. "Hey, Harry, check this out."

Harry, Kate and Taddy stopped also. Nelligan pointed to a half-cylinder attached to one wall. The black plastic cylinder was about seven feet tall and three feet wide, and was fixed directly into the wall.

"What is that?" Taddy asked.

"It's a dark room," Nelligan replied, grinning. "That thing's a spinning door. It let's people in, but not light. Hey, pal!" He caught the attention of a bearded man wearing soft moccasins and a leather apron, who had been tinkering with the solid-state mother board from a VCR.

"Yeah?" the man looked up, frowning to see strangers in his domain.

Nelligan flashed his press I.D., which for some reason tended to impress people. "Does your dark room have a freight entrance?"

"Yeah." The man continued to frown. "Are you folks supposed to be in here?"

Nelligan turned to his companions and grinned, then turned back to the man. "It's OK. We've got a plan."

CHAPTER FORTY

Makoto Takimura had joined the tour group, leather camera bag hanging from a shoulder strap, a Nikon F-3 camera body hanging from another strap around his neck, a third strap holding another F-3 with zoom lens. Makoto held the flash unit separate, connected to the camera body by a sync. cord and the whole rig connected by another sync. cord to a battery pack clipped to his belt. He looked more like a man on a portable dialysis machine than the photo editor of the school newspaper.

There were no summer issues of *The Pathfinder*, but the first issue of fall term traditionally was a summer wrap-up. Makoto honestly didn't know why Professor Bishop had asked him to listen to the cute translator. But as long as he was around, Makoto figured he'd grab a few rolls of black-and-white for the first fall issue.

Harry and Kate had rejoined the tour as they entered the audio-visual department. Lee pointed to the vast array of technical equipment and began describing the resources available.

"Jesus," L.C. Noraine cut in, thumbs cocked in the pockets of his leather vest. "When I went to school, you needed a pencil, a pad of paper and some books and you got all the learning you needed. All of these gizmos and doo-hickeys and I'm betting kids today aren't one iota smarter'n they were in my day."

As he spoke, Harry sidled close to Lee and whispered: "Take them into the dark room. One of the Secret Service men first, then Nakano."

"What?"

But Harry had moved on.

Frowning, Lee decided to do as he had been told. He brought the group around the repair station, displaying the latest laser disc players. These had been designed by a wholly-owned subsidiary of The Kuroshio Group, Ms. Sheppard pointed out.

Lee looked around distractedly but couldn't see Harry any longer. However, Agent McMurdo, whom he had met at the Trafalgar over the weekend, was standing with the A-V technicians behind the repair bench. Confused beyond hope, Lee decided to play ball. He turned to the tall cylinder embedded in the wall. "And, um, this is our state-of-the-art dark room. It's . . . quite impressive." Lee had never seen the inside of the darkroom and had no idea what was inside. "Shall we?"

"Wait." Agent Johnson stepped forward and frowned at the contraption.

"It's easy," Kate Fairbain piped in. "The outer cylinder is set in the wall and won't move. There's an inner cylinder which does. Spin that until an opening appears."

The agent considered this for a moment, then did so. There were hand-holds embedded in the hard plastic cylinder for grip. It spun easily at his touch and a hole, three feet by six and a half feet, whirled into view, revealing the inside of the cylinder.

"Now step inside, spin it one hundred eighty degrees, and step out," Kate explained. "It lets people come and go without letting in the light."

Agent Johnson stepped into the cylinder, removed his Foster Grants, and placed the palms of his hands against the inside of the tube. He disappeared from sight as the cylinder spun.

Kate waited a moment, then cut in front of the group. "Great. Mr. Nakano, if you would." She spun against the cylinder and the door reappeared. Like a stage magician's trick, Johnson's bulky frame had disappeared.

Kimiko Sheppard frowned. "May I go through with him?"

"There's not much room," Kate replied.

Sheppard smiled. "We're small people, professor." With that, she took Nakano by the elbow, whispered to him in Japanese, and led the wizened man into the cylinder.

A brief look of panic slithered across the old man's features. Sheppard squeezed into the tube, uncomfortably close to her superior, then spun the door closed.

The dark room was red.

Agent Johnson squinted at the overhead red lights which cast weird, unnatural shadows around the long, narrow room behind the cylinder. Both long walls were lined with arcane machinery – enlargers and duplicators and several things he couldn't identify. Large plastic tubs lined one counter, each half filled with liquid of different color.

The dark room was L-shaped, and suddenly bright, white light splashed from the short wing of the L, to his right, making him squint.

"Excuse me, sir," came a voice from the direction of the light.

Agent Johnson moved toward the light, rounded the corner, and found a door – a regular door, with a nob and hinges, but wider than most – hanging open.

He stepped out into another corridor. To his right and left the hallway stretched, all unrecognized. He was in a wing of the library building the tour had not reached before.

Before he could react, Tucker Nelligan stepped out from behind the wide door and slammed it shut.

"Hey!" the agent said.

"Watch it, pal," Nelligan shot back. "That's a dark room. You can't leave that door open, you know."

Agent Johnson grabbed the handle and yanked. Nothing happened. He thought about it a moment then turned to Nelligan. "It's locked," he pronounced.

"Natch. It's supposed to be locked. Regulations." Nelligan hoped the key ring Taddy McMurdo had helped him 'borrow' from the chief A-V techie wouldn't jingle in his pocket.

Agent Johnson tugged at the door again, slowly realizing he was cut off from the rest of the group.

Takeshi Nakano and Kimiko Sheppard almost burst from the cylinder and into the red-lighted dark room. Nakano appeared flustered and stepped quickly away from the young woman, barking orders at her, his voice a mixture of shock and anger.

Harry, who stepped out from behind one of the photographic enlargers, imagined that Nakano and Sheppard had never touched each other before. What little he knew about Japanese society suggested a rigid class system, in which a rich and elderly male executive would never be overly demonstrative with a young, female underling.

"Pardon me," Harry said, startling Nakano and Sheppard. He carried a clip board which he had borrowed from one of the work benches. Moving past the Japanese couple, Harry wedged the clip board firmly between the inner and outer cylinders of the door.

"What are you doing?" Ms. Sheppard asked, her voice rising in confusion. Nakano peered at Harry but said nothing.

On the far side of the concrete wall, Kate stepped away from the dark

Sheppard began translating and Harry raised a hand. "I don't think that'll be necessary, Ms. Sheppard. I suspect Mr. Nakano can understand every word."

She frowned. Nakano himself showed no emotion.

"What? Professor, Mr. Nakano speaks no English. That's why I translate for him."

"Friday night, at the reception the college hosted at the Trafalgar, do you remember that speech by our college president, Mr. Eckersley?" Harry asked. His voice had taken on a sharp tone. The door cylinder rattled madly and the pounding continued from the other end of the room.

Takeshi Nakano's attention remained firmly affixed to Harry. No emotion showed on the pale, leathern face.

"Y-yes," Sheppard frowned. "I remember President Eckersley gave a speech, but I don't remember what he said."

"That's because, alas, our President L. Charles 'Chuck' Eckersley is genetically incapable of making sense. I'm afraid his speech that evening was his standard mishmash."

Remembrance dawned on her oval face. "Oh, yes."

"You didn't translate the speech, because there was no rhyme or reason to it. Yet, when you gave your speech, Mr. Nakano," Harry addressed the man again, "you quoted from President Eckersley. Something about America and Japan gaining economic maturity, or some such blather."

"Oh. But I –" Sheppard tried to cover.

"If you quoted him, you understood him," Harry said softly.

Nakano didn't move; didn't blink. He stared calmly at Harry, a look of boredom crossing his face.

"You must tell me what you know about the deaths of Christopher Detweiler and Neil Keiter," Harry said softly. "It's vitally important, sir."

Nakano began to speak.

In Japanese.

It started quickly, a tight packet of words which he spat at Harry. Nakano's small but militarily straight body began to quiver and one bony, liver-spotted hand came up, pointing at Harry.

It was a flood of Japanese now, almost shouted. Harry stepped back, confused by the outburst. A trick of the red light made Nakano's eyes blaze inhumanly.

Kimiko Sheppard tried to cut in, to break off the harangue, but Nakano overpowered her, his voice rising to a full bark. He was shouting at Harry, waving his finger at him, true anger or something stronger – hate? – glinting dangerously in his eyes.

There was a cracking sound from the far end of the room and harsh, white light suddenly splashed against the work benches. Agents Johnson and Jensen entered together, guns drawn. The Portland Police officers followed, their weapons still holstered.

Kate, Lee, Taddy and Noraine brought up the rear, now jammed into the none-too-large dark room. Makoto Takimura, all but forgotten by the others, entered last, sensing some real news here that he might be able to free-lance out to the *Oregonian* or the *Post*.

197

And still Nakano shouted at Harry, spittle flying from his wrinkled mouth. Harry had backed up even farther, a look of complete, utter confusion crossing his face. He blinked once, then turned to Sheppard, eyebrows raised.

She glowered at him.

Johnson and Jensen stepped between the Japanese and Harry. With one shove, Jensen smacked Harry up against the far wall, the barrel of his gun against Harry's sternum.

"Hey!" Nelligan shouted. "No guns! He meant no harm!"

One of the cops stepped in quickly and forced himself between Harry and Jensen, shoving the gun aside.

Still Nakano shouted his bitter bile, his fists balled at his side, the knuckles bone white. He shook with rage.

"What the heck?" Makoto stopped taking photos and cocked his head to one side.

"Let's take this outside," one of the cops ordered, holding Harry by the upper arm. "Phil, get on the horn. See if you can get Wiley up here. I think he'd better sort this shit out."

CHAPTER FORTY-ONE

" 'Kay, the man's on his way," one of the cops stepped into the room and spoke to his partner. "Wiley says we're to keep everyone together till he gets here."

All the participants in that afternoon's mêlée had been sequestered in a large, airy library conference room, with one wall dominated by a bank of tall, narrow windows looking out over the sunny campus.

Taddy McMurdo had provided the required credentials to calm down Johnson and Jensen. They didn't know who he was or under which directorate he worked, but there was no doubting his bona fides. The two agents stood by the door, properly cowed by Taddy's ID.

A large oval table took up the center of the conference room, with several comfortable chairs and two couches strewn about. Nelligan, Kate and Harry sat in one corner, Takeshi Nakano and Kimiko Sheppard together in another. Lee sat at one end of the table, looking exhausted and utterly confused. L.C. Noraine had scrounged a deck of cards from his coat and sat at the other end of the great table, halfway into a game of solitaire. He was cheating.

No one spoke for a time. The air conditioning hissed.

"Pardon me," Harry spoke softly and stood. "I need a moment alone. I'll not bolt."

"Sorry, pal," one of the cops started. "Orders are—"

"Countermanded," Taddy cut in nonchalantly. "The professor here's fine, lads. He's not goin' anywhere. Are you, boyo?"

But Harry only smiled weakly at Taddy, saying nothing. Kate reached up and took one of his hands in hers. His skin was clammy. "Harry?"

"I'm fine, Kate. Right back. Officers?"

The two cops looked at Harry, looked at Taddy, looked at each other, and shrugged. "Okay. Five minutes."

Harry nodded mutely and one of the cops opened the door for him.

It was hard to believe that anything untoward had happened, ten minutes earlier and one floor lower. The usual array of graduate and doctoral students were milling about the library or were nestled down behind the study carrels, their minds locked onto their individual projects.

There was, perhaps, no place in Portland that Harry knew better, more intimately, than the library of John Jacob Astor. On the second floor, back behind the entomology section and a little forward of the pharmacopeias, there was an often-neglected study table. The light was bad there, and a continuous updraft from the floor ventilators was enough to annoy any student. So, as always, the carrel was unoccupied. It also was out of sight of any other library patron.

Harry sat down gingerly, his hands clasped in his lap like an obedient school boy. He stared down an aisle of books, not really seeing anything.

Some time passed.

He eventually crossed his arms on the table and bent over, forehead resting on his sleeves, eyes closed. By squeezing his eyes shut – as tight as they could be – Harry could see a wild, multi-colored, dancing aurora, just behind his eyelids.

He remembered reading once, what caused those lights. The trivia escaped him now.

Eventually, Harry sat back, breathing deeply. He scrounged through his pockets and found a paper Burgerville napkin; then wiped tears from his cheeks and blew his nose, stood and returned to the others.

"I demand an explanation!" Ms. Sheppard's hands were balled

into fists at her side. She was so angry her slight frame shook.

"That's not a bad idea," Detective Sergeant Wiley added softly. As it happened, Wiley had been driving toward the college when the call had come over his radio, asking for his assistance. He arrived at the college library less than ten minutes after the craziness in the photographic dark room. The two uniformed cops handed the situation over to the Sergeant and stepped back out of the way.

There was a soft rap on the door and Harry entered. He smiled at Wiley. "Sergeant."

"Professor." Wiley glanced innocuously at the two cops, who shuffled to their feet. But he didn't ask why his orders had been disobeyed.

"Would you mind telling everyone what happened, Professor?" Wiley asked softly, drawing a chair out away from the table and sitting down.

Harry took his original seat near Kate and Tucker. His color seemed better now, the others thought, and there was a bit of animation in his painfully thin face. That had been missing, when Harry had been there before.

He sat forward, elbows on knees, hands clenched in fists and chin resting on his knuckles. "I'm not altogether sure, Sergeant. I understand some of what happened, but not all."

"I see," Wiley said. He took no notes. His mahogany-colored face remained impassive, noncommittal.

"From the very beginning, this situation revolved around something other than wood," Harry continued, sitting back now and rubbing the fatigue from his eyes. "No offense to those who make their living from lumber, but I was unable to believe that the sale of timber products would lead to a double homicide. It simply is not the stuff of great controversies."

"Then what is it about?" Nelligan asked. Unlike Wiley, he was taking notes.

"I assume they were shipping something else. Probably drugs – cocaine maybe. Sergeant, over the weekend you mentioned how busy your department has been, especially with the increase in methamphetamine production."

"Yes," Wiley confirmed. "Oregon's become a center for that."

"Oh, hell!" Nelligan piped up. "I know where you're heading now, Harry. It's the precursor chemicals they use in making meth – or speed. A lot of that stuff has legitimate uses in the wood products industry. I know, because the *Post* did a big spread on meth a couple months back."

"Precursors?" Kate asked.

"Yeah, the chemicals that go into making meth. Stuff like, uh . . ."

"Acetone, M.E.K., phenol, a few others," Sergeant Wiley filled in the blanks.

Harry studied the sergeant for a moment, his eyebrows raised. "That's interesting. Kate, I don't know if you recall, but following the tractor explosion we were sitting on a number of barrels."

"Yes?" Kate frowned, trying to remember details of that insane day. "It was you, Lee and myself, but I don't remember much about the barrels."

"If memory serves, the barrels contained liquid phenol and acetone varnish," Harry provided.

"So what?" Noraine cut in. "Those're used in lots of wood industry sites. They use acetone to clean precision equipment and as a lacquer. And we've got liquid phenol at my nurseries back in Montana. We use it in making plywood."

"True," Wiley nodded. "But both products also are used in the making of methamphetamines. They're listed in the state police's summary of precursor chemicals. That's an interesting argument, professor. Not proof, mind you."

"True," Harry nodded. "Oh, before I forget, there's a student out in the library. An young, oriental fellow carrying several cameras. Makoto Takimura. Could you get him for us?"

Wiley thought about it a moment, then nodded assent to one of the uniforms, who exited.

"You were saying, professor?"

"I was saying, if there was a drug-exporting scheme, it would need several players. Some in the States and some in Japan. I suggest Detweiler was making methamphetamines on his property while The Kuroshio Group was shipping them to Japan."

"That's libel!" Ms. Sheppard spat.

202

"Slander. Libel's written," Nelligan cut in.

"Thank you," Harry reply wryly.

"Please go on," Wiley urged quietly.

"Detweiler was a businessman. He might have the contacts to establish international trade, but he wouldn't know how to get a hold of the – you should excuse the hackneyed phrase – criminal element necessary for such a scheme. And while I generally am pro union, we all have to admit that many of the major labor unions in America have held close ties with organized crime."

"Meaning Neil Keiter," Wiley said softly.

"Correct. Taking what little I knew, I surmised that Mr. Nakano, Mr. Detweiler and Mr. Keiter had been operating a large-scale drug shipping network. And now, they were about greatly to expand their operation. There was no good way to prove it, so I asked Agent McMurdo here to tell Mr. Nakano that a Detweiler shipment of timber showed up unexpectedly at the Port of Portland this morning."

"Which I did," Taddy added quickly, speaking directly to Wiley. "And once I'd mentioned it, he suddenly called off their oh-so-important flight to London."

"And while that's still not proof enough for a court of law, it convinced me," Harry continued.

Sergeant Wiley glanced at Mr. Nakano, who sat silently, staring at the wall opposite his chair. The elderly man had neither spoken nor moved since the sergeant arrived.

There was a knock at the door and the cop returned with Makoto, who looked scared witless. "Are you all right, professor?" he asked.

"Yes, thank you. Mr. Takimura, you were in the library's dark room during that, er, rather rowdy scene, weren't you?"

"Yes sir."

"This gentleman is a sergeant with the Portland Police Department. Could you tell him what Mr. Nakano here was shouting?"

Makoto looked uncomfortable and shifted his weight from cne foot to the next. "Whoa. I don't know, I mean, my Japanese is a little rusty, sir. I thought . . ."

"You don't have to quote him exactly," Wiley assured

Makoto, turning in his chair to face the student. "Please paraphrase or put it any way you remember it."

"Well," Makoto shrugged. "He was, um, accusing the professor here of . . . and like I say, I'm not certain, but—"

"Spit it out, boy!" Noraine barked, only to receive a withering look from Sergeant Wiley.

"He was accusing Professor Bishop of . . . attacking Japan," Makoto finally got it out, blushing considerably. "That's nutty, I know, but I'm sure he called the professor a murderer and a warlord and said something about . . . well, about Japan's right to Manchuria and the French Mandate islands. Look, I know this sounds crazy, but that's what I heard."

Wiley turned to the Japanese executive, sitting silently in the corner. Nakano was squinting, staring straight ahead, oblivious to the world around him.

But Kimiko Sheppard was afire. Her breathing was ragged and a vein stood out in her neck. "I demand to speak to our counsel immediately! And the Japanese embassy! And I mean right this instant, Sergeant!"

Wiley raised a hand, palm forward. "Certainly, ma'am. One moment please. Professor?"

"I'm afraid the Lion of Japan is hopelessly senile, Sergeant," Harry said, the fatigue palpable on his face and in his voice. "He's probably been this way for quite a while. Ms. Sheppard keeps him doped up enough to pass for the stereotypical 'inscrutable Oriental,' when in reality he's hopelessly senile, reliving his youth."

"I will not stand for this!" Sheppard was on her feet, but no one moved to stop Harry.

"So it wasn't Detweiler, Keiter and Nakano, but Detweiler, Keiter and *Ms. Sheppard*. Until, that is, Keiter got greedy. By the bye, Lee," Lee Connar's head snapped up as he shook off his reverie, "remember how Mr. Keiter stopped you from tape recording Nakano's speech Friday? I overheard him say it was because you were using a recorder from one of the Kuroshio Group's competitors. In retrospect, of course, he just didn't want anyone recording Mr. Nakano's dementia."

"I've got it!" Nelligan sat forward, grinning like the canary-fed cat. "Keiter tried to stiff arm his buddies, and they wouldn't budge. So he set that booby trap in the tree, as a bit of a warning."

"Right," Harry nodded. "Keiter knew the timber industry well enough to rig the explosion. And if we're right and he's connected to organized crime, then he'd certainly have the chutzpah to do it."

Nelligan was writing as fast as he could speak. "So following the explosion out at the farm, he confronts Detweiler and Ms. Sheppard here and says something like, 'That's just a taste of what can happen. Don't cross us.' So they killed him."

"At the farm?" Wiley frowned at the reporter.

"Sorry, Sarge, I forgot." Nelligan then proceeded to tell Wiley and the others about the tooth and bloody swatch of skin he discovered at the farm.

Wiley sighed melodramatically. "I wish you'd mentioned it earlier."

"We were kind of busy," Nelligan grinned at him.

"What next?" Wiley prodded, nodding toward Harry.

"I'll give you my best guess. One of our conspirators hit Keiter, killing him. They had to get the body off the farm before it queered the drug deal. Finally, one of them – you, Ms. Sheppard? – came up with a plan."

Sheppard was seated again, but the vein in her neck continued to throb and her nostrils flared.

"They went to the cliff near the Willamette River and threw Keiter over the edge, then drove to the bottom, using that Detweiler Farms van. They overlooked his wrist watch and didn't quite clean up all the blood, apparently. Anyway, they loaded his body aboard the van, then drove back to Portland and parked on the tree-lined side of the Trafalgar, away from most of the downtown traffic. You'll remember there's almost half a block back there reserved for the Detweiler Farms van and the limousine."

Wiley nodded.

"The rest is just a guessing game, Sergeant. You mentioned earlier that Detweiler had had a ball of fishing line in his pants pocket, which we agreed was rather odd. I suggest he and Ms. Sheppard waited until no one was about – you'll remember there was a brief but powerful rainstorm that afternoon – then dumped Keiter out of the van and, I suspect, rolled him beneath the vehicle, where he'd be hidden from passers by. Ms. Sheppard most probably stayed in the van while Detweiler ran up to his room and unrolled the fishing line, hanging it from his balcony down to the floor below: Keiter's balcony. Detweiler then went downstairs, used Keiter's key to get into the hotel room, spread Keiter's things about – shoes, wallet, jacket, what-have-you – then checked outside and, seeing that all was clear, undid the screws holding Keiter's balcony railing in place. Detweiler then attached the hanging fishing line to the railing and went back up to his own room.

"Once there, I would suspect Detweiler mussed up his bed and towels and called room service to complain. The maids arrived and went to work. While they were busy in the bathroom and bedroom, Detweiler went out to the front room of his suite and called room service, claiming to be Neil Keiter."

"Time out," Nelligan cut in. "Sorry, Harry, but I'll bet the hotel switchboard would know which room he was calling from."

"Beyond a doubt," Harry conceded. "Fortunately, Ms. Sheppard told me over the weekend that the Trafalgar management, in a display of generosity, allowed her to link a computer to their switchboard, which in turn allowed her to control the switchboard to some degree. Sergeant, I'm sure an examination of that device will tell you if it could scramble room numbers."

"It can," Taddy cut in, grinning at Harry. "We've got similar toys."

"What next?" Wiley asked. He sounded almost bored.

"When the maids left, Detweiler stepped out to his balcony, tugged at the fishing line and lifted Keiter's balcony railing up and out of its slots, letting it fall to the ground. He'd brought a pocket full of badly rusted screws along, to strew about the scene for effect. God knows finding rusted screws at the farm would be easy enough.

"The railing fell to the street several yards from the van. Taking her cue, Ms. Sheppard released the emergency brake and let the van roll forward, revealing the body that had died

206

as a result of a long fall onto cement. She was able to leave the van and circle the building before anyone noticed anything."

"Take us to our embassy now!" Sheppard barked at Wiley. *"Now!"*

Takeshi Nakano sat contentedly, staring into space.

"And Christopher?" Lee Connar spoke for the first time. He sat slumped in his chair, elbow on the table, his hand holding his forehead. His eyes were red and lined.

Harry sat forward and sighed, kneading a kink in his neck. He took a few seconds before answering. "Ms. Sheppard may have killed him or he slipped while trying to fake Keiter's fall. Probably the latter. I'm sorry, Lee."

No one said anything for a while.

L.C. Noraine let loose with a long, low whistle.

Nelligan scribbled madly in his notepad, grinning like the Cheshire Cat.

Kate touched Harry gently on the arm, smiling sadly at him.

Wiley stood and turned to his men. "Phil, could you get a court order to search that van, please? Also one for Detweiler Farms. Oh, and the communication equipment in the basement of the Trafalgar. That should do it. Thank you."

"Yes sir." The uniform left.

"Mr. Takimura, thank you very much," Wiley shook the student's hand. "I'm afraid you'll have to testify."

Finally, the sergeant turned to the Japanese delegation. "Ms. Sheppard, one of my men will escort you to the Japanese embassy, right away. I'll arrange for a doctor to look after Mr. Nakano, if you'd like."

"No," she almost hissed. "He stays with me."

"Fine, ma'am. Roger, will you drive them to the embassy, please?"

The other cop opened the door and motioned toward Sheppard and Nakano.

With a great display of self control, Kimiko Sheppard rose to her feet and touched her "employer" on the shoulder. Nakano stood also, beaming around the room. He began to speak softly.

Sheppard didn't translate.

"He's . . . uh, he's thanking the emperor for this most memorable honor," Makoto said, his voice catching in his throat.

Sheppard gently touched the old man on the elbow and led him to the door, exiting. Taddy nodded to the Secret Service agents to go along.

"She'd been the overseas contact for years, I imagine," Harry said after they left. "When Detweiler came up with this new scheme, she had to come over to arrange it personally. Nakano really was a giant in his day, I'm told. Now he's window dressing."

"That's sad," Kate said.

"Indeed," Wiley nodded. "Professor, we never did find anyone named 'Dodge.' I don't suppose you . . .?"

Harry shrugged. "Neil Keiter was raised in the States and moved to Canada around 1971. He came back to the state around 1980. I'm not positive, but he may have been dodging the draft. He probably returned after the general amnesty. Like everything else, I've not proof, of course."

Wiley sighed again. "And his fellow union workers tagged him with the nickname 'Dodge.' Seems plausible. Thank you, sir. I'll call you later for some clarification, if I may. If you'll all excuse me."

"I'm off, too," Noraine said, climbing to his feet. "This's been the damnedest thing I ever saw. But right now, and for about the next forty-eight hours, there's a hell of a void in the U.S./Japanese timber trade. If you'll all excuse me, I got some deals to cut." He beat a hasty exit.

"What about Joshua and Phoebe Pogue?" Kate asked.

Harry stood, his knees wobbling a bit. "From what I can tell, he thought she did it and she thought he did it, and we scared the living hell out of both of them. I'm not sure a marriage with that little faith will last."

Harry and Kate walked together to the door. They stepped aside for Tucker, who was making a beeline for the door, notepad in hand. Harry also noticed that Taddy was gone. He hadn't seen him leave.

"Coming, Lee?" Kate called.

Lee stayed slumped in his chair, resting his head against his palm. "No," he said softly. "I want to be alone a while."

Kate crossed the room to him and knelt, taking his free hand in both of hers. "We're truly sorry, Lee. I'll call you in the morning."

"Thanks, Kate. And Harry?"

Harry stood by the door a moment.

"Are you sure?" Lee asked, haunting pain pulsing behind his eyes. "About Chris, I mean. About . . . all of this? Everything?"

Harry seemed to visibly sag under the weight of the question. He didn't speak for a time and his eyes remained locked on the floor. At length, he nodded. "Absolutely, Lee. I'm sorry."

CHAPTER FORTY-TWO

Harry and Kate stepped out into the glorious blue of a North-western summer afternoon. Kate took his hand and squeezed it. "That was . . . damned amazing, Harry. I didn't pick up any of those things."

Harry blushed and squeezed her hand in return. "Ah, shucks." The tone was a bad mockery of his usual, playful mood.

"Will you be okay?" she asked. "There's something to eat at my place, if you're interested."

"Actually, Kate, I'm exhausted. That scene with Nakano took a bit out of me. May I take a rain check?"

She leaned close and kissed him on the lips, her fingertips touching the edge of his jaw line. The kiss lingered. Three passing students whistled cat calls.

"Take care, Henry Bishop," Kate said, turning and walking away.

Nelligan caught up with Taddy McMurdo in the administration parking lot. The older man was climbing into a rented sedan with a *U.S. Department of Education* parking sticker in the window.

"Mr. McMurdo?" he called out. "I'm Tucker Nelligan, *Port-land Post*. I was wondering if I might have a few words with you."

Taddy paused, one foot already in the car, and folded his arms atop the open door. "I don't think so, Mr. Tucker Nelligan of the *Portland Post*. I'm not at liberty to talk to the press. I'm sure Detective Sergent Wiley will have a statement shortly."

"It's not about these murders," Nelligan cut in quickly before Taddy could climb into the car. "It's about Harry Bishop."

Taddy studied the reporter for a moment, an off-kilter smile gracing his square face. Nelligan was a master of the waiting game and he crossed his arms over his chest, resting his butt against the edge of the hood.

Taddy started to chuckle, a high pitched, jocular sound, and his eyes crinkled shut. "And here I figured you for old Harry's friend," he replied, two parts cynicism to three parts indifference.

"I am his friend," Nelligan replied in an even tone. "His best friend."

"Then ask him what you will," Taddy suggested.

Nelligan neither smiled nor frowned and his gaze never left Taddy's eyes. "You two have history. I know it. It's in your body language."

Taddy said nothing, just grinned.

"I want to know about the Mad Hatter," Nelligan added, and that did it. Taddy's thick eyebrows climbed up his brow. The grin disappeared, replaced with a look of appraisal.

"Harry told you about that, did he?"

"Nope," Nelligan replied. "I dug it up."

"I see. And now you'd like me to fill in the details, is that it?"

"Yes."

Taddy climbed into the car and shut the door, then rolled down the window and leaned out. The idiot-grin was back. "Can't do it, Mr. Nelligan. If you're wanting information on Harry, then ask Harry."

He started up the engine and Nelligan stepped away from the car.

"You might ask him one thing," Taddy spoke up over the revving of the engine as he slipped the car into reverse and began backing away from the ivy-covered administration building. "Ask him about the grassy knoll. And you can tell him the March Hare sent you."

211

Nelligan stood where he was for quite a while, digesting what he had heard.

Later that evening, after taking to Marty, Nelligan would decide never, ever to mention the exchange to Harry.

Taddy stopped in a Motel 6 just outside Beaverton, far out of the way from his destination, Portland International Airport, and plunked down money for a room with a single bed, one night. The day manager smiled warmly and informed him there was HBO and Showtime at no extra charge. Ah, life in the sticks, Taddy thought.

Once in the room, Taddy checked through the balcony window to see if the adjoining room was empty. Seeing that it was, he picked its lock and entered.

Without bothering to go through the hotel switchboard, Taddy dialed a thirty-five digit number he had memorized.

His telephone call bypassed the switchboard, was routed through Lincoln City, Nebraska, on to Buffalo, New York. There, special circuits kicked the call to Laramie, Wyoming, which activated an automatic link to Boulder, Colorado.

From Boulder, the signal was forwarded via satellite to Washington D.C., where the Director's personal aide took the call.

"Did everything work out?" the aide asked, her voice metallic and inhumanly flat, thanks to the scrambling units.

"Not exactly," Taddy replied, speaking into his own scrambler, attached to the receiver by a rubber thong. "The deal with the Kuroshio Group is squashed, thanks to the Hatter. I told you he would be trouble."

"I thought you said he would *save* the deal."

"I did," Taddy replied, unflustered by any bureaucrat's bravado. "I figured he'd solve this crime and keep the Old Man happy. Little did I realize the Old Man was a drooling idiot. Never mind: I'll explain later."

There was a pause on the line while the information was digested. "I see," the aide finally replied. "Which means we'll have to find new buyers in Japan."

212

"And new suppliers here," Taddy added.

"This is problematic, Mr. McMurdo. I don't have to tell you the Board has been most concerned with keeping the drugs flowing into Japan."

"Not to worry," Taddy said soothingly. "There's more than enough meth being produced out here in the boondocks. We'll find us a couple of new players and resume shipments to Japan forthwith."

"I trust so. Keiter was most specific in his threats. I trust you were able to . . . lessen his potential damage to the project?"

"Ha!" Taddy laughed into the receiver. "There's a story for you. I needn't have bothered planning for Keiter. Someone else did him for us – Detweiler himself! I'll explain that in my report, as well."

"Fine," the voice returned over the line. "Please fly back immediately. Consider this operation closed. We're purging your 'Dodge' ID from the files."

"Understood. See you soon," he replied, hanging up.

Harry stopped by a liquor store on his way home and bought two bottles of Scotch whisky.

Once firmly settled in at home, with his comfortable slippers on and the cat fed, Harry put on an album of Duke Ellington music, opened one of the bottles, filled a glass with ice, and poured in three fingers.

CHAPTER FORTY-THREE

Harry drank until the bottle was empty then opened the second. It was almost two in the morning when the doorbell rang.

"S'unlocked," he roared from the comfort of his easy chair.

Lee Connar opened the door and entered. His tie was loosened and his face was haggard and lined. He sat heavily on the couch. "I thought you were going to give up the booze."

"Nope," Harry replied blearily. "Can't. Wouldn't want to anyway. You okay?"

Lee rubbed his eye with his knuckle. "No. Not okay." He leaned forward, elbows on knees, and peered at Harry. "Chris was my friend, Harry. From way back. I respected him. Admired him. How could he have been using his connections to ship drugs?"

Lee's voice caught once. His eyes were puffy with tears about to brim over.

Harry stared at the ceiling, sipping his drink.

"I'm thinking about quitting," Lee said, eyes fixed on the empty fireplace. "Getting out of academia. I wrote a resignation letter this afternoon."

"I see," Harry said.

"Harry, I . . ."

His voice simply died off. Neither man said anything.

Harry set his drink down and stood, walked to the couch and sat next to Lee, his arm around the dean's shoulder. Lee had started to cry.

"I'm sure it was an accident," Harry said. "It wasn't murder."

214

The tears came fast now, sobs wracking Lee's body. Harry held him tight and waited for the fit to pass.

"I just . . . I didn't mean to kill him," Lee said softly, leaning against Harry for comfort.

"I know."

"I just stepped out on the balcony and . . . I saw him, leaning over and yanking on this string and then the railing below fell and I didn't know what it meant. I didn't. He just . . . it was crazy."

"I know."

Lee sat forward again. Harry rubbed the dean's back and shoulders, his fingers digging into the knotted muscles.

"He saw me," Lee's voice was pitched unnaturally high. "There was this look . . . I don't know, Harry. It was anger and fear and embarrassment and . . . something like lust. Hate. Something. He went back inside the hotel room and I heard him storming down the hall, pounding on my door. I didn't know what to think. I opened the door and let him in. He . . . he asked me what I'd seen. I told him. Then I went out on the balcony and looked down and . . . there was this *body* down there. I . . . I couldn't see who it was, and I asked him, I said, 'Chris, what the hell's going on?'"

"And he told you," Harry prompted.

"He told me. All about it. Said he'd have to trust me." Lee sat hunched forward, his voice spiraling lower and lower, his energy drained. "He told me about the drugs and about the Japanese deal, and how with Astor's connections he could . . . the profits he was talking about were astronomical. Incredible. I just couldn't believe it. He'd been doing it for years and . . . now, now he wanted to use the school, *my* school, and I just couldn't have that, Harry. That just wasn't *right*."

The two men sat motionless for a time. "You hit him with the typewriter," Harry said at last.

Lee turned on the couch, his eyes questioning.

Harry almost smiled but couldn't dredge up enough strength. "You were using a typewriter in the hospitality suite Friday. On Saturday, Kate had to call down to the front desk and have one sent up. I wondered about it then."

They sat silently for a while. Harry leaned forward and retrieved his drink.

"I really don't remember hitting him," Lee said, then shook his head quickly, viciously. "No! That's not true. I remember. It's just . . . like it wasn't really me. He just . . . fell. And I remember sitting there, staring at him. Then dragging him out, throwing him over the balcony. Throwing Christopher . . ."

They sat for a while in the gloom.

"You never thought Ms. Sheppard killed Chris, did you?" Lee asked in a whisper.

"Made no sense," Harry slurred. "She needed him. And I doubted he fell over his own railing while hoisting the railing below. He had time to roll up the fishing line and jam it in his pocket. No, he fell later. The fact that he didn't make it all the way to the ground, but landed on the eighth floor, fooled everyone into thinking he fell *with* Keiter, not a minute later."

Lee nodded and leaned back. They sat for a while more, both silent.

"He wanted to use my school for drugs," Lee said at one point.

Harry didn't reply.

Lee gathered the strength to leave about an hour later.